THE BURNING HILL

A.D. FLINT

Copyright © 2024 A. D. Flint

First published in 2018 by Unbound. This edition published in 2024 by Ticcen Publishing.

The right of A.D. Flint to be identified as the author of this work has been asserted in accordance with Section 77 of the Copyright, Designs and Patents Act 1988. No part of this publication may be copied, reproduced, stored in a retrieval system, or transmitted, in any form or by any means without the prior permission of the publisher, nor be otherwise circulated in any form of binding or cover other than that in which it is published and without a similar condition being imposed on the subsequent purchaser.

This book is a work of fiction and, except in the case of historical fact, any resemblance to actual persons, living or dead, is purely coincidental.

ISBN (Paperback): 978-1-3999-7959-7

Design by Cherie Chapman

About the Author

The idea for this story came from a robbery that unfolded a few blocks from where the author was living in Rio de Janeiro. The young man involved had survived a notorious massacre of street children outside a Rio church years before, and what played out in the aftermath of the robbery on live TV news was an embodiment of the desperation of life at the bottom of the heap. An ugly thing in this beautiful city, shocking, even to a society inured to everyday violence.

The author now lives on the south coast of England with his Brazilian wife and two sons.

For my wife, Ruth. I could not have done this without you.

Chapter 1

1993

Vilson

Most people looked right through Vilson, like he was invisible. Sometimes he wished he were. The barely there kid stood alone in the afternoon shadows of the church, away from the others. He saw the cop car drawing up before anyone else did, and something cold and slippery moved inside him. Fear uncurling. Cops never came with anything good. He wrapped his skinny arms around himself, his shoulders rounded and hunched.

The Candelária church was in central Rio, an island with multiple lanes of traffic washing past, surrounded by modern office blocks. Over the last few months, it had become a safe haven for street kids, the sparse, dusty grounds at its front a patchwork of cardboard boxes flattened into mattresses.

The cop car pulled over at the kerb alongside the encampment, near a bunch of older kids kicking a Fanta can around in the harsh sunlight. The cop squinted through his open window and jabbed a finger at them. "I told you lot to clear out of this place," he shouted over the roar of the traffic.

Most of the kids carried on with their game, making a show of ignoring the cop. The eldest of them was a twelve-year-old named Gabriel. Even as Vilson was praying that his big brother would walk away, Gabriel turned to the cop.

"Oh yeah, sure," he shouted, puffing out his chest, "and make it easier for you to catch us and beat us? Makes you a big man, huh?"

"Watch your step or I'll make you pay for that tongue, you little shit," the cop shouted.

Vilson wanted to step from the shadows, to make Gabriel come away. He saw Gabriel give his friends a little smile that told them he wasn't going to fold up for some cop. He looked around and picked up a stone and threw it at the cop car. It thudded into the dull paintwork on the rear panel.

"One more, just one more, and see what happens," the cop shouted.

The other kids jeered, grabbing anything to hand, rubbish and stones, to hurl at the car.

The cop ducked his head back inside. Most of it missed the car, nothing hit him.

"You can't touch us." Gabriel forced a grin as he gestured at the traffic and at the church.

Gabriel had told Vilson often enough that they were safe on their island. Untouchable with so many eyes on their entrance. More and more kids were coming here, and Vilson watched them each time his brother led the celebration of another failed attempt to move them on. They were driving the cops nuts. Vilson and Gabriel and the others did what they had to do to survive and petty crimes appeared in the surrounding area. It was an embarrassment for the heroes.

Vilson could see the cop gripping the steering wheel, swallowing down his rage, taking control of himself. The cop revved the engine, rattling the loose exhaust pipe. Regaining his voice, he shouted, "You'll pay for this disrespect, I'm telling you."

The tyres squealed on the hot asphalt as the cop sped away. If there were any worries amongst the kids that the threat was genuine they were swallowed in bravado as they cheered and threw stones to finish.

Gabriel came over to the shadows, ruffling Vilson's thick of matted hair. "Don't look so worried, brother."

Vilson's round eyes stared up at him from beneath a permanent crease in his brow. "You made him really angry. He said he'd make us pay."

Gabriel sucked on his teeth. "Cops, man. Assholes who can't get any other job. They're the real criminals, not us." He reached out to Vilson. "Forget about him. They wouldn't dare do anything here, not under the eye of God."

The heaviness that Vilson often felt lifted from him. Gabriel could make everything better with just a word or a gesture. It made his heart swell to have Gabriel as his brother. Everyone loved him.

No one ever took them for brothers: Vilson was smaller and lighter-skinned. He wished he looked more like Gabriel. He stopped hugging himself, dropping his arms, pushing his shoulders back, trying to imitate Gabriel's confident posture.

When their *Mãe* – their mother – had brought them to the church two years earlier, she had hugged each of them in turn. Vilson remembered the warmth of her body. She had bent down to look at them and told them to look after one another. Her eyes filled with tears then and she had straightened and turned, quickly, to hide, away without looking back. Gabriel had put an arm around Vilson and pulled him close. He remembered feeling Gabriel's body shaking against his and looking up to see tears streaming down his cheeks. Vilson was too young to understand. He had put his arms around Gabriel. "It's okay, *Mãe* will be back soon. She said."

"That's right. She'll be back soon." They had held onto one another until Gabriel's body had stopped shaking. He had then pulled away from Vilson, wiped the tears from his cheeks with his fingers and put his hands gently on Vilson's shoulders, looking him in the eye. "Everything will be okay, brother." The smile came back then. The Gabriel who always had mischief in him, who was always fun. As the months passed and still their mother had not returned, Vilson had felt increasingly lost and afraid. And Gabriel always comforted him and said everything would be okay, and Vilson tried his best to believe him.

Gabriel ducked most stuff thrown his way with an effortless shrug or joke, and he never took a step back. Following his lead was harder than it looked. And sometimes Vilson caught Gabriel looking at him like he was wishing he had a better brother. That feeling was as bad as being scared. But Gabriel was always there come what may. Vilson always had his big brother.

Vilson awoke with a start late into that night, reaching out for Gabriel. The bed of flattened cardboard next to him was empty.

It felt as though the darkness had stolen something terrible from his nightmare, and it was still out there, crawling, its pale belly to the ground, coming for him. With the day's traffic gone it was silent, other than a low electrical hum from somewhere that made the silence even heavier. He sat up, hugging his knees to his chest. He tried to remember the prayers his mother had taught him. The words were jumbled and elusive, even the picture in his head of his mother's face was unclear. It was so long since she had gone.

A figure appeared through the low dusty haze. An adult. Another appeared a little further away. They were walking in a line.

Even though they weren't wearing uniforms it was obvious that they were cops. Vilson, like the other children who were awake, knew instinctively what was coming. And, like most of the others, he did nothing.

There was a shot on the other side of the encampment and then all the cops started firing. A handful of children jumped up and scattered, only to be pulled down by the bullets. One child fell very close to him, a little girl, head cracking hard on the paving. Dead before she hit the ground. Vilson flinched, the shock brutal. Numbing.

Without Gabriel, he could not snap himself into action. He needed his big brother. His eyes moved back to the cops and their slow, deliberate advance, his head barely turning, hoping that the faintness of movement might keep him invisible. One of the cops was less than ten metres away. Even in the smudgy glow of the street lights, Vilson could make out the grim concentration set on his face.

A shout went up from one of the cops further down the line. More shouts as a group of children bolted into the road, trying to make the safety of the side streets. The line of cops broke as they gave chase.

And still Vilson sat with his knees hugged to his chest. Someone grabbed his arm and hauled him to his feet. "Come on, man, let's go."

It was Babão, a twitchy pinball of a kid who was always telling tall stories that no one ever believed. A stone in someone's shoe, Gabriel had always said. Babão dragged him away, ducking behind trees and bins until they made the walls of the church and the deep shadow of a large stone buttress.

They tried to catch their breath, hearing the shouts of the cops and the cracks of gunfire and the screams of children.

"We've got to get away from here," Babão whispered.

"Not without my brother, I can't leave without him." The words came out of Vilson in a thin wail.

"Keep it down, man, you'll get us shot. Your brother took his chance, he ran, he probably made it, who knows? Now we have to take our chance. Let's go."

Vilson stood firm for a few moments and then let Babão pull him away.

Although there were other off-duty cops and vigilantes in other death squads, killing children to clean up the streets, the Candelária massacre gained instant notoriety. Only three of the cops that took part were ever convicted. The massacre weighed heavily on the country, shameful, hard to forget. But then no one liked to think too much about the children that survived it either.

Chapter 2
2004

Jake

Blend into the background. That had been Jake's priority when he'd arrived in Brazil. Copacabana wasn't the place to do that. Too touristy. Brazilians would never recognise him but a few Brits had given him a quizzical glance or a double take. He had moved on from his first stop and rented a little apartment in Ipanema and, in the following weeks, Copacabana's allure had started to fade. Eating in a restaurant near the beach one night, he had overheard a neighbouring diner, one of the sniffier residents of Ipanema, refer to it as *Cocô-cabana* – Cack-cabana. That hadn't helped.

He had cropped his hair and added some local shopping to the holdall of clothes he had brought from the UK. His fair skin had moved on a few shades and he was labouring to revive the latent Portuguese he had grown up hearing from his mother. He had found a teacher at a local language school willing to give him private lessons. He didn't want to get involved with a group and he kept his teacher at arm's length. But he was learning, and a couple of times he had even been mistaken for a Paulista, a native of São Paulo. And then his teacher told him about the bad blood between Paulistas and Cariocas. Paulistas wrote off their rivals as beach bums and, to Cariocas, Paulistas were a bunch of try-hards, so he was no longer taking it as a compliment. But it was a step up from *gringo*.

And blending in had another practical purpose: it made him less of a target. Beneath the vibrant beauty of the city there was always the undercurrent of violence. He never wore a watch when he was out, and only carried a small amount of cash. That frisson of danger livened things up though. The alertness to what was coming down the street brought the small things into pin-sharp focus. The smells were strong in his nostrils, the sounds of the city clear. He was still looking for that fix of adrenaline, even after everything that had happened.

All he had to do was avoid getting taken for a clueless day tripper with a pocketful of cash, just pass himself off at a glance. And yet he wanted to get in deeper, disappear altogether. He had reason enough, but sometimes it was hard work. A night out in Copacabana was easy.

Most of the time.

Over the noise of music and talk in the bar, he hadn't caught what the Dutch girl had said. He leaned forward.

"I said, give me a break," she shouted into his ear in her perfect English.

He tilted back to look at her face, trying to decide whether or not she was messing around. Pale-skinned, her cheeks were flushed with alcohol, her face screwed up. Had she misconstrued what he had said?

What had he said?

She was certainly fresh off the plane, ready to start ticking off her South American tour list. He wasn't sure if she'd told him that or if he'd made the assumption.

Copacabana was meant to be easy. Drinking caipirinhas was easy. Sweet and sharp, sugar and lime, masking the strong cane spirit beneath.

He was too many in to come up with a winning response, but he had to do something. He cracked out his best smile. She scowled and turned away, moving off through the crowd.

He wasn't big on smiling and forcing one didn't seem to have landed it anywhere near the mark.

He drained his glass self-consciously. He would get another. What was her problem anyway?

He joined the knot of people waiting to get served at the bar. He had exchanged a few words with a handful of locals in this place before, and he knew the girl behind the bar by name. She was at the other end of the bar but he managed to catch her eye, nodding and giving her a wave. She turned to serve someone without acknowledging him. His skin prickled. He told himself she probably just hadn't seen him.

The Brazilian hip hop thrashing the speakers and the white noise of shouted conversation around him were beginning to grate. He had less tolerance for noise these days.

He drummed his fingers on the bar. He wasn't near to getting served. Turning his head, he looked around the place, and then spotted the Dutch girl coming back through the crowd. She didn't look so annoyed now. It was only when he moved into her path that she noticed him, checking, the scowl returning. She made to step around him.

"Hey," he said.

She kept on going.

He just wanted to apologise. For whatever it was he had said. He held her arm, clumsily.

"Get your hands off me, asshole." She threw the remains of her

THE BURNING HILL

drink in his face, whipped her arm away and marched off. A few people looked on, nudging and chuckling. He wiped a hand across his face, the alcohol stinging his eyes.

"Okay, you must go now." It was a short Brazilian guy, speaking in English. The bar manager. He had an armful of empty bottles and a stack of dirty glasses in either hand.

"What?"

"You upset girls in my bar, you must leave," the manager said. Lots of people were looking now.

"You're kidding. I didn't do anything."

"You're drunk."

"Everyone's drunk."

"Go now or I get the security to make you."

Jake's angular features were unusual, they might belong here or there, difficult to place. In a nation of endless variety, he should have fitted in, but he felt alien.

He didn't belong in this place, or in Copacabana or Ipanema or anywhere. It was stupid to think he could just turn up, rent a place and make it his home.

"Okay, you win," he said. He stepped back, pushed his empty glass across the bar and walked out.

The day had been a winter hangover interfering with the start of summer: torrential rain in the morning, the afternoon cloudy and grey. Drains overflowed and raw effluent ran down from the favelas into the sea, turning it brown. Bathers and surfers replaced with a dirty froth and turds and sanitary products.

Colours that were more England than Brazil. That was unexpected. He had escaped England before, but not to get away from colours or even the shithole town he had grown up in. The place he had gone to then was a lot sweatier than Brazil, and not just because it was hotter. His short time there was made up of immovable slabs of poke-yourself-in-the-eye boredom, a healthy slice of exhilaration and a squirt of terror. He had thrived on the mix, until the day it had gone belly up. He could have returned to England a minor hero. Instead, he had chosen notoriety, before cutting out to Brazil to wash all that stuff away. Tonight, he had picked exactly the wrong place to do that.

He crossed the road and the famous black and white waves of the beachfront paving. The beach had been deserted all day. It would be deserted now. He wasn't sure of the time but it was after midnight when he had last looked at a clock, and that had been well before the evening had started to go south.

THE BURNING HILL

He held on to his Havaiana flip-flops, cool damp [sand] [under] his feet as he walked toward the crashing surf, wandering [out of the] glare of the beachfront floodlights. The dark side of Copa[cabana] [beach] was in his top three places to avoid, but there was a knot [inside that] had festered in his gut for as long as he could remember. [And he was] [le]tting it tighten. He wanted to push at the world a little, [see if it] [w]ould push back.

He kicked at the sand, watching the breakers for a [w]h[ile. He] [de]cided it wasn't such a bad place to be. Maybe he just needed [to see] [peo]ple. In a city. He smiled, and it felt genuine, even if it [wasn't] [much to] [lo]ok at. The smile broadened. The knot of anger was softening, [thanks] [in pa]rt [in] [tu]rned for the light and beauty of the city.

Two young guys strode out of the gloom, trying [to scare] [him] [with] the tension that was crackling off them into mena[ce. There] [wa]s no mistaking what they were, where they were from — [the kin]d [of fa]vela kids Jake was in the habit of crossing the road to [avoid. But] [here] [there] was no road to cross, no crowd to absorb him. The wor[ld] [had m]o[ved] back.

Jake knew nothing of the Candelária massacre, [but] [in the y]ears after Vilson and Babão had survived it, after [everything] [they had] thing thrown at them since, the world had driven them o[nto Copacab]ana beach on this night in search of an easy target. [Stea]ling, begging, stealing — they had done it all to work th[e streets] [o]f the street, ground it out to make themselves a home i[n the favela]. And, still, they were never far from the next beating, th[e next] [angry] gang member coming for them.

If Jake had known Vilson as a child, he wou[ld] [probab]ly have recognised the same skinny, round-shouldered kid [with a sho]ck of hair. But all he saw was a pair of random favela kids c[oming at him], the skinny lead kid pulling a revolver from the wai[stb]an[d of his b]aggy shorts.

Jake's blood instantly ran cold, the salty bree[ze] [nippi]n[g] [at] [bar]e his skin as he rapidly sobered. He was scared and his le[gs] [felt like rub]ber. His mind wasn't working, just berating him for bei[ng so stupid, f]or not making a run for it the moment he had seen them. H[e m]ig[ht have] made it back to the clean, safe light of the beachfront, [back to the] [tro]ubled stream of bar-hoppers and loose traffic. Stupid, stup[id].

And then he was through it. Like a plane climbi[ng through a s]torm, engines screaming, bursting clear of the black cloud. T[he no]i[s]e was all around, every nerve end in his body fizzing, but h[e wa]s [al]l [c]lear. Sighted. He dropped his Havaianas in the sand an[d raised his han]ds to shoulder level in surrender, palms turned slightl[y in]w[ard]. B[o]d[i]ly to strike.

He saw Vilson's skinny hand shaking as he pointed the revolver at his face. Jake could sweep the barrel away with one hand, chopping the other into the kid's wrist, and he would be disarmed before he even had a chance to think about pulling the trigger. Action is quicker than reaction. They had drummed that into him. And he was stronger than this kid, but there was also the one behind him.

The revolver was a spindly relic. Serious players, the kind that might pull the trigger just because there was no good reason not to, would at least carry something chunkier, more likely a semi-automatic. This kid was no psycho. Let it play out a bit more. No need to go hero yet.

"*Passa a grana*," Vilson rasped, scragging the front of Jake's shirt as he rammed the revolver into his cheek and then forced it into his mouth. The sight on top of the barrel chipped a front tooth and gouged the roof of his mouth. A flare of pain. He felt the sliver of tooth on his tongue and caught the taste of the barrel, sour metal and salty dirt, before the blood doused it. Jake's eyes narrowed. Anger. Always there, like a dozing pack of dogs ready to stir. But he had to hold onto the dogs. Just let them pull a little. That was when he functioned best. Right on the edge.

The kid looked maybe seventeen or eighteen, less than a decade behind Jake. His bootleg Flamengo AFC shirt, with its horizontal red and black stripes, smelled of cooking oil and smoke. His partner stood back a little, shorter and twitchy-looking.

"*Passa a grana*," Vilson repeated, followed by a helpful translation in a thick Carioca accent: "Give the moh-ney."

The menace was sliding away from the kid, the tremor in his hand rattling the barrel against Jake's teeth. He had guessed right. This kid just wanted to get his money and get home. Jake's eyes softened a little. The dogs quietened. He was going to be okay.

Babão spoke for the first time, "*Puxa o gatilho, 'lek! Mostra pra ele que 'cê tá falando sério.*"

Jake's alcohol-fugged brain had to extract the words and reassemble them, Vilson catalysing his translation as he pulled back the hammer with its double-jointed click. Babão had instructed Vilson to show he was serious, and he was becoming more agitated. But if he was carrying a gun he would have pulled it by now. It was still okay.

The blood was still surging around Jake's body but rationality was in full control. The dogs lay down. He almost felt regret. He went for his pocket, slowly, and pulled out his scruffy fold of notes for the skinny kid to snatch. It was an acceptable amount and there was no one else silly enough to be out on the beach to panic them.

Vilson turned slightly to address Babão over his shoulder, the gun barrel rasping over Jake's teeth. Adrenaline was twitching Jake's muscles, but he resisted the urge to make any movement, even swallowing. Blood and saliva were pooling at the back of his throat. He was struggling to control his gag reflex, the overflow dribbling from the corner of his mouth. He swallowed.

The gun went off.

A brutal kick, Jake's world exploding in a violating blitz of colour and noise. Blackness.

Swirling light. He was coming to, his grip on consciousness weak.

This was death, or the very last moments of life.

Hollow, sick ribbons of vertigo only anchored by the cool sand he found himself lying on. Burning snaps and sparks tracing across the dark, cloudy sky. His ears were ringing.

The right side of his face was pulsing, throbbing, burning. He could smell cordite. He moved a hand toward his face, the nausea hitting before he even touched the slick of sticky, hot blood and smashed flesh.

Faces were looking down at him. People. Gasping. Shocked. Rapid talking. Talking amongst themselves. *Gringo*. Talking to him.

A calmer face. A bright light shining in his eye. "*Você está me ouvindo?*" Can you hear me?

He thought he could hear gunshots, distant, from an unreal world. Shouting. More shots. Screaming.

The sounds rolled and stretched. It was all very far away now. He was dropping away into darkness, the light no more than a distant star. He was going.

Chapter 3

Vilson

The two boys ran in the shadows along the beach for a couple of hundred metres before dinking back up onto the beachfront paving.

"Stash the piece, man," Babão hissed.

It was only then that Vilson noticed its weight in his hand. He was in shock. He had stuck the revolver into the back of his shorts.

"And slow down." Babão tugged at his shirt. "We're out for a walk, just like anyone else."

Vilson Bonfim de Lima knew they weren't fooling anyone but he forced himself into a stroll alongside his lifelong friend, his trusted friend, Jose Carlos Machado da Silva, better known by his nickname, Babão. Babão – the dribbler – because of the spittle that came from his mouth as he spoke.

There were cars behind them, people stopping to see what had happened on the beach, giving other people the confidence to stop and stare. Brake lights flared in the loose traffic as people started to stream across the road from the bars.

Rolling along the beachfront toward Vilson and Babão was a worn-out 4×4, a police patrol truck marking a beat along Copacabana, Ipanema and Leblon. A nice, quiet evening for the three cops riding in it. Bright lights and pretty girls.

"Christ, it's the cops," Vilson said. The patrol truck was less than a hundred metres away, approaching the braking traffic, the supply to the opposite carriageway now choked off.

"Don't stare," said Babão. "They haven't got the lights on, they don't know. They'll just pass."

Vilson kept his eyes fixed on the little mosaic tiles of the Copacabana paving, the black and white waves drifting and swelling in his nausea. He had to keep his eyes down.

The truck must have passed now. He couldn't help himself, glancing up. It was drawing level. The big cop in the passenger seat wasn't looking him in the eye, he was focused on the uneven bulk at the back of his shorts, where the butt of the pistol was just poking out from under his loose tail shirt.

Vilson was already moving as the cop pushed his arm out of the open window, twisting around as the truck rolled past. The cop fired without issuing a challenge. The angle was awkward and the shot snatched, fizzing harmlessly into the soft sand somewhere between the road and where the big Atlantic rollers were crashing into the beach.

Vilson and Babão split wordlessly, running into the three lanes of traffic that were backing up to a halt. The truck swung around, bouncing violently over the kerb, scattering a handful of pedestrians, who were yelping and screaming having shrunk to the ground at the sound of the gunshot. There was no space for the police truck to weave through the oncoming vehicles. It was stuck. The youngest of the three cops burst out the back of the vehicle and came after Babão. The big cop booted open his door and got off another shot at Vilson.

Less wayward than the first, it thunked into a car radiator a few strides behind Vilson's legs, steam blowing from the cracked grill.

Vilson jinked through the oncoming traffic, running a line between the second and third lanes. Cars swerved and crunched into one another like crazed bullocks in a pen.

He scrambled over a bonnet blocking his way, a bullet buzzing close by his head. Another punching into the windscreen. Dropping low, he made fifty quick metres, almost at the outer range of the cop. He was able to run flat out now. The dread of the thump of a round in his back charging him.

He cut across the wide, tree-lined central reservation and the emptying lanes of the opposite carriageway, and he was away, sprinting down a street alongside the Copacabana Palace Hotel.

Four hundred metres of hard running got Vilson to an entrance to the favela, an alleyway at the end of a street of expensive apartment blocks, with their high, spiked railings and security guards. He waited for as long as he dared, but there was no sign of Babão. He had maybe taken a different route into the favela.

Panting for breath, he slowed to a walk on the hard dirt of the alleyway, a pungent mix of urine and rotting garbage on the cool evening air. There were still lights on in some of the shanty homes with their corrugated-iron roofs and ramshackle hollow-brick-and-concrete construction, the bright slabs of light only serving to deepen the surrounding shadows. The needs-must housing sprawled up the lush hillside above the city in a shambolic pattern. Sanitation and water supplies were rudimentary, with electricity tapped off the grid, crazy tangles of lumpy wires twisting away from electrical arteries on the fringes of the favela.

Vilson passed one or two people in the dark alleyways. Sheathed in sweat, it was a struggle to control his breathing as he laboured up the steep path. He couldn't have any gang members seeing him looking like he had run from something. But no one challenged him, there weren't even any kids on lookout duty.

He passed some of the better places, satellite dishes and water tanks on the roofs, air-con units lodged in the walls. They would have more good things inside, fridges and cookers maybe. These people most likely had jobs down in the city. A wage. This was the good stuff that Vilson and Babão might one day be able to buy – something real sitting above the city with its untouchable riches, a fantasy place.

They talked all the time about making a better life. "You're a worker," Babão would say. "Man, you're a worker."

Vilson would take on anything to make a wage. Babão stuck to collecting his cans and bottles and cashing them in for recycling, while he dreamed up bigger ideas. They thanked God for the good days and got through the bad, always scraping the pennies together. And it was never enough. Babão could never quite break with his need for crack.

"Quit bitching and nagging at me. I'll get a wife if I want that," he would say. "I work long hours, man, I only do a little bit to kick me on."

Always a little bit.

Their shack was amongst a collection that was the lowest of the low. The irony that they were perched at the very top of the favela with the greatest views of the city was not lost on them.

Vilson flopped inside, not even making the pile of old sacks they used for bedding. They were beyond the reach of electricity up here, a makeshift paraffin burner their only source of light. There were a couple of ruined pans and a tin of cooking oil in one corner. Alongside them was a plastic washbowl that contained a thick tablet of soap. The door was a scuffed plywood board that was pulled across the entrance.

Vilson knew the cops wouldn't be following but he was still too scared to light the place. He sat on the dirt floor in the darkness, breathing in the rank air as the sweat ran from him.

An hour later he noticed his heart was no longer pounding and the roar of blood in his ears had faded. The sweat had dried to an uncomfortable stickiness on his skin. His anxiety for Babão was a hot stone in his belly and the words of his regular prayers kept darting into the dark corners, hiding from him.

When exhaustion finally overcame him, he slept fitfully in the couple of hours before dawn.

On waking, he shuffled to the door, trying to stretch the stiffness from his joints, peeking out into the half-light. This was the safest time of day, there was hardly anyone about. And there was still no ...ão.

Vilson lit the paraffin burner and stared into its ... tried to still his mind, to get a clean grip on faith, praying ... nt he could remember. But something cold kept snaking in ... ould they even hear his prayers after what had happened ... on Copacabana? Hugging his knees, the tears came silently in the ...ering gloom. *Que coisa* – What a thing.

The knock on the door made him jump. His heart ... – he was back. Another knock – a playful rat-tat-tat. Babão ... insist a joke even after a night like that. That was Babão. Vilson ... silently to the entrance and hauled open the makeshift door ... th the joke, a big grin on his face, ready to hug his friend ... had heard, and they had answered. *Graças a Deus.*

Terror slid through him. He tried to hold his grin, but his facial muscles betrayed him, twisting it into a withered grimace.

In front of him stood the boss of *As Formigas Vermelhas* – The Red Ants – the drug gang that ran the favela. Anjo was propping himself against the door frame with a sinewy forearm, a gun held casually in his hand, a laconic smile belying the joy at seeing Vilson. His black eyes glittered. Vilson knew that fear was the reaction that Anjo most prized. Fear was respect.

Vilson had known Anjo before he was in a gang, before he had murdered his way to the top spot. He wasn't sure if Anjo had grown paler over the years, making the contrast with his eyes more stark, or whether he had just become more terrifying. Anjo's features were almost sleek, small ears flat to his skull, but there was a tautness, a simple cruelty fixed in his expression, like that of a young boy bent on doing nasty things to small creatures. Behind Anjo was Franjinha, his second in command. A vacant, unreadable face topped with lank hair.

"Hey, *Canela*," Anjo said affably. "That dopey kid tells me you don't have my money."

Anjo was not quite out of his teens, just a year or less older than Vilson. *Canela*, the skinny bit of the ankle – Anjo had called him that since they were kids. Vilson hated it.

"I've got some," Vilson said, struggling to keep his voice even. He pulled out the money they'd taken from the *gringo*. He'd counted it several times and knew it was short.

Anjo passed the money over his shoulder to Franjinha, keeping his smile on Vilson. Skewered by the intense gaze, Vilson braced himself, shoulders hunched, eyes darting about.

THE BURNING HILL

Franjinha thumbed through the notes carelessly. "Fifty *Reais* light." The shortfall was less, but Vilson dared not protest.

"Where's Babão?" Anjo enquired, tilting his head to look inside.

"He's just— He'll be back soon."

"Not trying to run out on me, I hope?"

"No, no way, he knows better than that."

"You know, I was up all night worrying about you." Anjo was joking but there was no smile. "I've had no sleep, and I climb all the way up the hill to your shithouse shack and he's not here. And then you tell me you don't have all my money. It's a lack of respect."

"We'll get the money, I promise. If you can just give us until the end of the month."

"Listen, I'll do you a favour for old times' sake. You've got until the end of next week to get busy and find the rest." Anjo shifted himself off the doorframe. "Plus, let's say," he continued, looking over his shoulder, "what, fifty percent interest?"

Franjinha nodded impassively.

"And tell Babão it's no use trying to hide from me," Anjo said. "There's nowhere I won't find him."

He lifted his handgun and pressed it lightly to Vilson's forehead, a ring of cool metal against his skin.

Anjo made a show as he cocked the hammer, savouring the click-clack of the metal ratchet. "*Entendeu?*" Understood?

Vilson acknowledged him with the slightest of nods and bug-eyed terror, "*Entendi.*"

Chapter 4

Marinho

Early that same morning, the pair in the upstairs apartment woke Marinho thirty minutes after he had finally managed to get to sleep. He could hear muffled shouting as they thumped around on the thick floorboards of the old building. It was daylight but it was too early for this. He reached for his handgun lying on the bedside table and wearily knocked the butt on the metal downpipe between the bedside table and bed. The pipe ran through all three storeys and everyone would hear the hollow bang. It went silent for a moment upstairs and then there was more shouting. He couldn't tell if they were shouting at him or at each other or both. He wasn't getting back to sleep now. He should get up and get out for his fifteen-kilometre run, and later in the morning he was due in the gym. A good training partner was lined up for a sparring and groundwork session before his shift later in the day. He was disciplined with his training but he really didn't feel up for it today. His arms, his legs, everything felt heavy.

His apartment was in the Jardim Botânico district of the city, although not in the good part. It was tiny, the bedroom barely accommodated a small double bed. He was the only one sleeping in it. It had been that way for too long – the unsociable hours of his job and the fight training that he stuffed in around it kept it that way. He had to get where he needed to get to before he could think about that kind of stuff. Marinho wasn't born-and-bred Carioca, he was from the state in the very south of the country and hadn't lost the accent. He had come to Rio for the opportunities. *A cidade maravilhosa* – the wonderful city – was glad that he had insisted that his parents and younger sister didn't follow him. He was as vague about his family with his colleagues as he could get away with.

Kicking the sheet off, he got out of bed and went to the pokey bathroom. There was a bucket of discoloured water sitting in the tiled shower cubicle. Pulling his uniform shirt from the bucket, he held it out for inspection as the water cascaded from it. Some of the blood had lifted out but he was going to have to scrub hard to get rid of all the stains. Marinho was *cabo* – corporal – Marinho Palmano. Wiry and agile, he had the poise of an athlete. He had a fighter's nose, thickened at the bridge, and yet his eyes, smudged with scar tissue, had a tranquil quality. It was adrenaline that had kept him from sleep almost until morning. Adrenaline and the images from the previous night that he could not shake.

The reel started running in his head again: as Vilson was making his escape from Copacabana with Marinho's lumbering captain firing shots after him, Marinho was chasing down Babão. He was the only one of the three cops armed with an FN carbine, its dated, slender build lacking the snap of modern assault rifles, but it was accurate enough. He had squeezed off one round as he exited the truck and then made a quick decision, lifting the barrel.

He watched Babão plunge across the lanes of traffic, only just skipping clear of a collision of two cars that would have crushed his legs. Making the central reservation, Babão cut back past the patrol truck. He crabbed along behind the protective line of cars before straightening and running onto the opposite carriageway. Marinho could see him again. Babão glanced over his shoulder now that Marinho wasn't firing on him. He ran blindly into an oncoming taxi that had just turned onto the main drag from a side road.

The taxi braked and swerved but the wing mirror and windscreen pillar clipped Babão, spinning him away and dumping him on the asphalt of the middle lane. The yellow taxi didn't hang around.

Babão was back up on his feet in an instant. Marinho could see the kid was running on instinct, staying in the lane for a few metres before his wits kicked back in, then veering toward the pavement and the sanctuary of the side street ahead.

All the while, Marinho was moving. Picking his way through the chaos of the first carriageway, loping along the central reservation, sticking close to cover. He dropped to one knee beside a thin tree, leaning against it to steady himself. He hadn't put himself in a foot race – heavy, ragged breathing would disrupt his rhythm. He had just wanted to get to a clear line of fire.

He drew the butt of the rifle into his shoulder, hooked his left elbow through the shoulder strap and pulled tight to keep the weapon steady. Lifting the barrel above Babão's head, he took two slow, calm breaths. He let the barrel feather down until he was sighted on the centre of Babão's back, over a hundred metres away and stretching rapidly.

Marinho's mind emptied of everything beyond his connection with his rifle, its bullets and their target. He squeezed off a round. He saw it snag Babão's tee shirt at the shoulder. He didn't see the small plug of flesh and bone fragment twisting away in a puff of pink spray.

Babão was again taken off his feet in a grotesque pirouette. Again, he managed to pick himself up, his will quicker than his body this time. He was facing Marinho for an instant as he rose and staggered back, trying to fix his balance. The second bullet hit him in the gut. He folded, falling to the pavement, five metres short of the side street. Agony stiffened and curled his limbs.

He was on his side, keeping off his shattered left shoulder, when Marinho got to him, rifle still locked in, head cocked into the sight. Marinho shifted his grip to pat him down one-handed, the barrel propped in Babão's back.

The kid was clean and Marinho rested the rifle in the crook of his elbow to take a closer look at the wounds. It was only then that the kid seemed to become aware of his presence, eyes wide, pain searing his body. He stared up at Marinho in silence. Fear in his face.

Marinho's captain, Nogueira, arrived and immediately doubled over, chest heaving. Nogueira was powerfully built, with a gut that had been testing the lower buttons of his shirt long before he had hit middle age. Sweat was beading up on his balding pate and soaking into his shirt. He swore through snatched breaths.

Marinho had heard Nogueira's shots, counting at least seven. "Did you hit the other one?" he asked.

"Not sure." Nogueira looked up. "This one still kicking, uh? Why haven't you got the cuffs on him?"

Arguing that the kid was no longer a danger to anyone and in no condition for cuffing would do neither him nor the kid any good. Marinho complied, Babão screaming as his wrists were pulled together behind his back.

"Your friend ran out on you," Nogueira said flatly. "He's probably back up the hill already, dug into whatever hole in the dirt you two crawled from."

The patrol truck, lights on and honking plaintively, barged slowly through the clogged lanes of the opposite carriageway, bumped over the central reservation and rolled the wrong way up the carriageway to them.

The driver, Branca, ambled over from the truck. "Chief, heard on the radio that some *gringo's* been shot on the beach."

"Dead?"

"Still alive when the ambulance got to him, but they blew his face off, so not for much longer, I guess. Bet your friend there could tell us all about it."

"Well, let's take a little trip and find out."

Babão's eyes rolled in fear. "No, not that. Put me in the ambulance,

I'm begging. Take me to hospital."

"Hospital, huh?" Nogueira said. "And who's go... you up?"

Babão's eyes drifted and then locked on Marinho... them kill me, man, please don't let them kill me."

"Take it easy, no one's going to kill you," Marinho... ...ldn't swear to it to the kid though. He noticed a fleck of ... kid's lower lip as he lay there on the Copacabana pavement ... the painful breaths rattled in and out.

"Open the tailgate," Nogueira commanded Mar... ...ed to Branca, dipping his head toward the truck.

Branca nodded and tried to haul Babão to his f... ...tting blood on his uniform. Babão screamed and c... ...thing giving inside, more blood gouting from his stom... ...king his shirt. Branca cursed and kicked at him.

"What are you doing?" It was a shout of alarm, t... ...ng in surprise, a young woman running from a loose gro... who were keeping their distance.

"What is he to you?" Nogueira squared up.

She took a breath, composing herself. "I'm a la... ...eeds an ambulance."

Marinho was on the back foot, as was Branca, ...was unfazed. "He's a murderer. The ambulance people a... ...n the beach right now, picking up the brains of the *gring*... ...don't worry, we'll get him to hospital."

"Was he even armed? Did you shoot an unarm...

"He and his gangster friend shot at me and m... ...ullets flying all over the place. Do you get that? Putting ... the public in danger. People like you."

"Where is his gun?"

"I think you need to be careful."

"I'll take all your numbers right now – this is n... ...eyes were ablaze, but Marinho could see that she was w... ...e to the danger in Nogueira's stony face.

Nogueira made the slightest of movements to... ...h to show intent. "You've said your piece, you can go ... tell your rich friends how you stuck it to the underpaid c... you safe. Go on, we'll clear up the mess here. Go on. ...

His eyes still fixed on hers, he issued an order, ... out with a slow, deliberate calm. "Get him in the back."

He had called her. There was no bluster, and M... ...oped

that she could see that this was not a man to back down. She stood her ground, chin set, but she couldn't hide the first tremors of suppressed anger and frustration. And fear.

She might not like it but it was better for her this way, Marinho thought, shouldering his rifle. He got Babão up again, sticky blood daubing his hands and uniform. Branca grabbed his legs and they heaved him into the back of the truck. Babão moaned before passing out on the scratched metal floor. Marinho climbed in to take one of the fold-down seats lining either side.

"Let's go – I'll ride in the back with our friend," Nogueira said to Branca, his eyes never leaving the young woman. "Goodnight," he said courteously, his face ghoulish in the milky glow of the street lights.

Marinho was concentrating, trying to run through the full reel from the night. If he went through every part in turn, he felt he might be able to reassure himself that there was nothing else he could have done, that there was only one way the thing was ever likely to go. But his mind kept cutting to the worst parts and looping them over and over. He needed a distraction. Wringing out his sopping, stained shirt, he stepped from the shower. There was a stiff wooden brush under the kitchen sink and a big bar of laundry soap. Laying the shirt out on the stone drainer, he rubbed the soap bar into the stains, and then scrubbed. It was how his mother had washed the family's clothes in their outside sink all his life. His parents still didn't have a washing machine and neither did Marinho. If he didn't get the stains out of the shirt, he would have to buy another out of his own pocket.

Chapter 5

Jake

Jake awoke two evenings later with the nasty sensation of having overslept or of arriving at the end of the line. Some bleak, abandoned place. His eyes felt as if they had been grilled and then welded shut. There was a chemical taste in his mouth, like insect spray.

He could only get his eyes open as far as slits. It was a white room. The light burned his eyes but he could see enough to know he was in hospital. Dread turned through him, and confusion, and he had to crunch his mind through the gears before he was clear. He wasn't in *that* hospital. That had been a bad place. He had difficulty dragging himself away from the memory.

Terror jabbed him. The beach. The gun. Then he remembered the ambulance. This must be the place after that. It seemed like he had made it.

He was thirsty, his mouth dry and furred. Dabbing with the tip of his tongue, he explored the injured side of his mouth, finding smooth holes in his upper jaw — the spongy sockets of missing teeth. He could feel the notches and prickly stubs of fine stitches everywhere. A deep channel cut cleanly through his upper jaw, the path of the bullet, he guessed. It was, as was the smooth network of ridges inside his cheek. The kid had shot through the side of his face. He had kind of missed.

His eyes were beginning to function properly. Turning his head for a look around sent a bolt of agony through the top of his skull to the base of his neck. And nausea spat up from his stomach. He brought his head back in painful increments and stuck to a survey of the room within the range of his swivelling eyes.

"*Acordou.*" The voice was deep, a man's, beyond Jake's vision. He couldn't remember what the word meant. Maybe he'd never heard it before.

Light, squeaky rubber soles on the floor. A female nurse appeared above him. She spoke in a high voice, too quickly.

He tried to line up some words in Portuguese, but nothing would come. He was struggling to remember anything. He started to panic. "Am I okay?" he asked in English.

His voice was distant and unfamiliar. There was pain where

previously there had been a dull ache around his jaw. And it felt like he was speaking with a mouthful of cotton wool laced with needles.

He could see out of both eyes and he was breathing. He was grateful for that. But what he really wanted to know was what was left of his face.

She spoke again.

He was sluggish from the sedatives, a freight-train headache compounding his inability to make any sense of her words. He caught the word *cabeça* – head. She said it a couple more times. Maybe the bullet hadn't exited cleanly? Maybe it had ricocheted off bone, lodging somewhere deep in his head? He felt around his face and head. It was a mass of bandage. Why had they bandaged his whole head?

She told him off, trying to pull his hand away.

"Tell me what's wrong," he said in English, the pain making him wince.

He heard the man's voice again. His face appeared. Salt-and-pepper hair, a dog collar and black shirt.

Jake lost it, oblivious to the pain now. He wasn't going to lie there while some priest gave him the last rites. He had seen priests standing over beds before. He wasn't going to let it happen to him. He wasn't going anywhere until someone told him what had happened.

He tried to push himself up with his arms. He could feel the IV tubes pulling at his skin.

The nurse gave an instruction.

The priest grabbed Jake's arms and held them down. He was too weak to resist. He felt the prick of a needle.

"No," he was trying to shout but only managed a weak croak, "don't you put me out."

He was already sinking through the bottom of the mattress. He couldn't fight the darkness as it closed over him.

It was angry voices that started to shift the blank empty darkness. Recriminations. And with them came the colours. The flashes and psychedelic whirls that were woven into nearly every dream. Numbing terror. It clung to Jake, morphing into cold dread as he came up through a fog of sedation into the white room.

It took him a moment to again confirm that this wasn't the other white room. The other hospital. The life they had forced him to leave behind. Fury and shame swarmed his insides.

At least he was still alive. He was a survivor. He had learned that

THE BURNING HILL

much about himself. He moved his head gingerly to look around. There was pain but no bolt of agony this time. And the chair by his bed was empty. No priest. Maybe he was out of the woods.

He realised that the angry voices from his dreams hadn't stopped. There was an argument going on outside the door.

It burst open and a young woman entered, a classic Brazilian blend of smooth brown skin and blue–green eyes. She looked like she had stepped out of the Brazil of his imagination, even though the curls of her long, dark hair were tied back in a severe, not-so-Brazilian manner.

She was followed by a nurse. "You cannot come in here."

"You can't stop me," the young woman said evenly.

"Do you know this woman?" the exasperated nurse asked Jake.

"Of course he does." The young woman spoke in English, with an American lilt. "I was with him the night he was shot, wasn't I, Joaquim?" She nodded at him, encouraging.

Dim places within his memory began to flicker unpleasantly, a vague recollection of something ending badly in a bar. But he would never have introduced himself as Joaquim. He was wary; she might be a journalist.

"We met that night?" he asked.

"He doesn't know you," the nurse cut in. "You're taking advantage. You must leave now."

"I'm not leaving."

"Then I'm getting a doctor and he will make trouble for you."

The nurse left and the young woman pushed the door shut.

"My name is Eliane, I'm a lawyer. I'm sorry for coming to see you like this, but I was there on the beach. I need to piece together that night, to build a case against the police – have they been to see you?"

"I haven't spoken to anyone."

"You mean to anyone official?"

"I mean I haven't spoken to anyone."

"But your family – they know you're here, right?"

"No."

"Maybe I could contact them for you?"

"I have no family."

She tried to hide her surprise. "Then, is there someone else I could contact for you?"

"There's no one." It took him a moment to realise that he had said it in Portuguese. The words were coming back to him.

She seemed unsure where to go next. Uncomfortable. "I don't believe the boy they took was the one who shot you," she said, switching to Portuguese. "I saw him, he was·········· you remember?"

The pain was a hot wire threading around his ········· you talking about? Who took who?"

"Have you been told anything?"

"All I know is I was shot. I don't even know h········ been here."

"Three days. But I thought Padre Francisco ca·············· you."

"The priest?"

"Yes. He knows the boys who robbed you."

"Oh. I thought he was here for – for something············id.

"The police shot one of the boys and took him············ trying to find out what happened to him. The other esca·········

"No one calls me that any more." It was the on········· ame to him. "It's Jake."

The door opened and a young doctor swept in··········· in tow. "You have no right to be here," he said to E······

"Why haven't you told him what's happened to···········ame back, without missing a beat.

"He has been sedated. We were waiting until h············fully understand."

"So tell me now," Jake said.

The doctor cleared his throat self-consciously an················for a few moments. "The injuries from the guns···········ostly superficial," he said in English, carefully making his············ the words. "Although I must say that you will certainly··········ow."

Jake hoped that he had just overcooked his··········pick. 'Disfigured' didn't sit well.

The doctor ploughed on. "Most of the bullet exi·········· were some small pieces that were left behind in your jaw········ one. They are not a problem right now so we left them h·········eded to deal with something more dangerous. We made············ brain as a normal procedure and there was no injury from th········but I must tell you that we did find an aneurysm. Appro··········" He touched a forefinger to a point just above and behi···········was almost as large as…" He searched for a word, gave············ated the size of a cherry stone with his thumb and forefing····

"We operated. The aneurysm was very bad, very b···········wing for a long time in your head. You will live now, I th············w, if that boy had not shot you and we had not made············ you would die sometime. You are walking along an············day suddenly," he popped his lips, "it burst like a balloon, and *fuhm*." He tipped his forearm from upright to horizontal. "Quick, like this. Dead."

The doctor looked at Jake, seeming to have momentarily forgotten Eliane. She was also looking at Jake. Expectantly.

He didn't know what he was supposed to say. The doctor had spoken in English but Jake was still struggling to process the information. He wanted them to go away, to leave him alone.

"That boy saved your life," Eliane prompted. "Do you understand?"

"He tried to kill me," Jake said.

"No, Jake, this boy went to the priest afterwards – it was an accident, he didn't mean to pull the trigger."

"You shove a loaded gun in someone's face, there's a good chance it's going to go off," Jake said. Take responsibility for what you do. He believed in that. It was carved into him from bitter experience.

"But you will live because of this," Eliane said. "These things happen for a reason, Jake. Maybe you can help these boys in return."

"I don't owe anything to anyone."

"The shooting was in the news and people are interested. They think it's like a miracle. The media want to talk to you."

"No way." He had gone to the media once before. It wasn't a beast you could tame.

"But the publicity would put pressure on the police," she said.

"No," he said, anger flaring. It was always tucked in there, ready. Her eyes dropped.

The doctor stepped in front of Eliane. "Okay, no more. He should not be made upset like this. You must leave right now."

"Okay, but if you remember something – anything – it might make all the difference," Eliane said to Jake, darting around the doctor and placing a business card on the bedside table before allowing the doctor to usher her out.

"My number is on the card," she said. "Just in case."

Chapter 6

Vilson

Blazing hot day had followed that night on the beach, winter giving way to summer. Everything had changed; it was all connected, Vilson knew it.

The hard barely was beginning to soften as he walked into the late-afternoon shadows cast by the Candelária church. That day, many years ago, was when everything had changed, a tear in the fabric of the world. When the off-duty cops had killed Gabriel.

He shivered and quickened his step. The spirits of his long-dead brother and the other children drifted unhappily around this place.

Stepping into the cool air of the cavernous interior with its soaring arches, superstitious awe pressed down on him, every molecule of the massive interior laden with it. He felt almost as tiny and insignificant as he had on his first visit.

At the font he made a shallow bow and dabbed his fingers in the holy water, crossing himself and touching a finger to his lips, as his mother had taught him.

He saw Padre Francisco beneath the statue of *Nossa Senhora* – Our Lady – clearing away dead candles to make room for more amongst the banks of flickering votive flames.

Padre Francisco finished his task before straightening at Vilson's approach. Unhurried. In all these years Padre Francisco hadn't changed. Maybe there was more grey than black in his hair now but, as far as Vilson could remember, he had always had the grey. Strong features and good skin made his age difficult to place.

"Peace be with you, Vilson."

"And with you, Father." The words came out of Vilson automatically, but he left the pleasantries at that. "Is there any news?"

"The English man will be okay. He knows it was an accident."

Vilson had never liked handling the decrepit old pistol. Babão always said it was as likely to blow up in your face as hit a target.

Padre Francisco continued. "The lawyer is trying to get him onside to help your case."

Vilson wasn't holding out any hope on that score, he had no faith in the system. It was made for people like him. "What about Babão?"

"Vilson, I am praying for him, but you know that the police took him away."

They both knew what that usually meant.

"I know he is alive, I feel it," Vilson said defiantly. He had repeated this to himself a hundred times or more. He had to make it true. "Can I see my mother's letters?" he blurted. He needed some comfort. Something to hold onto.

"Of course."

Padre Francisco's cramped little office was barely more than an alcove, a rickety desk and a metal filing cabinet, the beige and brown paint chipped. Padre Francisco removed his vestments. The sacred words that went with the ritual had a potency that Vilson was unable to resist. An instant spiritual high, unbinding a little of the tension.

Now in his plain black shirt and dog collar, Padre Francisco rattled open a drawer of the filing cabinet and pushed back the hanging files to retrieve the bundle for Vilson.

These were the letters that Vilson's mother had written to him every few months since he was a boy. Since he had last seen her. There were runs of stationery in differing colours and sizes, shades of washed-out pastels. The letters were the only record he had of his mother, and the chunks of colour also reminded him of significant periods and events in his own life. The letters were everything to him.

He had studied every cheap biro stroke, the welts of uneven ink, the folds and creases and the marks and stains on the paper. Unable to read the words, he understood the patterns, the regularity of the shapes, and they formed a sort of language for him, one that reflected the readings that Padre Francisco gave him.

Vilson picked out his favourite and unfolded it carefully for Padre Francisco. With so many hours in the pulpit, Padre Francisco's reading voice had a particular quality, practised and yet somehow natural, the deep tone rising and falling, emphasising in all the right places. As soon as he started reading the letter, his voice flipped a switch in Vilson's brain. It took him straight there, brought out all the images in vivid detail. It gave him a good feeling that he rarely felt in the outside world. This letter described the humble, broken-down *rocinha*, the small farm that his mother had found and hoped to turn into a home for Vilson and his brother, Gabriel. They would leave behind the grinding fear of their lives in the city, maybe farm some cattle and a few pigs, grow some maize, maybe even a little coffee or sugar cane. But even broken-down farms cost and Vilson's mother would dedicate herself to working jobs in the nearby town to make the rental deposit on the patch of land and its abandoned farmhouse.

THE BURNING HILL

The letter was one of the oldest, written not long after Vilson's mother had left them on the steps of the church.

Padre Francisco reached the end of the letter and folded it. Even with Padre Francisco falling silent, Vilson was still far away on the farm that inhabited so much of his imagination, a place he could almost smell, working alongside his mother under a hot sun with a sweet stream for them to dip in and cool their skin and quench their thirst. He withdrew slowly and reluctantly from his place. "Father, it's not just the police who are after me."

He couldn't meet Padre Francisco's eyes as he told him about Anjo and his gang. "I must have somewhere safe," he pleaded. "Can I stay with you?"

Padre Francisco had known Anjo from childhood. Anjo was vicious and unbalanced even then.

"We'll have to find a different way," Padre Francisco said, shaking his head. "I'm so sorry, but that boy is too dangerous. The church takes care of people in the favela, vulnerable people, but we can only do that with his permission. You know what he is capable of if he discovered we were hiding you. But don't worry, we will think of something."

Vilson would have begged if he had thought that it would move Padre Francisco, but his head dropped, beaten. And then something occurred to him and he grabbed at it. "Maybe this is a sign, Father?"

"Sign?"

"Yes. Telling me that this is the time to go to my mother."

"Vilson, you know what the letters say. She is not ready yet."

"But it has been so long. When will she be ready?"

"I don't have an answer for that, I'm sorry."

The regularity of the letters had dwindled in the last few years. Vilson was starkly aware of that. The hope had leached out of them, until they were little more than logs of the hardships that his mother was enduring, instructing Vilson to stay put, to make a life for himself in the city. The farm was a dream preserved only in his imagination.

"I will go to her. I have nowhere else," Vilson said.

"But we only have a postmark on the letters. We have no idea exactly where she is."

Now it was Padre Francisco's eyes shifting away, unable to meet his. Vilson didn't understand. "The postmark is from the town though, isn't it? I could find her if I went there."

"Vilson, I think it is a big town. I can make enquiries, but you must wait."

"I cannot wait." It came out in a strangled shout, his desperation tempered by the surroundings and company. "They will see if I wait."

Chapter 7

Jake

He was sitting propped up in bed. He could do that for a few hours at a time. He had even managed to totter down the hospital corridor to the toilet, wheeling the mindless little trolley that held his saline and morphine drips.

When he had looked in the bathroom mirror the first time he had almost laughed. He'd have won a Halloween fancy-dress competition hands down. They had only shaved one side of his head for the operation and, with most of the bandaging now removed, he was stuck with a half-baked Mohican. They had pulled a lot of stitches out of his face but, inside and out, it was a puffy mess of livid scar tissue, the remaining dressings and surgical tape stiff with dark scabs of dried blood.

He was glad when some of the long, empty thinking hours were sponged away with the arrival of a TV on a tall, ungainly stand. Cutting a swathe through prime-time Brazilian TV, *novelas* – the soaps – dominated his viewing.

He was hooked on the self-aware humour of the frothier *novelas*. His favourite was a kind of arch spin on Tarzan, with the primped faux-feral blond hero emerging from the comfort of the jungle into the craziness of the modern world. It was called *Uga Uga*. He still couldn't quite believe it when the title came up on the screen. The characters often spoke too fast and the more opaque idioms left him baffled, but the nurses were able to fill him in. They were also fans.

The evening news had just ended and *Uga Uga* was next up. The previous evening's episode had finished with the younger of a pair of hairy, and resolutely shirtless, brothers getting into yet another potentially fatal fight. Before he had a chance to discover the outcome, the police had arrived.

"Good afternoon, *Senhor* Jake," Captain Nogueira greeted him.

He and his *Cabo* Palmano had visited a few days earlier when the morphine was turning the inside of Jake's head to glue and scrambling his perception of time. He could scarcely recall anything from the meeting, other than feeling wary.

The big captain might be all expansive bonhomie and lame jokes, but he was chest-thumping alpha all the way through, rank or no rank.

Jake couldn't quite figure the *cabo* – the corporal – though. He could see the marks of a fighter on his face, but there was plenty going on behind his eyes. Jake decided to pay more attention to him than to his captain.

Nogueira was into his stride, lobbing plenty of *gringos* and *caipirinhas* into his spiel about why silly drunken *gringos* shouldn't wander onto the beach late at night.

"What happened to the boy you shot that night?" Jake cut in.

"You don't need to worry. You are protected by us. And we will get the other boy, you have my word on that."

It occurred to Jake that the captain had a habit of answering a different question or just starting a new conversation in response to anything that didn't suit him.

Jake didn't owe either of the kids. He owed dumb luck. But in the hours spent staring at the ceiling and at the TV, the pain swirling with narcotic relief, all kinds of things kept intruding. The expectant face of the lawyer. Other faces from before. Bodies. Broken and bloodied and burned out in the desert. Accusations. The images had followed him to Brazil, and with them came the swarm of shame and anger.

"But why shoot him if he wasn't armed?" Jake persisted. He had time on his hands, and a streak of belligerence.

"He was armed," Nogueira said. "Both of them were."

"No, that's not right—" Jake checked himself. He wanted to reveal only what was necessary. "I'm sure only one of them had a gun."

Jake saw something shift in the *cabo* then, barely noticeable. His expression was set, but maybe it was something in his eyes or in his body language. He didn't know exactly what it meant, but it meant something wasn't right.

"*Senhor* Jake," Nogueira said, trying to sound bored, "it's all in your statement."

"I gave a statement?"

"Of course. The last time we came. We typed it up and brought it for your signature," Nogueira said, presenting it with a flourish.

Jake had trouble focusing on the print and read through it twice to make sure he hadn't missed anything. "There's hardly any detail in this and I never said they were both armed. This isn't right."

"*Senhor*, when we came to see you last time it was just after it happened. You were tired but your recollection of the events was very clear. After that, when you start reading stuff and seeing stuff on TV, and talking to other people, the events can become confused. And when you take morphine over a number of days it can make the unreal seem real. I have seen this many times."

Jake hadn't known which way was up at that last visit. He had been incapable of giving a clear account in English, let alone Portuguese. Afterwards, to get a foothold in the narcotic fug, he had started measuring his recovery in units of pain, holding off for as long as possible before topping himself with a bonus squirt of the morphine pump. He soon lost interest but the eights and nines on his pain Richter scale were registering less frequently. There were fewer squirts of morphine, and his mind was more lucid.

"Only one of them had a gun," Jake repeated slowly.

"I can assure you when we intercepted them they were both armed. My officers and I were involved in a firefight with them. We saw it first-hand."

Jake had to keep control of the anger. He had to remember more.

"*Senhor* Jake, excuse me, but we are short of time," Nogueira said. "We need your signature."

A crisp image jumped from the jumble of murky figures and flashes and psychedelic swirls that had churned through Jake's head countless times. "The kid who shot me – he was wearing a Flamengo shirt," he said. The dark red and black stripes of the Rio football team on the skinny frame. "Was he the one you caught wearing a Flamengo shirt?"

Nogueira looked like he'd just got a parking ticket. "You realise these kids tried to murder you, don't you? What does it matter about a football shirt?"

"I want to have my statement to include it. And I want it to say that only one of them pulled a gun."

"We don't need to do that," Nogueira growled. Catching himself, he redialled joviality mode. "You've had a big knock on the head and you have all those drugs washing around inside you. You need to rest. Let us deal with this stuff."

"I'm not signing that statement," Jake said. "It's your version of events, not mine."

The stick-on charm evaporated, Nogueira's face turning to stone. His eyes narrowed, flashing with anger. "We're not just a bunch of dumb hick cops, *Senhor*. I did my homework. I looked you up, found out that you made a bit of a name for yourself back in England."

Jake shifted uncomfortably in the bed.

Nogueira had a nasty smile. "That touched a chord, uh? You've been in this territory before and it didn't work out too well then, did it? You learned nothing from that, no?"

"You're going to have to try harder than that."

Nogueira's smile disappeared and Marinho put a cautioning hand on his arm. Nogueira shrugged it off and lunged forward to stand over Jake. He thrust an index finger close to Jake's face. "This is not England, remember that. We play by different rules. No one has your back here and bad things can happen to *gringos* who step in the wrong places."

Marinho put a hand on his shoulder. Nogueira took a breath. Recovering a little composure, he allowed himself to be drawn away. Marinho guided him to the door.

Nogueira turned back on Jake at the threshold. He kept his voice calm. "You're in the wrong place, *gringo*."

The anger and adrenaline buzzed on after the cops left. Jake felt alive, the pain in his face forgotten. Sure, his recollection could not be litmus-tested, but there were one or two certainties, even if the truth was a drifting cloud, changing shape as it went. And it felt like there was something hidden behind it. Something he needed to know. Maybe the favela kid was the only one who really knew what had happened. Maybe he knew who owed, and who was owed.

Nogueira was right on one thing, though. Jake had been in this territory before. He had refused to put his name to someone else's version of events before and he wasn't about to roll over this time either. Screw the consequences.

No one was going to tell him what to do.

Chapter 8

Marinho

Marinho knocked on the door and entered on Padre Francisco's 'yes'. The priest was sitting at the desk in his tiny office, trying to rub the tiredness from his face with the palms of his hands. "Confession is done for today, son."

"I know, Father. I needed to see you face to face."

The priest looked at him more carefully. Marinho was in tee shirt and jeans, but he could see the priest clocking that he was a cop now. "Father, I believe you know those boys from the shooting on Copacabana?"

"I can't give anyone up to you."

"That's not why I came, Father. I was on the beach that night. I want to put something right but it's difficult with my boss."

"You took the first step, coming here."

"But my boss has a hold over me. I am tied to him."

"In what way?"

"He knows something that no one else can know." His eyes dropped and his head followed.

"You can lessen your burden with me," said Padre Francisco. "Sharing a secret reduces its power."

Marinho bit his lip and then nodded. "Maybe you are right, Father. Let me think about it. But I need to tell you about what happened to the boy." He gathered himself, setting his face, trying to push the emotions away. It was the first time he had spoken to anyone about what had happened, and it was harder than he had imagined. "It was terrible, Father. What passed after the shooting troubles me far more than what passed before." Hesitant at first, the images then began running in his head and it all came tumbling out as he described the events following Branca driving them away from Copacabana: Marinho was sitting on a fold-down seat on one side of the patrol truck, Nogueira on the other side. The truck bumped over a pothole and Babão's eyes fluttered open. His eyes were blank only for a moment before he looked up, first at Marinho and then across to Nogueira. Marinho saw the fear return to his face. It was still strong, even as his life was ebbing.

"That's right, friend, this is it," said Nogueira.

It seemed to Marinho that hopelessness then and his eyes started to close again. He was drifting a   med an open-handed blow at his face to snap him back,   truck rolled on its ruined suspension, throwing him off

"Slow it down, idiot," he barked at Branca. A   med across Babão's shorts, the urine sliding into the   lood that was filling the runnels in the metal floor. "   ugh gangster now, uh, piss-pants?"

He laid a foot on Babão's throat and gradually   ure. "You shouldn't have crawled out of your hiding   into my beautiful city tonight. And murdering a *gringo*   how bad that is for business? Which is your gang?"

"Boss," Marinho implored, laying a hand   arm. Nogueira swatted it away irritably and drew clo   bão's weak reply.

"I'm not with any gang, sir. I swear it."

"Is that so?"

Branca had the lights on and jinked through   early toppling Nogueira from his seat. He roared at him   wn.

"Let's make it simple for you then, uh? Which   m?" Nogueira asked, pressing hard on Babão's windpi   off for the answer.

Babão coughed and retched. "*Morro da Babilôn* "

"Just a regular kid from the favela. No gang, n "

"I swear it."

"Maybe I should call in back-up," said Nogueira.   ngry cops with grudges and big guns to drive into your F   t the place up a bit. Sweep the filth back up the hill, you

Nogueira shifted his weight back onto Babão's   bão writhed in his own bloody mess on the metal flo   ging and filled with terror.

"Boss, come on," Marinho said. Firm this tim   d a finger in warning, not even looking up from Babã

The kid's eyelids fluttered, a shudder running   Life slipped away and his last breath rattled free, his bod

Nogueira shook his head. When he finally lo   inho, he was stony-faced. Daring him to say something.   quiet.

Pulling up round the back of the station, Branca   back to open up. "What happened?" he said.

"Our suspect has suffocated," said Nogueira   g at Marinho. "I think you forgot to open a window,   u're going to have to take another little drive with him."

Marinho knew that this was Nogueira's way of getting the body out of his precinct. Dump it in someone else's territory. Let them deal with the paperwork headache.

"No, boss, please, I can't do that."

"Oh yes, you can, *cabo*, and you will."

Marinho was powerless. Nogueira either bent subordinates to his will or blackmailed them. With Marinho, he could use the latter tactic. And Marinho had heard about a cop before his time who had turned on Nogueira. He had ended up dead.

Chapter 9

Vilson

It was a boxy old television. Someone had left it overnight in the dumping ground at the bottom of the favela. What a find. It looked pristine amongst the rubble, tins, plastic and rubbish sacks. This early in the morning, kids hadn't even smashed in the screen yet.

Vilson's best screwdriver didn't fit the screws in the back. He hammered at the edge of the plastic with a piece of brick and levered it with the screwdriver. He managed to get his hands into the gap, tearing skin on the jagged broken plastic, and wrenched some more. A big flap of plastic snapped off. Now he could get at the copper wire wound around the tube.

He could sell it.

Selling the wire from fifty televisions still wouldn't get him the money he needed, but he didn't know what else to do. And it was better than squatting in the dust of his shack, knocking his head against the wall.

"What you got there, Canela?"

Four kids were lined along the shaded side of the dumping ground, none of them more than twelve.

"Don't call me that, you cheeky little bastard," said Vilson, stuffing the coil of wire into the pocket of his shorts.

"The boss is pissed with you," the kid said. "He's getting heat from the cops because of your stunt on the beach."

"Your boss? Don't make me laugh, you're not soldiers," Vilson said. This bunch just fed off scraps from Anjo. They added eyes and ears to his official lookouts and sentries.

More than a week had passed since the robbery, and cops had entered the bottom of the favela the previous day and kicked in a few doors. Anjo had put the hill in lockdown. He wouldn't do anything to Vilson until his deadline was up – that was one of the things he liked to make a show of, sticking to his word – but he didn't want Vilson disappearing.

"You owe him money," the kid said, "so hand over what you got there."

Vilson had to stand firm. He couldn't let this bunch push him around, that would be total humiliation. Scared of a bunch of kids.

41

The kid picked up a broken chunk of brick, his friends following suit. "I said hand it over."

Vilson wished he had escaped the favela when he had the chance. He told himself that he had hung on for Babão, hoping for the return of his friend. He should have set out to find his mother. But locked deep within him was the fear of pursuing a dream that was as remote as a fairy-tale castle.

He knew what shape the fear would take when Anjo came for him. Fear of the unknown was paralysing.

"You're testing my patience," the kid said, drawing his arm back, loading it to hurl his brick.

Vilson pulled the coil of wire from his pocket and tossed it over, his hands shaking with humiliation.

The kid relaxed the arm holding the brick. "Is that it?" he sneered. "A piece of dumb wire. If you're still empty-handed come Sunday night the boss is going to do you up on the Burning Hill, you know that, don't you?"

Vilson didn't answer.

The kid flicked his shoulder back and dummied a throw, laughing as Vilson shrank back.

"Hey, you boys, what's going on?" It was Padre Francisco, coming up the hill toward them.

"Just playing, Father," said the kid, moving away, his posse following.

"Vilson?" Padre Francisco asked.

Vilson nodded. "Sure, they're just fooling around, Father."

"You boys remember that I know your mothers," Padre Francisco said after the kids.

"I'll give her your best," the leader said quietly over his shoulder, the others giggling.

Padre Francisco spoke when they had gone. "A policeman came to see me today."

Vilson's eyes narrowed. "Don't ask me to turn myself in to those animals, I won't do it."

"It's not that, son, it was about Babão. I'm so sorry, it's bad news."

"No. He is alive. I feel it," said Vilson. "Thanks be to God." The words had become a constant prayer in the week since Babão had disappeared. Babão, his only friend. But his stomach churned. His body knew.

"Son, this young policeman was on the beach that night. He saw Babão die."

Vilson's breath caught in his throat. "No, it's not true. They do nothing but lie. How can you believe him?"

"He told me that he took no part in the killing and that he wants to help you. I believe him, Vilson. I looked into his heart."

"He tricked you – it's a trick – the cops have already been knocking. They just want to kill me too."

He caught himself saying it – 'kill me too'. Even as he tried to deny it he had acknowledged the truth about his friend.

The grief flooded his body but there were no tears. In his experience, crying in front of others only drew more cruelty.

There was a long silence before Padre Francisco spoke. "This tourist would have died if it wasn't for you – you know that. Vilson, something good came from this terrible thing. Perhaps this is the sign that you were looking for."

Vilson stiffened, something sharp cutting through his grief. "This thing in the *gringo's* head was destined to kill him, the bullet should have killed him. That was his fate. The *gringo* cheated death. Babão was taken in his place."

"No, my son, you're not making sense."

"Babão was not meant to die, it was the *gringo's* time. It's as plain as day."

"You're upset. This doesn't make sense."

Vilson took a step back from Padre Francisco, almost stumbling on the rubble. How could the priest not see it?

There was only one way back from all of this. One way to rebalance fate. To clear the path for him to find his way back to his mother.

The *gringo* had to die.

Chapter 10

Anjo

The slightest breeze came through the window to the young boss of *As Formigas Vermelhas*. It felt almost cool in the first light of the day. Anjo's house was larger than most in the favela, better finished than most, but the money was in the electrical gadgetry – a giant TV, the best sound system, the latest games consoles.

He was curled in a huge leather beanbag, his soldiers draped over sofas, lying on cushions on the floor, some on the hard tiles, sleeping the fitful sleep that follows a two-day cocaine binge.

Anjo – Angel. An ironic nickname picked up in childhood, his mother having cursed him with her dying breath as she gave birth to him. It was just a story, one that had grown from a cruel jibe in early childhood. But it had dug itself in and become reality for him.

An aunt had taken him in for a few years, but she was hardly ever there, always working her cleaning jobs for rich folks down in the city in return for stingy wages or the sack if their place wasn't left spotless. There were no older brothers or sisters to protect him whilst she worked. Bigger children had taunted and bullied him, and the overriding feeling he remembered from his early childhood was fear. He also remembered the day when he had changed everything. A couple of older boys started picking on him, he was maybe only seven years old at the time, and the other young kids he was playing with backed away and went silent. They didn't have the guts to stand with him. Anjo was frightened but the pinch of anger made him talk back at the older boys. They chased him through the alleyways of the favela, shouting and laughing, enjoying the sport. It didn't take them long before they had him cornered. Desperate, he unfolded the rusted little penknife that was his prized possession and waved it at them with all the threat he could muster. They taunted him. They didn't believe he would do anything. He remembered feeling terrified, paralysed, feeling that they were right. And then one of them tried to grab his arm. Anjo lashed out instinctively and opened the boy's face with the little blade. Blood poured down his face in a sheet from the long, deep wound across his cheek and nose. The cut boy and his friend panicked at the sight of so much blood.

The joy in that moment was every bit as intense as any fear Anjo had previously felt in his short life. He was able to just walk away, and those boys never came after him again. No one did. Over time, the boy with the cut face had grown to like his scar. It was a badge of honour, made him look like a tough guy, and he started to tell a different story about how he had got the scar. A few years later Anjo shot him. His first kill.

Anjo had grown up telling himself that his mother's curse was the blessing that had made him strong. He still told himself that. Sometimes he believed those words. Sometimes the fear of dying badly, dying in agony, dying alone was overwhelming. When he was unable to contain it, when it threatened to suck him into the abyss, he took cocaine. He was taking more and more these days. Only the powder though, he never did crack. That was for the customers, the addicts.

Even in the enveloping comfort of his beanbag, sleep still would not come. He looked down at his bony chest, his heart racing and stuttering in turn with frightening palpitations. He could see his heart pulsing beneath his sweating skin, rippling the thin material of his shirt. It felt like it was about to burst. He was desperate for the oblivion of sleep, resisting the urge to do more coke to rid himself of the crushing headache and the insistent whine in his ears, piqued by the hum of the large upright fan that shuddered and ticked as it made ungainly sweeps to and fro.

His body twitched and he noticed the weight of the gun in his hand. He almost broke into a smile, turning it over affectionately. Just a tool, easily replaced, but in his hand it was an extension of him, part of his identity. Most of his higher-ranking soldiers ran with Glocks; he went for the elegance of his Beretta.

He lifted it and squinted down the barrel as he swept it across the room, over his snoring and fidgety soldiers, keeping pace with the fan, amusing himself. He came to a juddering halt on Franjinha, his second in command.

He wondered.

They had come so far and now they had reached a crossroads. Anjo was ambitious. He needed to strike out, seize more territory, break the shackles of the cops. He paid the cops to leave him alone, but now they were trying to tell him how to run his own show. And they had raided the hill without his consent. That was a step too far. He was the law here. He would bring them a war if he had to.

And always he had Franjinha at his shoulder, the calm in a storm, always canny, weighing up the odds.

Franjinha snorted and rolled over on the thin sofa, burrowing his head in a cushion, an arm flopping to the floor and knocking over a beer bottle. The ring of glass on the tile floor disturbed the others for a few moments, before the broken rhythm of snoring struck up again.

Anjo's hand began to shake with the heaviness of the Beretta. He let it drop away from Franjinha. They had been through so much together.

And still he wondered.

Chapter 11

Jake

His place was just a block back from Ipanema Beach and a couple of hundred metres from the bar where Tom Jobin had watched a beautiful girl walk by and then written a song for her that became a worldwide hit.

Jake's apartment was on the ground floor of an old house making up two sides of a courtyard, with another house divided into apartments on the other side. The courtyard was paved with tiny grey and white cobbles arranged in an obscure pattern, and pointy enough to make walking over them in bare feet an ordeal. It was planted with stunted trees and vines and flowers, and closed off from the road by a tall gate with ugly spikes and sheets of welded-on metal painted prison grey. It felt isolated from the busy avenue that ran parallel to the beach; calm. The apartment was small and modestly furnished, with a few cockroaches for company and scrolled wrought-iron bars on the windows, which were pretty but had a purpose.

While trying to avoid looking too far into the future, Jake had at least decided that this little patch of the city was home. The beach was just a short stroll. There was a smoothie bar on the corner around the block where he got his granola with pulped açai fruit and guarana syrup in the morning – the breakfast of champions, according to the garrulous man behind the counter. Jake liked the smells in the little supermarket where he picked things to try out, not always sure what they were even after he'd eaten them.

He had always fantasised about escaping to Rio. Escaping. Like an old-school bank robber. He had never taken much interest in finding things to spend his money on and he'd banked a lot of his army salary. It had given him something to fall back on in Brazil.

The cab Jake had taken from the hospital dropped him outside his apartment and he scurried in. He was home. It felt safe back inside. But only inside. In the afternoon he had to force himself out into the harsh sunlight. He needed to snap the thick cord of choking dread. The vibrant city that had so beguiled him now seemed distorted and alien. It didn't look right, it didn't sound right.

The duty doctor had been furious when he had discharged himself. With good reason. The right side of his face was a lumpy mess, scored with purplish–red scars. He was off the morphine, and the painkillers he was popping were playing havoc with his emotions too and even minor physical exertion left him drained.

He bought a mango smoothie at his regular place and perched on one of the stools lining the front of the bar on the street corner, watching people walk by. People stared at him. They couldn't stop at the barber to get his head shaved on the other side. It was a had a proper Mohican now, close-cropped, although it wasn't a great improvement. He put his baseball cap back on gingerly.

He picked up his stride as he headed toward the beach, determined to shake off the timidity, trying to recalibrate.

A gaggle of young favela kids came around a corner, coming in his direction, and his chest ratcheted to a crushing tightness around his heart and lungs. Slewing away from them, his legs failed and he slumped to the pavement, craving maximum contact with the ground. It was the same sickly vertigo that had taken hold of him as he lay bleeding into the sand that night.

Anger was usually on hand to burn away the fear but he couldn't get the sparks to catch.

Light, running footsteps came up behind him.

"Hey, are you all right?"

It was the lawyer.

She was early.

"Uh, yeah," he said. "I'm fine. Just a dizzy spell. I'm getting up."

"I think you should have stayed in hospital."

"You're not the first to say that," he said with his narrow, lopsided half smile.

She helped him up and they crossed the road. The place where they were supposed to meet was on the distinctive Ipanema part of the paving at the edge of the beach.

The lawyer. Eliane. Was she part of the reason he was here? He took a moment to think. No. There was something about her that flagged a warning to him, but it was Nogueira and his brand of justice that had lit the touchpaper. Jake wasn't going to help put a line through a kid's life for the sake of neat paperwork.

At Eliane's insistence, he seated himself beneath a large beer umbrella with matching plastic table and chairs. The little kiosk alongside the seating area was done in the same yellow.

"What can I get you?" she asked.

A cascade of big green coconuts hung down the front of the kiosk. "One of those, I think."

The bartender retrieved two cold ones from a cool box. Hacking with a short, broad machete, he spun it expertly in his other hand between each cut until he had parted a lid. Eliane came to the table with a straw poking out of each.

Jake ate the fresh, cold jelly coating the inside of the lid before he drank the sweet liquid inside. "Man, they don't come like this in England," he said, enjoying the moment.

"You feel better?"

"Better."

Out on the sand there was a set of iron parallel bars and a high bar concreted into the beach. There were a handful of bare-chested guys working out on and around them. Most were preening as much as sweating, and the vainest of them had stopped altogether. Pulling off his shorts to reveal tight Speedos, he held his arms out and started turning slowly on the spot like a rotisserie chicken, trying to crisp his skin evenly.

But it was another guy who really stood out in the group. He was more dedicated, lean and strong, no pumped-up gym bunny. He was an athlete.

It was Marinho. Dips, chin-ups, hanging from the high bar and pulling up his knees to one side and then the other. Energy-sapping sprints in the soft sand.

Padre Francisco had fixed the meeting.

"You really think we can trust this guy?" Eliane asked.

"I honestly don't know. This priest thinks he's straight up."

"Has anything more come back to you from the night on the beach?" Eliane asked.

"Only enough to put my word against Nogueira's."

She rubbed at her temple. "They'd play on your injury – even if we could get him to court – and question the reliability of your memory."

"But he completely made up my statement."

She shrugged. "He'll wriggle out with lost in translation, lost paperwork, lost something."

"What about getting him on the lost body?"

"They can make that another paperwork error. It would make them look stupid, but that wouldn't bother them too much and it wouldn't count for much." She rubbed her temple some more and looked at him sideways. "The point is, Nogueira is covered because the city wants to keep a lid on shot tourists. The only way to make them squirm is through the media and you are the lead into that."

"I already said I can't do that, not even as a sideshow."

"But if the media lean hard enough on the police department, Nogueira's bosses might cut their losses and sell him out."

"Look, I've been there before. I know it will backfire, trust me."

"What happened?"

"Uh. Another time, maybe." He wasn't going to rake over that one. He looked over at Marinho. "What about him? He told the priest he saw what happened in the back of that police truck."

"We can't use him. If he is straight he'd be dead before anyone even thought about setting a trial date." She puffed out her cheeks and put her head in her hands.

"Are you sure you really want to do this?" he asked, managing to avoid making it sound like a challenge.

It seemed as though she had to wrestle with a decision before she looked at him again. "I live not far from here with my parents. It's a nice place. I've never lived anywhere else. Out in the world, I'm that regular middle-class young woman from a comfortable middle-class family, carving out a successful career. On the other side of the door to the apartment there's not so much certainty."

She looked like she couldn't quite get enough oxygen, that she couldn't quite fill her lungs. The brusque lawyer veneer was falling away in front of Jake's eyes, and it was clear that it wasn't an easy transformation for her to make. She indicated Marinho out on the beach. "You tell him nothing of this, okay?"

"Of course."

"Okay then," she said. She gulped in some air. "I still remember the day they brought my dad home from the hospital – I was just a little kid. He was in a bad way. He had been beaten and left for dead but I didn't know that, I was just told that he had had an accident at work. I think I knew even then that it wasn't true. When they settled him on the sofa, he asked me to draw the blinds because the light was too harsh. You know, it feels like they were never fully opened again for him. My dad had a factory – a printing business – back then and he was attacked by some favela bad guys trying to rob the place. So." She stopped for a moment, her guard down, and Jake could see she was searching for another memory. "My parents moved out of their bedroom at the back of the apartment so he wouldn't have to look out onto the favela – it runs up the hill behind our block – and I swapped my bedroom for theirs. It always felt to me like the favela was almost close enough to touch. I think it maybe still does. From then on, I was the little girl staring into a different world from her bedroom window, but no one would talk to me about what happened in that world. I was never allowed me around my father, and with my mother – well, she just always changed the subject until in the end I gave up asking."

She sighed and shook her head before continuing. "My dad was overjoyed when I told him I was going to study law. He assumed I would become a prosecutor. He didn't speak to me for weeks when I told him I wanted to work on the defence side."

She told Jake how in the end she had opted for corporate law as an unhappy compromise. She had a duty. The once-successful printing business for which her father had nearly sacrificed his life to protect had drifted off course and eventually folded. Her father rarely left the apartment and had never worked again. There was very little money left after paying for her law degree and she was now the family breadwinner. "Getting involved in this is not good for my career," she said. "My company likes its lawyers to be invisible. And what is not good for my career is not good for my family. And the last thing I can do is tell my family what I'm doing." The steel came back into her eyes as she looked directly at Jake. "So to answer your question, no, I'm not sure I want to do this, but it's something I have to do. Even if I am totally unqualified to go up against this police captain, even if I am totally out of my depth."

Jake said nothing. And he was glad that he had kept quiet about his experience back in England. It wouldn't have made her feel any better. He watched as Marinho finished his circuit, cooling his head beneath a communal shower ahead by the workout area. He soaked a small towel and put it over his shoulders. Walking past without acknowledging them, he bought a bottle of water at the bar and came back to sit at an adjacent table. Close on to them, he leaned forward, head dropping down. Sweat and water dripped from him. He rolled the ice-cold bottle around his neck and then took a drink. "The boss of the favela, Anjo, is throwing one of his big parties tomorrow night," he said, staring out at the ocean. "It will be a distraction, and it's the only chance I've got to pull this kid, Hector, out. They are due to kill him the day after."

"Wouldn't it be better for the priest to get him out?" Jake asked. He still wasn't convinced about this young cop. With Marinho hunched over and Jake only able to see the side of his face, it was hard to read anything from him.

"Throwing these parties is part of Anjo's *Godfather* thing, you know. He likes to think he's old school. He hands out sweets to kids and sometimes he even pays hospital bills for sick folks. But he'll kill anyone he even suspects of crossing him. Priests included. Padre Francisco will be the prime suspect so he has to be somewhere public tomorrow night. He has to have an alibi."

"Then I'll come," said Jake. "I can help."

"Are you out of your mind?" Marinho said it with feeling but kept still. "You can barely put one foot in front of the other. No way." Although his head was down as if he were staring at the ground, he was looking out the corner of his eye in Jake's direction. He seemed determined to keep up the pretence of not knowing them if observed from afar.

Jake drew breath, ready to kick off. But Eliane touched the back of his hand, giving the slightest shake of her head. This wasn't the moment.

"You understand it's difficult for us to trust you given who you work for?" she asked Marinho.

"You don't know the half of it with my boss," said Marinho, turning his head to look at her for the first time. "But I am not my boss. Call this a penance, if you like. I have one condition though."

"Which is?" she asked.

"You stop coming after him."

"He murdered a boy."

"That happens every day in this town. Saving the other one is a win – why not just take that?"

"I can't."

"But you're not even the right kind of lawyer for this, are you?" Marinho said.

"Why would you protect him?" she asked.

"That's not what I'm doing. I just know it's a fight you don't want to have. Not unless your family is powerful."

Eliane glanced at Jake before looking away.

Jake could see that Marinho had his confirmation from her lack of response. "Then what world are you living in?" Marinho said. "Even if you do take my boss down there'll be another guy just like him to take his place, or maybe one even worse. There always is."

"And hopefully there'll be another disillusioned corporate lawyer to take him down too, maybe even a proper lawyer."

"Leave my boss alone. I'm warning you," said Marinho. "Otherwise I can't be held responsible for what will happen."

"I can't do that." She was calm but said it firmly.

Marinho looked down at the ground between his knees, head in his hands. "Goddamn," he said. "If you only knew what you're getting yourself into, I swear you'd be running as fast as you could in the opposite direction."

He stood and walked away without another word.
Live with something on your conscience or risk not living at all. It struck Jake that most guys in Marinho's position would be sorely tempted to go into the favela, grab the kid and turn him in. Get a pat on the head from the boss and put all this crap in a drawer.
Jake had to make sure that didn't happen.

Marinho

Marinho came out of Nogueira's kitchen door with a platter of skewered chicken hearts. Across the backyard, Adalto Osório de Farias Nogueira was salting cuts of good beef for the *churrasqueira* – the barbeque. The sun was bouncing around inside the high white walls and the huge spread of charcoal had burned through to a papery grey, beating out a ferocious heat.

The *churrasqueira* was part of a brick-constructed lean-to topped with terracotta tiles in a corner of the yard. It was the only shaded area. Small paving tiles, a well-watered flowerbed and a tiny swimming pool made up the rest of the yard. There were plastic toys in the pool, some floating, some bumping the slimy bottom. Nogueira's guests were taking refuge in the cool of the house.

Out in a coastal suburb to the west of the famous beaches, it was modest enough to stay off the radar. And like all the houses in the neighbourhood, it was a fortress, electric wire topping the yard walls.

Marinho laid his platter on the counter next to the barbeque. A young girl came out of the kitchen, stepping daintily over the tiles with a bottle of ice-cold beer in either hand. Her dark hair was loose and un-styled, her skin starting to break out, adolescence coming early.

"An angel sent by God." Nogueira grinned, wiping his hands on a cloth and taking one of the beers from her.

"Sir?" the girl said, offering the other beer to Marinho.

"Thank you."

Nogueira wiped his sweaty face on the sleeve of his tee shirt and put an arm around her. "This is Ana Lucia, my eldest grandchild. Say hello to Marinho, child."

"Hello, *Seu* Marinho."

"*Tudo bom?*" All good? Marinho asked.

"*Tudo bom,*" she replied.

"She's just got herself into one of the best schools. Smart as a whip is my beautiful girl," said Nogueira. "She'll probably end up a judge."

"Being a judge sounds boring, Grandpa. Maybe I'll be a

policewoman or a lawyer."

"A lawyer?" Nogueira laughed. "What are you tr[...] your poor old grandpa? And you won't make any money [...]. No, you study hard, become a judge and help your gra[...] the bad guys. Deal?"

"Deal."

"Good girl," Nogueira said, kissing her on the t[...]. He handed her a used plate. "Can you run in with [...] your grandma that I'm putting the meat on now?"

Marinho stepped back from the heat of the [...] while Nogueira watched his granddaughter for a few mom[...] lked back to the house. "That young bitch lawyer ha[...] g in people's ears like a mosquito."

"She can't really do anything, can she?" asked M[...]

"Doesn't seem like her family has any juice. B[...] king enough noise about the kid we got to irritate peopl[...] and the Commissioner is kicking that shit downhill," [...]. "It looks like she's snared that dumbass *gringo* too."

His eyes were fierce. He tilted his head slightly [...] give him a clearer look into Marinho's soul. "I need t[...] thing from you."

Nogueira broke eye contact, laying strips of bee[...]que, the fat hissing and spitting through the smoke. He w[...] work silently and deliberately, standing back when he w[...] rinho knew that all the while he was trying to extend the [...] him.

"Are you with me?" he asked, turning back to M[...]

"Of course, boss. Always."

"Then why am I hearing whispers about you [...] ople without checking in with me?"

"I was just trying to shake something out on the [...] ay," Marinho said, fighting to keep his manner casual. [...] had Nogueira found out? Who would have told him?

Nogueira turned the meat on the barbeque, usin[...] ain. He looked sidelong at Marinho. "And?"

"Well, I found out a little about the kid, but I thi[...]

"Marinho. Some friendly advice: never take me f[...] been on the force twenty-five years on shitty pay with on[...] t of a shittier pension as long as I don't take a bullet be[...] We all need to make a little, but whatever game you pla[...] e in, understand?"

"Yes, Chief, I'm sorry."

THE BURNING HILL

"That holier-than-thou brigade, assholes with too much money and too much time on their hands, they have no idea what it's like for us. I've seen too many people killed, buried more of my friends than a man should. Killing makes me sick, you know that? For real, right here in my stomach." Nogueira rubbed his round belly and swallowed, grimacing. "I don't like it, but I will get my hands dirty if I have to. I protect myself and my family and the guys who stand with me. That's it. That's all that matters. Understand?"

Marinho nodded.

"Good. So what about Anjo? Did you speak to him or any of his guys?"

"No, it was all real low level." Marinho's relief at telling the truth was at painful odds with his previous answers.

"Well, Anjo is another one who's forgotten the rules. The little shit is still refusing to cough up this getaway kid, Vilson, and I know he's holed up in his favela. Our friend is eating turkey and burping pheasant these days."

Nogueira pressed his heavy barbeque fork into a lump of steak, blood oozing out, each drip onto the coals beneath producing a puff of steam and ash. He turned the fork on Marinho. "I need a result to take the sting out of this mess. You're going to bring me the getaway kid – actually, any kid that you can fit up will do. That's decided," he added, his shoulders relaxing. "And then we'll take care of Anjo."

"But, Chief, I can't just march into the favela and grab him."

"You'll have to figure a way. The Commissioner wants a head on a stick. This is how you learn your lesson. I look after you and for that I only ask loyalty in return. You do your time and I'll put the word in with *BOPE*."

Marinho was desperate to make it into the elite police unit – *Batalhão de Operações Policiais Especiais*. BOPE guys were the special forces of the cop world. When regular cops were outgunned or too scared to go into a favela to shoot it out with a drug gang, they sent in BOPE. Feared in the favela, BOPE was respected outside as a unit of honest fighting men, free from corruption. But his only chance was if Nogueira protected his secret. If Nogueira chose to reveal it he would be thrown off the force altogether. Nogueira could cut the strings and let him fall any time he chose. And he could cut far more than strings.

"Go get another beer, or have something stronger if you want – I've got some good whisky inside – enjoy yourself," Nogueira said, immersed again in his sweaty barbequing. "Oh, I almost forgot to ask, are you training?"

"Just light stuff and a bit of sparring, Chief."

"You might need to step it up – I'm talking to some people, trying to get you a good fight, understand?"

When Marinho climbed into the octagon – or the cage as it was better known – he did it to build on his meagre savings, but he was going to have to line Nogueira's pockets again. He nodded a show of gratitude.

Chapter 12

Vilson

The party was dying down, but Vilson could still hear the thump of bass behind him as he crept down the darkest alleys of the favela. The bolt of fear that struck him each time he saw someone sitting in a doorway or walking toward him barely subsided before he saw the next person.

He was near the bottom of the favela, the glow from the city's street lights like a mist breaking over the line of corrugated-iron roofs. One more turn and he would see the exit of the alley onto the end of the smart residential street. He had chosen the quietest exit, the one least likely to be manned by one of Anjo's lookouts on a party night.

He saw a shadow move ahead. His legs jellied and he almost faltered. He forced himself to saunter on – he could not let himself look suspicious.

It was just a kid, no more than ten. He had something in his hand. Vilson guessed – he prayed – that it wasn't a gun. The young ones usually made a show when they had one, waving it around and swaggering.

He nodded to the kid as he approached. He could see now that it was a walkie-talkie. The kid lifted his chin in response, only one side of his face lit up by the sickly light washing up from the city street below. Vilson didn't recognise him. He had a chance.

"*Oi Comandante,*" – Hey Commander – Vilson said breezily, surprising himself. His jokey salutation had sounded pretty natural. He was a regular, a local guy doing his thing.

The kid tutted a relaxed brush-off.

Vilson was past the checkpoint. Just a few more metres to go. The grubby little alley, rubbish rolling down its sides, ended and he was on the paving of the street. He turned right, his self-conscious saunter turning stiff and mechanical, like a smile held too long. He turned his head, eyes swivelling everywhere, looking for the cop.

This was the agreed place. This street, only a short street, and the cop was nowhere. He went on a little further, stopped and ambled back awkwardly. He knew there would be security guards behind the spiked railings of the apartment-block lobbies watching him and silently urging him to move on from their strip of pavement before they were obliged to come out and confront him. He kept on moving up and down the street. At some point one of those security guards might just get twitchy enough to call the cops. Anjo's sentry kid also might suddenly remember that he should have stopped and checked on Vilson before letting him pass. Every minute that went by increased the danger and Vilson was aware that there were a lot of minutes now. He chided himself. This was a bad place to meet. So close to the favela. He should have chosen a street a few blocks away. A volunteer worker for the church had come into the favela during the day and sought him out to tell him that Padre Francisco was arranging his escape. Both Vilson and the church volunteer had been terrified of being seen together, and this meeting place was the only one that Vilson's scrambled mind had come up with in the few seconds before he had hurried away from the volunteer.

Yes, this was a bad place to meet, but Vilson had got himself out of the favela clean, and now this cop was a no-show. It could be that the volunteer had got mixed up or maybe Padre Francisco had been suckered, and Vilson had been stupid enough to go along with it. It was always the same for people like him. And always hard to swallow.

He caught a shadow on the corner thirty metres away. A movement. His heart skipped. A guy, moving quickly, hurriedly. The guy checked when he noticed Vilson, approaching more slowly now.

He wasn't dressed like a cop but he had the look. He stopped ten metres short of Vilson, his features hollow beneath the street lights.

Vilson's nod to the cop's guarded greeting was as much code as was likely to pass between them.

He saw the cop's shoulders relax a little.

There was a noise behind Vilson. A disturbance. He turned to look back toward the alley.

Three figures spilled onto the street. One of them spotted him.

"There! There he is." The shrill cry came from Anjo's sentry kid. They surged forward as one, the difference in heights making them look like a row of odd-sized bottles until the tallest pulled a pistol from his shorts and the other two fell back.

Vilson recognised the point man striding toward him, an outstretched arm levelling the pistol at him. It was Franjinha, Anjo's lieutenant. He felt something inside him collapse. He was done.

He turned his head to Marinho and that seemed to stir the cop. He started toward Vilson.

Franjinha halted and shifted his unsteady aim, the barrel weaving a confused little pattern like a moth around a light bulb. "You stop right there, fucker, or I will shoot you down," he shouted at Marinho.

Marinho obeyed, holding his hands up, palms out.

"*Bom menino*," – Good boy – Franjinha shouted. "Now turn around and walk away while you still can."

Marinho fell back, but only as far as the shadow of one of the trees. Vilson quailed as Franjinha stepped up, but he didn't move from his spot. He was rooted. A dead man. He knew that the fate awaiting him up on the Burning Hill was infinitely worse than a bullet in the back, but still he could not run.

Franjinha cocked his head, smiling his blank smile. He gave Vilson a backhanded flick across the face with his pistol, the sight catching Vilson on the outer edge of his brow.

Vilson let the blow carry his head around without even wincing. The blood gathered for a moment in the split skin before running down the side of his face.

"Let's go, you sack of shit," Franjinha said, steering Vilson toward the favela with a series of lazy kicks, sniffing and twitching his head. He looked back a couple of times to check Marinho wasn't following and then mussed the hair of Tôca, the sentry kid. "You did well – sharp eyes, quick thinking, soldier."

Anjo

Franjinha and the kids got busy on mobiles and walkie-talkies as they climbed through the favela. By the time they broke out onto the scrubby hilltop bordered by tall grass and thorny bush, Anjo and most of his soldiers were there. There was no music in the favela now. A different kind of party was about to start. A couple of soldiers were staking paraffin torches in the ground. Anjo liked the spiritual feel they added.

There was nothing spiritual in the things piled at his feet, but they would provide the theatre. Theatre that had gained notoriety well beyond the Babilônia favela.

Any tiny, mangled vestige of hope that Vilson might have clung to was stripped away when he saw the things. He bucked and thrashed, his eyes rolling back.

Franjinha had to kick the back of his knees to put him on the ground. A few kicks to ribs and kidneys and the fight was gone. Vilson lay still.

"Good evening, brothers." Anjo greeted them with a slack grin. As high as most of his troops, he was also mellow from the half bottle of *cachaça* he had drunk to take the edge off the coke. He␣␣␣␣␣␣␣␣␣lend spot on tonight. Even so, he felt detached,␣␣␣␣␣␣␣␣␣tely, deliberating every movement.

They pulled Vilson to his feet, the blood from␣␣␣␣␣␣␣␣␣cing jagged streaks down his face. Anjo placed a fri␣␣␣␣␣␣␣␣␣his shoulder.

"Vilson and me, we go a long way back," Anjo␣␣␣␣␣␣␣␣␣way through the words. "We have taken different pa␣hs.␣␣␣␣␣␣␣eved much, become powerful, despite the tests that God␣␣␣␣␣␣␣␣me. Vilson is not so strong, but I always tried to help␣␣␣␣␣␣␣␣␣ow I am." He shrugged self-deprecatingly.

He was getting a little lost in the eloquence of␣␣␣␣␣␣␣␣␣ling a genuine camaraderie toward Vilson.

Vilson was a friend. Anjo's eyes drifted off to␣␣␣␣␣␣␣␣␣␣p of Copacabana beach far below them. Another world.␣␣␣␣␣␣␣␣iend.

"I was generous, I gave Vilson time to pay his de␣␣␣␣␣␣␣␣hose to run. You don't run from Anjo and his Red Ants."

A couple of the younger kids were beginning␣␣␣␣␣␣␣␣␣had plenty more to say, but the thread had gone. And␣␣␣␣␣␣␣␣the kids to miss anything. It was the first time for som␣␣␣␣␣␣␣␣d he was keen to see which of them had the stomach␣␣␣␣␣␣␣␣. He looked around, a slow sweep to acknowledge them␣␣␣␣␣␣␣␣gave the signal for Franjinha to get started.

Franjinha picked up two small jerrycans of p␣␣␣␣␣␣␣␣␣␣e of the stronger teenage soldiers, Lagarto, to carry a l␣␣␣␣␣␣␣␣nd a bald old truck tyre, worn down to the canvas.␣␣␣␣␣␣␣␣ldiers followed, dragging Vilson between them toward␣␣␣␣␣␣␣␣␣runk and branches on the facing side charred, the folia␣e␣␣␣␣␣␣, the other side somehow still living. There were waxy s␣␣␣␣␣␣␣wish human fat on the blackened trunk, streaky gobs␣␣␣␣␣␣␣␣the charred crusts of rubber, bone and flesh at the ba␣␣.

Victims were bound to the tree with the chain,␣␣␣␣␣␣␣␣ound and round the tree trunk and the torso and l␣gs.␣␣␣␣␣␣was Franjinha's idea after the rope they had used the firs␣␣␣␣␣␣rned through, the guy collapsing in an unsatisfying hea␣␣␣␣␣␣␣into a rage.

Securing the torso while leaving the arms free,␣␣␣␣␣␣␣␣␣the spectacle as they jigged and clawed at the air ar␣␣␣␣␣␣␣␣ead against the tree trunk. Usually there was screami␣␣␣␣␣␣␣. The entertainment rarely lasted long. But there was on␣␣␣␣␣␣␣sion with a tubby old guy, a community leader who had␣␣␣␣␣␣␣␣␣inst the Red Ants. He had burned fiercely, and had gone for some minutes with one of his fists beating at his chest. Although weakening, this pathetic repetition had continued even as his living flesh burned off and charred. Even when he had finally become still the fist stayed at his chest until the gristle of the shoulder joint burned right through and the arm fell away.

It had fascinated Anjo. He guessed it was probably some sort of death twitch, but he had made sure the story that was put about had the guy living through those horrific minutes.

It wasn't just the gruesome detail that had scored that burning into the local consciousness. The copious body fat had acted like tallow around a wick, still going long after the petrol had burned off, the thick, greasy stench of burning pork overpowering the acrid rubber smoke. It caught in the throat, as if the tiny droplets of fat in the smoke were congealing like a smear of gritty floor wax. It clung to every fibre of the surrounding homes for days. No one had craved meat that week.

Lagarto was wrenching at the lid of one of the jerrycans, Franjinha squatting with a rag in his hands. He would douse the length of rag in petrol before tying it round Vilson's head. With the tyre lying on the ground at the foot of the tree, they would slot his feet in and sluice it with petrol. The chain securing his legs against the tree trunk would stop him from kicking the tyre away. With experience, Anjo had figured out all the details to make it go just like he wanted.

A halo of flame and something to get him cooking down below.

"No, no, no," Anjo murmured. Franjinha was putting the cart before the bull. The cutting came first. It was Anjo's latest refinement. Franjinha should be making a show with the blade, terrorising Vilson, taunting him, until finally he sliced off what made him a man. Would he bellow, or shriek like a girl? You could never tell. Whatever, he wanted the screams to ring around the corrugated-iron roofs of the favela, and they hadn't even chained Vilson to the tree yet. The fools were too strung out to remember even a simple sequence.

Irritated, he was about to step in as Lagarto finally jerked the lid off the jerrycan and clumsily tipped it. A modest glug soaked the rag, trapped air stalling the flow before petrol spouted over Franjinha's arms and the front of his shirt.

No one was certain how it happened but, somewhere between Franjinha jumping up and cursing Lagarto, the petrol ignited. Flame licked prettily across the scrubby grass, a lazy, curling exhalation. Then it leapt to the rag and to Franjinha.

The jerrycan exploded with a low *whump*, engulfing Lagarto in a coruscating spray of burning liquid. He fell to his knees, tipped sideways and rolled soundlessly onto his back. The flames whooshed in a muted roar, tracing the movement of his arms as they flailed mechanically.

Anjo watched in astonishment as Franjinha stared goggle-eyed at his own flaming arms and chest, the cocaine dulling his pain response. A few of the really stoned soldiers guffawed. It was only when the repellent stink of burning hair and the first sickly whiff of roasting flesh reached Anjo's nostrils that Franjinha started screaming.

The tearing, high wail finally spurred them into action, but there was little at hand to smother the flames.

Lagarto's flailing arms slowed and then dropped to his chest, wrists and fingers bending into claws with the heat. There was nothing more.

Anjo shouted ineffectual orders as Franjinha screamed, his hands flapping at his arms and chest, trying to turn his face away from the searing flames lashing up his throat.

Scrabbling about in a nearby rubbish heap, a soldier named Drago got hold of a torn chunk of old floor lino. It took Anjo a moment before he understood Drago's intention. "That's right, smother him," he shouted at Drago, wanting to regain command of the situation.

"Get down on the ground," Drago yelled at Franjinha, but he just screamed and flapped at himself more. Drago knocked Franjinha down and smothered him, rolling him and beating at the flames until they were eventually out.

Smoke was rising from the burned shreds of Franjinha's shirt and he was holding his arms up in front of his chest protectively, hands shaking uncontrollably. His arms and chest were a blackened crust with plasma oozing through the raw patches of flayed skin. His face wasn't so bad, but the lank hair that his sister had once cut in an embarrassing fringe in his childhood, earning him the nickname Franjinha, had burned off up to his crown, leaving just a thin cap of crinkled hair against his reddened scalp.

He was helped to his feet, yelping and squawking each time his injured flesh was touched. A soldier tried to take hold of an arm to support him.

"Leave it! Leave it, you idiot, it's agony," Franjinha yelled, breaking down in a series of pitiful whimpers. Plasma was beginning to drip steadily from his skin.

"Come on, man, let's go," Anjo said gently. "I'm going to give you a shitload of powder – the really good stuff – and then you won't feel a damned thing. And I'm going to get a doctor, a real expensive one from the city, to is you up."

Franjinha nodded. "It hurts, Christ it hurts." He shuffled off with Anjo.

"And bring Lagarto," Anjo called over his shoulder. "I don't leave any of my soldiers behind."

No one was eager to carry Lagarto, not least because they had only just managed to put him out and he was still hot. And when they tried to grab a wrist or ankle the sheaths of blackened crust came off in their hands to expose the oily, slippery flesh beneath.

"Hey, boss." A young voice called out behind Anjo. "What do we do with him?"

Anjo had no patience for obtuse kids right now. He pulled the Beretta from his waistband, ready to make a statement. But the kid was pointing at Vilson, who was still standing in exactly the same position. He could have slipped away in the chaos, but there he was, wearing the same idiot expression of blank terror. Anjo despised it.

Tôca was the kid who had noticed, the same one who had spotted Vilson trying to escape the favela. A good kid. Anjo nodded approval, lifting the Beretta and taking casual aim. He fired three shots in quick succession. Vilson crumpled to the ground.

Anjo tilted his head in satisfaction. He had shown them he was decisive. A man of action.

Chapter 13

Jake

Going along with Marinho, Jake had agreed to hang back beneath the trees at the corner of the road. Marinho hadn't wanted to spook Vilson. Jake had remained hidden, watching as Vilson's fleeting salvation was snatched from him. The world had slowed horribly when the gangster kid had started waving his gun around. Jake was transported back to the beach with the gun in his face, but it was worse somehow, fear sucking the life from him, breath by shortening breath. He fought the overload of flashing alarms that seemed to want to shut down his body. He had never felt anything like it before, not even in that bad time out in the desert. All the terrors, all that stuff that he couldn't forget, smashed together into a lump and rammed down his throat.

Marinho came back to him, shaking his head. He took a deep breath, composing himself. "Okay, friend, show's over. Let's get you home."

"We can't just leave him." The words were catching on Jake's taught, snatched breaths. "We've got to help him."

"Don't talk crazy, you shouldn't even be here. Look at you, you're shaking."

Only now did Jake realise that he was gripping the iron railings so hard his fingers were cramping, sweat pasting his shirt onto his skin.

"Let's go," Marinho said.

Jake heaved himself off toward the favela.

"Not that way," Marinho hissed.

"I've got to help him."

"Help him what? The kid that took him away, he's the right-hand man to the favela boss. I'm lucky it was dark enough and he was high enough not to recognise me."

"You know him?"

"My boss has a deal with them I met that kid once on a cash drop. Look, Vilson is a dead man, and I'm sorry for that, but we walk away with our lives tonight."

He steered Jake past the entrance to the favela and across the road, but Jake came to a stubborn halt by some grubby unlit shop windows at the corner of the street.

Marinho was remonstrating in a coarse whisper. Jake wasn't really hearing, the dark entrance of the favela he   his consciousness, dizzying, hypnotic.

He had no idea how much time had passed before   that Marinho was no longer speaking. The last of the   Jake up drained away and he had to sit down on the   a minute," he said.

His backside was aching before he felt ready to   ain.

"You okay?" Marinho asked, helping him up.

Jake nodded.

"Come on, man, let's go, there's nothing you can   said, coaxing now.

There it was. He couldn't do anything. They wou   They would destroy him. Finally, a surge of anger. That's   said. Well, screw them. Screw them all.

He was just about in touch enough to realise   was shorting out, stripping him of the capacity to deal   night play out on that hillside.

But he found himself starting back toward the al

Pop, pop, pop. The reports of pistol shots up in

Marinho caught him by the arm. "That's the end   The same gentle tone.

Jake was transfixed, staring so hard that the black   alley became a flickering, shifting spot. It seemed to have   an offer of rebalancing the scales, maybe even an escape   noise in his head. Its pull was as irresistible as it was terrifying.

He broke away from Marinho and entered.

"Fuck," Marinho rasped. "Stupid. Fucking. *Gringo*

Jake turned and saw Marinho pulling his   the waistband at the back of his jeans.

"You stay behind me," Marinho said, pushing   less tempted to shoot you that way."

They crept up the alley, flattening themselves in   st of the shadows.

The favela was quiet, holding its breath in the   the shots. Jake fought to control the harsh whistle of   ing. Every shuffle and cough that came through the win   omes they passed froze the sweat on his skin. And then,   his mind was clear. He burst through the dark cloud   He was in the zone.

Marinho headed left at each junction and they   k in the low buildings, the fringe of the favela. There   path working up the hill through thick, tall grass and brush.

"Somewhere up there is the gang's execution ground," Marinho whispered. "I don't know exactly where but this place is famous."

The grass hissed in the breeze and a half-moon poked through the clouds, the unwelcome light pressing them into a crouch as they laboured upward. Jake sucked in lungful after lungful of air, his leg muscles burning.

He smelled the paraffin before he saw the lapping yellowish glow of the torches. They tucked into thick brush and scoped the area, letting the minutes grind by.

It wasn't until they broke cover that Jake spotted Vilson's body by the tree. The flickering light of the torches gave no hint of what horrors the outline held. Dread crawled through Jake's skin as he reached down to touch his fingers to Vilson's neck to confirm the obvious.

Jake flinched as if from an electric shock. Vilson jerked his head and gasped. He was suddenly breathing hard, very much alive.

"What the fuck, man?" Jake whispered hoarsely. "I thought you were dead." He caught a flash as Vilson's eyes rolled back. The kid was in shock.

"I thought I was." Vilson looked at Jake, wide-eyed, recognising him by his scars. Then he noticed Marinho and recoiled. "Who are you?"

"I'm Marinho, you fool, it was me who came to meet you earlier."

"You let them take me away," Vilson said, "to kill me."

"And we came for you," Marinho said. "Although you'd need to ask your saviour here why. How badly are you hurt?"

"I'm not hurt."

"Then what the hell happened here? Actually, save it – we have to move."

Marinho got Vilson to his feet, bustling him away from the exposed ground. And then his shoulders sagged. "Shit. My boss and the boss of this place have to believe you're dead."

Just under the waft of warm paraffin was the faint but cloying smell of decaying flesh, the flesh of victims of less formal executions out in the undergrowth.

Marinho pursed his lips. "We need a body."

Jake followed his lead. He felt squeamish, the nerve endings in his hands jangling, hoping not to touch slimy flesh as he groped around in the dark gaps and unidentified lumps and blobs amongst the hissing grass. He was better at dealing with the known quantity, however grim.

Vilson hung back, constantly looking around to see if anyone was coming and shuffling from one foot to the other. "We need to go," he said. "Those guys could be back any minute."

It probably made sense for Vilson to keep a lookout rather than get his hands dirty, but that didn't stop Jake putting a bit of resentment to boil.

Marinho was the first to locate a body, tugging gingerly at a leg. Jake stepped in, steeled himself, and hauled on the other.

Something gave way, sending out a bigger wave, an overpowering stench of putrefied flesh. Jake tried breathing in through his mouth in little gasps but still it infiltrated and he retched again and again. Quietly. Eyes running, slimy ropes of saliva and vomit hanging from his lips as the spasms hunched him over.

The torchlight in the clearing confirmed what their noses had already told them. The body was heaving with maggots.

"This is no good." Marinho's voice was edgy. "It's too far gone. We can't pass this body off as his."

Chapter 14

Anjo

Franjinha had persuaded the TV news crew to come for the interview through an established contact in the favela, a fixer. They had only agreed because it was a slow-news day – a throwaway remark from the female reporter over the phone, Franjinha had told Anjo. His black eyes had glittered at that.

Franjinha was coming back up the hill now. "They're all set up and ready down there," he said to Anjo. "Pretty chilled out."

There was an unwritten code of conduct for these things: the gangsters got their platform and no one misbehaved. Anjo knew this was why the reporter and her cameraman felt safe. They might also say that they were only here because there was nothing better for them to do, and they would feign boredom – that was guaranteed with these people. But Anjo also knew that gangsters excited them. All the folks down in the city savoured that close-up experience, a bit of danger without real danger. It was like those people he had seen on a TV show who went down in cages to see the Great Whites swim up and nudge the bars. Anjo wanted to see the change in their expressions when they realised he was coming through the bars.

Flanked by a select guard of soldiers, Anjo wrapped a thin scarf round his head and face, just his eyes showing. When he was given the signal that they were filming, he strode down the hill to the entrance of the favela where the crew was set up on a corner.

Ticking, twitching, he got to the reporter and waved his Beretta in her face. She backed out of shot, forgetting her cues. Terrified.

Anjo thrust his face into the camera lens, launching into a tirade. "I am boss of Morro de Babilônia. I am the police up on that hill. Justice up there is quick and fair, not like you have down here."

He turned to the other three soldiers bringing up the rear, dragging a heavy blue trunk down the hill. He beckoned them on with the Beretta. "There is no corruption on the hill, no one gets robbed. Everyone is safe. Why? Because of me. And if one of my people comes into your city and does something bad, I take care of it."

He had to pause for a moment, the words were outrunning his brain. He had to make sure he said it all right. Franjinha had run through this speech with him but he wasn't here to prompt.

Anjo's black, glittering eyes narrowed and the reporter went absolutely still. She maybe thought he was going to shoot her. Maybe he should. He had his words lined up again now. "When a *gringo* gets robbed and shot on Copacabana your cops can only catch one guy, and then they somehow forget what they did with him. The second I found out those guys come from my hill I began hunting down the other bad guy. I never rest until I find him. I am judge and jury. And executioner."

He snapped his hand down, the signal for the three soldiers. Moving uphill of the tarpaulin, they let go of the top edge and hauled on the bottom. The heavy lump within slid and flopped onto the cracked concrete.

It was a charred body, the limbs bent up and stiff. The death grin of the skull beneath the blackened crust.

"Oh my god," the reporter gasped.

"And I don't lose the body. I am justice, I am order," Anjo shouted, thumping his chest. "Me."

Chapter 15

Jake

Vilson was sitting on the thin rug laid over the tiled floor of Jake's small living room, hugging his legs, his chin resting on his knees. Jake switched on the early-evening news ahead of *Uga Uga*. In the two days since they had pulled Vilson off the hill the *novela* was the only thing that had half raised the kid out of a kind of resentful, skulking daze.

He glanced at Vilson as they watched the news report. Vilson's eyes widened and he hugged himself closer. The footage cut away as the body was rolled out of the tarpaulin, but there was no doubting what it was.

Up on the favela hilltop, with Marinho despairing as they had stood over the stinking unknown corpse, Vilson had conjured a jerrycan of petrol. With the corpse alight, they had torn down the hillside as quickly as Jake's feeble stamina allowed with the yellow glow from the billowing flames at their back. In that moment Vilson had gone from being no use to anyone, from *zero-a-esquerda* – a zero-on-the-left – up to a one, as Marinho sarcastically put it. That had been the high point. Figuratively as well as literally.

Jake turned off the TV.

"Why did you do that? The *novela* is going to start," Vilson said. He avoided eye contact most of the time and when Jake did catch him looking at him it was with something between mistrust, fear and hatred. Right now it seemed like outright hatred. It was time to start talking. Properly.

"What happened up there with that gangster – you said he shot at you?"

Vilson looked at the floor. "I just want to watch the *novela*."

"Me too, but I want you to answer me first."

Vilson shook his head in frustration and stared at the floor for a few moments. "Most people think his eyes are not too good and he can't shoot straight. Most people he kills are close-up, you know, like executions." He shivered involuntarily and scoped the room like it might be bugged.

"Not a great reputation for a badass gangster."

Vilson shrugged. "He still scares people."

Jake turned the TV back on. Vilson was immersed [...] the opening credits for *Uga Uga*.

Experience had taught Jake that it was in th[ose ...], scary moments that the unbreakable bonds were made. [...] wasn't sticking here. It looked like this was as good as it wa[s going to ...]. He had pulled the kid off the hill either because it wa[s ...] to do, or because Nogueira had needled him into it. [...] in-between. He hadn't really given much thought to [...] be supposed to feel afterwards or what would happe[n. ...] first time he had had to deal with the fallout from a lack [...]

Vilson ate Jake's meals with a strange mi[xture ...] and resentment, like a last supper on death row. And Jak[e ...] stop him washing himself under the outside tap. He wo[uld ...] of the clothes Jake offered, stubbornly sticking to h[is ...] of ragged shorts and faded Flamengo AFC shirt. He [...] ablet of soap the colour of earwax under the kitchen si[nk ...] to washing his outfit by hand.

The ageing landlady lived in one of the apartme[nts ...] side of the house. She had spotted Vilson washing ou[tside ...] day and was straight on Jake's case. "I don't know wh[at ...]g up to in there but he has to go," she had said.

"He's only staying for a few days," Jake had as[sured her].

"Where's he sleeping?"

"There." Jake had opened the door wider to sh[ow ...] heets on the couch.

"I know where he's from, what he is."

This place was less of a drain on his very finit[e ...] the budget hotel he had started out in, but his ini[tial ...]ding somewhere so close to the beach had been chi[pped ...] the following two days of traipsing round the city, gett[ing ...]pers verified, stamped and signed and then getting [...]fied, counter-stamped and countersigned. Brazil did a go[od ...]ous bureaucracy.

He didn't want to go through that again. Thi[s ...]ome. Something needed to happen.

He turned the TV off again when the *novela* en[ded ...] we now? I mean, I never went in for that miracle-and-f[aith ...] that's not why I got involved…"

Vilson got up while Jake was still talking and w[ent ...] the kitchen. Jake followed to find him picking a papay[a ...] owl.

"I thought that would make us straight," Jak[e ...] "but

you're acting like I've done something wrong."

Vilson ignored him, rattling through the drawers for a knife.

"I asked you a question."

Vilson grabbed a paring knife, turning it on Jake. "Fate wasn't served on the beach."

Jake looked at the small knife. The handle and blade were worn but it was sharp. Jake had sharpened it. Was this for real? The kid hadn't had it in him on the beach that night, and he doubted he had it in him now. Jake stood his ground, but he was ready. Adrenaline, fear. And then the anger. The dogs wanted to go. "Go on, do it," he said.

Vilson's arm was tensed, shaking with effort. He was staring at the knife, like he was willing it to do something. His eyes were shining. Fear and anger and frustration. Jake could see all of it swimming around in there.

Vilson let out a big breath and his arm dropped. Beaten. He turned to the sink, his head dropping as he stared into it, before picking up the papaya, slicing the soft skin from the fruit with shaking hands.

"What did you mean about fate?" Jake said, catching the tension in his own voice.

"Nothing, it doesn't matter."

Jake wanted to understand what was going on with this kid, but patience didn't come naturally. He touched the puckered scars on his face; it was becoming a habit. Yes, the bullet had saved him but it had also half killed him. And Jake had then climbed the hill to drag this cryptic little mute off it. He deserved at least a thank you. Or something other than this.

There wasn't going to be any buddy movie here. He needed to move this kid on. "Do you have anyone you can go to?"

"I'm going to find my mother."

"She doesn't live in the favela?"

"She had to go away when I was a child. I never saw her again."

The hairs lifted on Jake's neck.

That changed everything.

He instantly saw a way to erase things that were stuck on him as permanently as the scars. Ugly, hidden scars he had carried his whole life that had festered and suppurated. He couldn't bring himself to accept the intervention of a higher power, but something had opened up, something he could really hit for.

Marinho

Nogueira slammed his fist on his heavy desk, making the stuff on it shudder. "Just one simple thing," he shouted at Marinho. "That's all I asked. Get it done. And now I have this shitstorm to deal with."

The door to the small office was closed but everyone outside would have heard.

Marinho knew it was deliberate and now Nogueira breathed, composing himself, his face turning to stone. This was when he was most dangerous. He spoke quietly now. "I would shoot you right here, right now, if I didn't need dead gangsters more than I need dead cops."

He still had the face on a few minutes later when Marinho followed him through to the cramped room he had chosen for the press conference. Nogueira settled himself behind the long table with a fan sitting on it that blew cool air into his face. Marinho had to stand to one side. Journalists were still taking up the rows of plastic chairs and jockeying for position in the spaces at the sides and back.

"Close the door, *cabo*," he instructed Marinho once they had all crowded in.

The atmosphere was close. Just how Nogueira wanted it, Marinho realised. Everyone bar Nogueira was hot and fractious, the journalists squabbling with one another and complaining about the lack of air-con and mobile-phone signal.

"This press conference started five minutes ago." Nogueira quietened the room with that. "You have ten minutes left."

One of the journalists started to protest. He dried up the instant Nogueira flicked his eyes over to him. There was only the sound of journalists fiddling with notepads and recording equipment now. They preferred softer prey.

Nogueira hadn't said it in his rant back in the office, but Marinho was guessing he had called the press conference ahead of having his hand forced by the Commissioner. Nogueira would want to take control before the fallout from Anjo's star turn on the TV news became a runaway train. Marinho had met the Commissioner a couple of times in Nogueira's company and it was clear that he was intimidated by Nogueira. A bureaucrat who just wanted his take and to be left alone, he didn't bother Nogueira if he could help it. But he was the type of guy that would swing whichever way the wind blew him, and this thing was becoming a stir that was too much to ignore.

A journalist cleared his throat, a new member of the pack. "Is the police force now so inept that it has lost the right to protect the city? Or is there something more sinister at the heart of this – corruption perhaps?" He wanted to make a mark, but his voice had a slight crack.

Nogueira fixed him with a stare. "I'm guessing you had the benefit of a good education, you should be ashamed that you've wasted it."

"It's a valid question."

"It's soft, liberal stupidity." His eyes and face were hard, impenetrable, immovable.

The journalist reddened and a few others chuckled. If they could smell blood it wasn't from on the other side of the table.

When more questions came, they were watered down, easily dealt with by Nogueira. Marinho looked around the room impassively, the sweat pouring from him as it was from all the journalists. Nogueira was bossing this thing and his audience knew it.

A journalist put up his hand, determined to get some kind of score, to restore a little professional pride if nothing else. "Why does no one know what happened to the boy that you arrested that night?"

Nogueira didn't miss a beat. "I can only tell you what we know. We took him to a hospital when it was clear that his injuries were serious. We are still trying to find out what happened to him after that, but it could be that a criminal gang targeted him. We think he might have been involved in a feud." He looked at the sweating faces in front of him and at his watch. "Time's up, folks."

"Captain Nogueira." It was a female voice tucked away in the corner of the room. Marinho's stomach lurched. He had somehow missed her coming in.

"I don't know if you remember me?" Eliane continued evenly to Nogueira. "I know what happened that night. You murdered the boy."

Chapter 16

Vilson

That afternoon, Vilson was perched on a little wooden stool in Jake's sitting room. He was staring at nothing in particular on the TV in the hope that the lawyer would do the same and stop talking at him. It wasn't really working. She had told him that she had come straight from some press conference. It was all about the fight for him and the fight to get justice for Babão she had said, and then she had gone on to batter him for the last hour. "What do you remember? Tell me again. I need every tiny detail. It might not seem important but it could be vital. Tell me one more time. There might be something you missed."

What did it matter? What could she do? "We have to believe that the system can be fixed," she kept saying. "If we don't, we'll never get away from the corruption and injustice. It can only change from the top down and that's where we must put the pressure. It has to be done the right way." On and on she went.

It seemed like she actually believed what she was saying. A comfortable bed and a safely locked door probably made it easier to believe. Vilson carried on staring at the TV without watching. He wasn't going to be her pet project. Or the *gringo's*.

The *gringo*, the crazy goddamned *gringo*. Vilson had meant to kill him. He knew that he had never had killing in him, but this was to rebalance fate. It was the *gringo* who should have died on the beach, not Babão. The balance had to be restored to clear the path for Vilson to find his mother. He was sure of it. He had to kill the *gringo*. Next time he would not fail. He must not let another chance in life get away from him, like so many others had. His body twitched. He wasn't sleeping at night.

A buzzer went by the door. Someone was at the metal entrance gate.

Eliane came from the kitchen. "I'll get it."

Vilson hadn't moved.

She went out the front door and across the courtyard to open the gate.

The young cop came in behind Eliane, out of uniform. That didn't make him any better. A wolf in sheep's clothing. Vilson hadn't figured his angle yet, but he had to have one. Everybody wanted something.

Eliane went to the kitchen. "Coffee?" she asked over her shoulder.

Marinho closed the front door behind him and [...] it. Even without looking directly at him, Vilson could [...]. The cop didn't even acknowledge him. "Coffee?" [...] low, controlled, but the anger lit him up. "You thoug[...] wasn't angry enough before? Is that why you crashed his p[...]?"

Eliane came back with a Thermos of coffee, s[...] small cups with saucers and spoons on a tray. She place[...] heap coffee table.

"I'm sorry I didn't tell you," she replied. "I thoug[...] less risky if your surprise was genuine."

"It was definitely that all right."

"And I wanted to try to catch him out in front o[...] sts."

"And how did that one work out?"

"Not great. It doesn't feel like we're any further [...]

"Apart from making him angry enough to want [...]

"He can't come for me. I made sure that all th[...] knew my name and why I was there. Although that's ge[...] uble at work."

"Your job is the least of your worries, believe m[...] inho. He's got a million ways to get to you. You [...] reful everywhere you go now, in everything you do. Bef[...] an annoyance – a fly in his beer – now you're in hi[...] he doesn't allow people to stand in his way."

Marinho shook his head in frustration and for t[...] oked at Vilson in his baggy shorts and football shirt. "[...] be dressed like that, not even in here. Neighbours pa[...] see, rumours get around, connections get made. Get t[...] you some stuff."

Vilson finally looked up from the TV. "I'm going [...] ght."

"No way," Marinho said. "She's stirred up a ho[...] one catches you out on the streets and we're all dead. B[...] re is the *gringo*?"

Vilson shrugged.

"You need to give me a bit more than that beca[...] my patience here," said Marinho.

"He took off. Said he needed to go away for a c[...] Said something about family."

"He went back to England?"

Vilson shrugged. "Didn't say."

"You knew about this?" Marinho asked Eliane.

She shook her head. She was also shocked. "H[...] didn't

have any family."

"He's split then," said Marinho. "That's it. It got too hot for him and he left us sinking in the shit. Selfish son of a bitch."

Chapter 17

Jake

"You're lucky to get one at such short notice," the woman at the ticket office said to J...

Turning up at the Novo Rio central bus terminal in the city in the late afternoon with no idea of the schedules, it was a long wait for his bus. Low-lit girls of concrete and diesel fumes and uninterested queues for marathon journeys. Jake's destination was a nineteen-hour ride away. The map on the wall by the ticket office showed it as no more than a finger's width across the vast splayed hand of the country.

"Mum, look, a small boy in a queue said, pointing at Jake in horror. "What happened to his face?"

The mother pulled the pointing hand down and told him off in a whisper. Jake still held his crooked half smile. The kid was only saying what everyone else was thinking.

He wasn't experiencing the head-spin and breathing-through-a-straw feeling amongst the milling queues in the enclosed space, but the aftershocks of the shooting were still rolling through him. People tried not to recoil when they saw his face but it was definitely a kind of buffer. It kept them at arm's length. That wasn't a bad thing.

Night had fallen by the time his bus finally nosed its smoke-spewing way into its designated bay. It looked long on mileage and a little frayed around the edges. And, like most things in Brazil, it was spotless. The driver stepped off the bus to check everyone on board before reversing it out of the parking bay, out of the station and away into the evening.

There was enough of a gap left in the drawn curtain for Jake to watch the roads go from his aisle seat. Buildings and advertisements and road signs flickered past, the colour leached from them by the endless dull street lighting. The bus pulled through the night to the growl of engine and the whine of transmission.

Jake reclined his seat the few degrees it allowed. Whichever way he shifted and rearranged himself, his knees were still wedged against the seat in front. He couldn't get comfortable, the air-con nozzle only creating a chilly layer in the musty hot fug. The other passengers looked comatose, many wearing sleep masks. They were used to these journeys, it seemed.

Broken roads bumped and shook him from snatches of sleep that seemed to last no more than a few seconds. His backside and legs cramped and twitched and ached. Right through the night. He was too tired to even switch on the overhead light to read. And then the uncertainty started to gnaw at him.

Dawn came, grey, bleeding through the thin curtain. He needed to relocate the feeling that had put him on the bus.

When Jake had told Eliane in the hospital that he had no family, it wasn't the truth. He had had two families, and he had broken with both.

The arguments and fights between his mother and father were the only consistent thing in his childhood, until the day his father had walked out the door to go to the pub and never came back. And then Jake's mother had turned her venom on him. She was probably a manic depressive, maybe schizophrenic, he didn't really know because she would never go near a doctor who might tell her something was wrong with her head. What he did know, most definitely, was that she was a drinker – about the only thing she had in common with his father. And she was not a good drunk.

He could have grown into one of those saintly types that took on the burden of carer; he had been through phases when he had tried. But his mother had never warmed to the role of grateful, bedridden invalid. He could never get anything right when she was in her bad places. Sometimes she would flip to exuberant affection, and he had craved those moments, but he also learned to distrust them because they were never more than a brief sunny spell. Anger and frustration grew up with him and he couldn't stop fighting her. He became a shit of a kid. He became what she kept telling him he was.

He had wandered into an army recruitment office at eighteen on a whim, joining up to get away from home. An easy escape. A permanent way out. Forever in trouble at school, he had been heading for more out of it. The army had taken him in, saved him. The army was a predictable, solid family. Routine and order. Jake had baulked when he had first joined up, but it soon began to fill a gap that he'd never even realised was there. Joining as a squaddie, his CO told him he had potential and he was put forward for officer training within a few months.

When the cancer had come for his mother the army had given him leave, even though he wasn't sure he wanted it. That wasn't a great feeling and it was made worse by her genuine delight at seeing him. He experienced an unsettling reversal of his childhood, the warmth and affection prevailing over the moments of her lashing out when the pain consumed her wasting body. She told him she was at peace with herself, ready, but at the end she clung on for as long as she could in an unwinnable, grim wrestle with death. It was four weeks from diagnosis to the funeral.

"So fast," his father had said, shaking his head. "It's just you and me now, son. I want to make up for all those lost years." He had barely been in touch in the last fifteen.

"What for?" Jake had asked. The man was a shambles at the wake, in tears for most of it, maudlin and drunk and falling over. But he had at least managed to say nice things about Jake's mother, even if he hadn't meant them.

The army had offered Jake the escape from his childhood before and he wanted to escape it again. He reported for duty the day after the funeral and hadn't seen his father or heard from him since.

As an officer, Jake had better money, more privileges, but he was no longer just one of the lads and neither did he feel totally in step with his fellow officers – he came from a different place to most of them. It only really started to bother him after his mother died. It grated more and more, and he let the doubts creep in over nailing his colours to a career that was based on the whim of an eighteen-year-old Jake. He could feel the anger and frustration and resentment beginning to bubble up again. And then Iraq Part Two arrived. He was cynical enough to lack conviction about the war but he had always wanted to be in one. It wasn't bloodlust. He wanted to see action, to experience what he had trained for, with everything that went with it. And it was about the lads around him, the determination to keep one another alive. Surviving. Forging the brotherhood that had slipped away from him since becoming an officer. An unbreakable bond.

Amidst the headlong flight of the Iraqi forces in those opening days of the invasion they had hit patches of fierce resistance, and Jake had most definitely felt fear as his troop of three Warrior armoured vehicles pursued a ragged column of Iraqi vehicles flanked by two heavy tanks. But there was also raw exhilaration. Pure, mainlining adrenaline. There was nothing like it, blasting across the desert with his guys in their safe metal box, cocooned in the constant throaty roar of the engine. A throwback to cavalry days, the vehicles charging three abreast through a haze of dust that made the sun a deep, dirty orange, the leftover of the giant cloud kicked up by the column far ahead. It settled in a fine white layer on everything, on the metal skin of the Warrior, on the skin of the soldiers, on their uniforms. Their own cloud of dust billowed out behind them, blocking out everything they had passed. It was like a solid wall, like there was no going back. On[...] [...] hose moments were worth all the long hours of b[...] [...] river, Sammo, head peeping out of his hatch in front of [...], [...] to whinge about anything and everything to do with I[...] bu[...] was quietly enjoying this. Dave, the gunner, head and ch[...] [...] of his turret hatch alongside Jake, had a wide snaggle-[...] [...] nted in the middle of his dusty face.

Jake's troop were only meant to harry the colum[...] [...] k off a truck or an armoured car if they got the ch[...] [...] no intention of engaging the heavy Iraqi tanks. Ther[...] [...] on the vast, rocky plain where the terrain started to [...] [...] nore broken. It was there that the two tanks turned to [...] [...] the rest of the column continued. No longer boun[...] [...] ocky terrain, the tanks were able to take proper aim a[...] [...] ame smashing into the dirt ahead of Jake's troop, b[...] [...] and stones at the skin of their vehicles. The enemy wer[...] [...] range quickly. The next shells might obliterate Jake['s] [...] box. Commanders and gunners dropped down inside [...] [...] were about a kilometre from the enemy, well withi[...] [...] the Warrior's 30-mm cannon, but it was no more than [...] [...] inst the tanks. His troop were suddenly in a very hairy pla[...] [...] ared and his mind was racing, but it was also absolutely cl[...] [...] what to do. And he did it calmly. He could hear the sh[...] [...] mo's voice as he responded to his command for the Wa[...] [...] heel around on their sharp turning circle. As they started b[...] [...] into their own dust cloud, he called in the air strike. M[...] [...] ir of A-10 Warthog tank-busters swooped over.

The American planes flew over the static Ira[...] [...] ame around in a wide arc. The Iraqi tanks stopped firin[...] [...] oop, concentrating on getting away from the planes no[...] [...] his troop around again, called a halt, and came out of [...] [...] h to look through his binoculars as the dust cleared. O[...] [...] pass, the A-10s dropped altitude and kicked up lines of du[...] [...] ound the Iraqi tanks with their rapid cannon fire. The[...] [...] once more to finish the job. Thick black smoke began to [...] [...] ward from the pale dust cloud that was shrouding the d[...] [...] And then the A-10s tipped their skinny wings to wh[...] [...] ke's troop. These planes were wildly popular with the A[...] [...] ops; they had often come to the rescue and his lads w[...] [...] the pilots were going to give them a flypast. Maybe eve[...] [...]

He saw the stuttering smoke from the nose of [...] [...] efore

THE BURNING HILL

he heard the cannon. It was a dull buzz, like a screwdriver ripped down corrugated plastic. Jake saw white flashes all around him through the thick dust blasted out of the desert by the explosive rounds.

He dropped back inside the turret as a round struck the dirt next to the right track of his Warrior, the explosion bouncing the men around inside the metal tin. Jake's helmet smacked hard into some surface or other. He was disoriented for a moment, his ears ringing, dust and smoke blinding him. He couldn't feel any injuries. He shook himself into action, flailing around inside until his hands hit the semi-conscious body of Sammo. Dave swore as he groped around for the button for the electric ram to open the rear hatch of the burning vehicle before they managed to haul Sammo out.

"We've got a blue-on-blue," Jake said into his radio. He stopped himself from shouting. "I repeat, blue-on-blue. Abort the air strike. Abort, abort."

But the A-10s came around a second time before the message was relayed through Central Command. The intensity of Jake's terror was something he had never felt before. It was the feeling of death. He wasn't yet helpless in its grip, but it was coming for him. The A-10s strafed them again, the dull buzz tearing dispassionate strips across the earth, reducing everything in their path to dust, splintered metal and bloodied flesh. In the immediate aftermath, Jake's terror turned to fury. If he could have somehow got to the pilots in those moments, he felt like he could have killed them.

Sammo made it. Two lads from his troop died out in the desert and a third died a few days later in hospital. Paul Vincent was from Devon, crazy about rugby and the fittest in the troop. He had only just turned twenty when he was left with a body that was just a hunk of smashed meat, a machine inflating and deflating it, until his parents gave permission to pull the plug. Jake had never wanted to set foot inside another hospital.

All the vehicles in Jake's troop had carried orange marker panels to allow easier identification by Allied pilots. The A-10 pilots should have seen. But the line from Central Command was that Jake had called in the attack without correctly identifying the location of the friendlies. Jake's senior officers went along with it. No one wanted to rake over the coals.

Bad PR might compromise the mission, damage trust, endanger more Allied lives. Jake heard it all.

His CO told him his record would be unaffected. He had a promising career ahead of him, if he kept quiet. It had been a confused situation out in the desert, the CO said. Just one of those tragic things that was inevitable in the course of a war.

A confused situation. That was true. Jake's fury with the A-10 pilots had subsided – they would know they had killed friendlies that day, it would stay with them for the rest of their lives and it may not even have been their error. The fault might have lain anywhere along the line from Jake's mic through British comms to American comms and into the helmets of the pilots. Someone knew. Someone had got it wrong. Take responsibility, pay your dues, move on.

Knowing he wouldn't be able to pack it away into some tidy compartment, Jake went back to his CO. "I'd like to hear the comms recordings from the engagement, sir." Jake was willing to take whatever he deserved on the chin, but he was convinced he had called in the coordinates correctly and identified his own position. His mind had been clear out there in the panic and confusion. He had been in the zone.

His CO was sitting behind a cheap, modern desk in a small office with equally modest furnishings. It wasn't the same army he had joined as a young lieutenant. But some things didn't change. "You have to put your personal feelings aside and think about your responsibilities to the regiment," he said to Jake. "We're soldiers and we have to accept whatever comes our way in a war. We all signed up to that."

Jake went to see the parents of each of his lads who had died. The visits were unofficial, his CO had told him not to contact them. Knocking on a door to tell a mother and a father that he had played a part in the death of their son was hard. Photos on the mantelpiece. But he found himself unable to stick to the army version. He told them what he knew because he felt it was the right thing – he wasn't seeking their forgiveness. Paul Vincent's parents got angry with him anyway, they wanted to lash out at the army, at anyone in the army. But they wanted to get to the bottom of it. All the parents did.

Jake got nowhere. The army pulled down the shutters and his CO summonsed him. "Last warning. Don't throw your life away on this. You won't get a win."

Jake saluted, walked out of his office and went straight to a tabloid journalist.

He really had seen the army as a second family, a consistent, reliable contrast to his first. But retribution was final and ruthless. Caught out by the scale of media attention, the British and American High Command reacted swiftly. The PR people went into overdrive; they really did a number on Jake. At least someone had got a career boost

THE BURNING HILL

out of the wh... ...rry business. An edited transcript of the radio comms from the incident was handed to the media, with sole responsibility pointing to Jake. His brief, unwanted celebrity turned to notoriety. He ... ...d to split the moment they announced he was under investigation. He was on the plane to Brazil by the time the army had left a suitable delay between that announcement and the one for the charge of court martial.

Brazil hadn't worked out as the fresh start he had imagined, but it was only now the murk, like a damp winter morning, was lifting. He was going to do something. It wasn't a reaction provoked by anger in the way that the needle with Nogueira had driven him to rescue Vilson from the hill. The kid had been beaten with the shitty end of the stick his whole life. And now Jake was going to make something right for him. He was going to put what little family the kid had back together.

Marinho

Marinho stood with Nogueira, across the road from the main entrance of *Morro da Bõa Vista*. Anjo's TV news performance had gained spectacular, if brief, notoriety. The media had gone crazy over it until the horrific kidnapping and murder of a family up in the north had gripped the country, along with a new corruption scandal involving a government minister. The heat might not be so intense now, but Nogueira was still getting some.

Marinho stood at his shoulder as Nogueira breathed in an air of confidence and crossed the road, ambling into the favela like he was taking a stroll along the beachfront on a Sunday. Marinho had a decent poker face but he wasn't in the same league. Even though they were fooling no one with their plain clothes, they went unchallenged. The word had been put out; they had a pass.

Climbing the hill, Nogueira stopped at a small shop that had its metal window shutters pulled down. The sign on the door claimed that the shop was a world leader in used electrical goods and repairs. Nogueira took a breath to recover from the climb, using the heel of his hand to push the sweat from his brow.

The city was less than two hundred metres below them. Safety and sanity seemed a very long way away. Marinho wished to hell he was back in the unmarked car on the street where Branca was waiting at the wheel.

Branca went along with whatever Nogueira told him because he

89

knew what was good for him. Marinho wondered if Branca ever saw that dying kid curling up in agony on the Copacabana pavement in his dreams and every time he closed his eyes. Give Vilson up and the dead kid might haunt him forever. Helping him was inviting a death sentence. And the worst of it was that Marinho needed Nogueira. If Nogueira got put away or got put down, all hope of the career that Marinho wanted so desperately would be gone forever. He was between a rock and more than one hard place.

Nogueira gave him the slightest of nods. You ready for this?

Marinho nodded back. His stomach was churning. Nogueira had told him he was along for the ride because of his ability to set his face cold when it mattered. And because he was useful in a fight and kept a cool finger on his trigger. Marinho knew Franjinha was on the other side of the door. If he or any of his kids remembered him from the night with Vilson, he was dead. And he knew that Nogueira might put a bullet in his head before anyone else got a chance, just to make a statement to Anjo. Nogueira always had a backup plan, an out, if things went to shit. Whatever Nogueira had up his sleeve, Marinho had to go through the door and meet his fate. And show not the faintest trace of fear. Even if his guts had turned to water.

Nogueira loosened his shoulders, put his own face on and knocked. He looked like a hit man on his holidays. Marinho had to give it to him: he was a tough son of a bitch.

A kid opened the door enough for them to move into the hot little electrical shop, the weak strip lights giving it a sickly pallor.

Anjo was leaning against the long shop counter, Franjinha at his side, other soldiers crammed in against shelves stacked with cardboard boxes containing electrical flex, plugs and components. There were untidy piles of TVs and stereos and kitchen appliances in various states of repair on the counter and on the floor.

Marinho followed Nogueira's lead, keeping his hands slightly away from his body, palms turned out. A very deliberate, unthreatening gesture. Coming in peace. He could feel the uncomfortable bulk of his handgun tucked down the back of his trousers. No one would expect them to walk into the favela unarmed. Anjo and his soldiers kept their guns similarly holstered. An all-round show of good faith.

The sweat was suddenly pouring from Marinho. In that stuffy, cramped space, everyone was sweating. Every asshole in there knew that every other asshole knew that if it all went to hell no one was walking away without having lumps shot out of them.

Marinho avoided catching Franjinha's eye, whose burns were

peeled and red-raw shiny. He had a kind of cap of stretchy medical gauze smeared with grease on his head. There was more of the gauze wrapping the taut, raw skin of his arms. He shifted on the spot, tensing different parts of his body to distract from the pain that was etched into his face, even with its customary blankness. The burned skin of his hands was too tight for him to fully clench his fists. Marinho could see that he was twitching for a line. But there was nothing else coming from him, no hint of recognition. It was one thing crossed off the list that would stop Marinho from getting out of this place alive.

Anjo pushed himself away from the counter to command attention. "O *Capitão*," – The Captain – he said, grinning. "What an honour."

Nogueira bowed his head, playing up to Anjo's dig. "The honour is mine, to be with the most famous guy in Rio."

Anjo liked that.

Nogueira immediately changed gear. "But you know your television stunt is still making a lot of trouble for me." He was straight to it, punching the wasp's nest. Fearless, thought Marinho.

Anjo's grin disappeared. "I thought we were here to talk business? Why are you still going on about that?"

"Because when you go mouthing off about bad cops and your favela law and corruption in the city you make it my business."

Anjo was still. Deciding which way to go. Nerves were getting the better of some of his soldiers, their eyes darting about.

Marinho willed his breathing to remain even and tried to contain the tremor in his muscles. His body was ready for the fight.

"I do what I want in my favela. I am boss here," Anjo said slowly.

"That's right, we don't step on one another's territory, that's how it works, but you came and trampled on mine."

Anjo shrugged. "I cleaned up your little mess."

"By leaving a fried corpse in the middle of the road? Was that even the right kid or just someone you didn't like the look of that night?"

"It was the right kid. I put the bullets in him myself. Some little hoodlums must have decided it would be fun to torch him afterward." Anjo chuckled. "Kids, uh?"

Nogueira glanced at Franjinha's burns. "Not just the kids who should avoid playing with fire, uh?"

Anjo pulled the Beretta from the back of his shorts. He was quick. He might be a lousy shot, but he was quick.

Other kids went for their guns. There was a murmur around the room.

Nogueira and Marinho moved their arms further out from their bodies in unison, palms turned out.

"This is a lack of respect," shouted Anjo, his voice ⸺ ⸺ ⸺ ⸺iting in the small space. "You remember where you are r⸺l ⸺ ⸺ ⸺ ⸺ This is my place. I might think about taking your shit if ⸺ ⸺ ⸺ ⸺ ⸺ ⸺ ig me a wage. Except last time I looked, I was paying yo⸺ ⸺.

His soldiers laughed on cue. There was a nasty ⸺ lp⸺ ⸺ ⸺ ⸺ new Anjo well enough to know there was a kill coming.

Nogueira shrugged graciously, no hint of tension ⸺ n ⸺ h⸺ ⸺ face. "You are a businessman, as am I. But this has ⸺ ⸺ ⸺ ⸺ ⸺ r my business. I know you can see that. It's making life d⸺l ⸺ ⸺

Franjinha moved and Marinho tensed. Nogueir⸺ ⸺ ⸺l⸺ ⸺ ⸺ ⸺ ⸺.

Franjinha placed a hand on Anjo's forearm ⸺ ⸺ ⸺ ⸺ ⸺ ⸺ eyes glittered as he kept on staring down Nogueira.

"It's okay," Franjinha said. "It was just a bad jol⸺ ⸺ ⸺ ⸺ ⸺ op?"

"Sure," Nogueira said, keeping his voice deep a⸺ l⸺ ⸺ ⸺ ⸺k, to show there are no hard feelings, maybe I can put s⸺ ⸺ ⸺ ⸺ way. My *cabo* here is fighting soon, a big fight – I can he⸺ ⸺ ⸺ l⸺ ⸺t of money on it."

Nogueira had held his nerve and kept them al⸺ ⸺ ⸺ ⸺ new that. He rumbled on with languid confidence as if ⸺ ⸺ ⸺ ⸺ ⸺d the Sunday stroll by putting his feet up in a beach b⸺ ⸺ ⸺ ⸺ ⸺ ⸺ ⸺ his hand.

He hadn't cut any kind of deal but he had ha⸺ ⸺ l⸺ ⸺ ⸺ome into Anjo's backyard and piss against his post. Witho⸺ ⸺ ⸺ ⸺ far, Nogueira was the biggest dog in the room and eve⸺ ⸺ ⸺ ⸺

Chapter 18

Jake

The early-morning sun was streaming through the gaps in the curtains, carving golden slashes across seats and slumped heads. The bus whined through the gears as it slowed to pull off the single carriageway to a roadside café for a breakfast stop and driver switch.

A couple of hours after the lunch stop, struggling to tell whether his backside was aching or numb, Jake saw the first signs for Cruzeiro, his destination.

This was where the priest had said he should start looking for Vilson's mother. He had contacted Padre Francisco through Eliane and stopped to meet him en route to the bus station. His mother's lucky-dip Catholicism had never rubbed off on him and he didn't have the highest opinion of priests, but Padre Francisco had projected a sense of calm that had settled over him like a blanket. In the cramped little office in the Candelária church, everything had seemed clear and simple.

"I think it is better that you go without Vilson," Padre Francisco had said. His eyes had clouded then, Jake recognising a look of regret. He had seen a fair few of those in his life.

"Please don't expect too much," Padre Francisco had said. "A lot of time has passed. I don't even have an address for his mother, just a town, and she may have moved on by now."

Seventy-three kilometres to go, the latest sign said. The town was north of Rio and inland, somewhere out in the heartland of Brazil beneath the thick, green crown of the Amazon. Vast fields of sugar cane, tall and strong under the fierce sun, rolling away on either side of the road. The tarmac was black and shiny in the tyre tracks, covered everywhere else in a fine, red dust.

The bus chugged up and then ran down a series of hills along a stretch of straight road before finally turning off. It wound down a slope through the edge of town, bridged a dried-out riverbed and climbed through a newer, more sparsely populated area. The driver announced Cruzeiro's bus station as he pulled into what was little more than a big concrete shelter. It was completely deserted.

"I hope you're here somewhere," Jake said to himself, the baked air sucking the moisture from his lungs as he stepped from the bus.

Small town, smaller pool of people to trawl. That was a plus. But the reality was he had no photo to go on, little in the way of description and no fixed address. He did, at least, have a starting point. The church. An overheated horse and cart plodded past; he hadn't seen a moving car yet. It looked like a taxi was out of the question.

He started back down the hill, over the dried-out riverbed and up the other side into the centre of the town. He resolved to stop any middle-aged woman he saw and ask her name, but he only passed a couple of young mothers with covered buggies protecting their babies from the sun, and a few old folks, gently desiccating in the heat as they hobbled from one patch of shade to another.

The modest church was in the central square. An oasis of greenery and trees surrounded by a parade of shops and the town's older, colonial-style houses. The whitewashed church walls were scrubbed free of the red-earth stains that were splashed up the skirts of many of the houses he had passed.

He had to wait a good hot while in the square before the old priest turned up. He was still looking blank after Jake's introductory spiel. "Father, Padre Francisco from the Candelária church in Rio, he said he would be contacting you?"

The priest squinted and looked away, as if his recollection was written on some distant board. "Yes, I heard from your Padre Francisco, but I have not heard of this woman, this…"

"Goretti Lima, Father, her name is Goretti Lima."

"Yes, yes, that's it. But like I told your Padre Francisco, I don't know this woman. I only came to this diocese in the last six months."

"But this is a small town. Surely it couldn't be that hard to find her?"

The priest looked surprised, as if unused to being questioned. "Are you sure she still lives here?"

"I know she *was* here, so this is where I've got to start looking."

"Well, I don't know everyone in town yet, but I will make enquiries for you."

Jake used his frustration as a spur, going on to buttonhole every shopkeeper and customer in the parade running alongside the square. He probably would have caused a stir as the only *gringo* in town even without his car-crash looks.

An hour later he was slumped against the wall surrounding the square, drinking cold bottled water. The shops were beginning to close as the sun dropped behind them, shade enveloping the square. No one knew Vilson's mother. He had learned nothing other than that he could get a room in a motel on the edge of town.

He started putting one sweaty, cooked foot in front of the other, ignoring his empty, cramping stomach, instead focusing on the goal of a long, cool shower. His scars throbbed, his legs were weak.

The motel was about half a kilometre out of town on the main road. He hoped his first impression from a couple of hundred metres away was wrong.

It wasn't.

The building was a low, shabby, concrete job in an approximation of Wild-West-style-Mexican-stroke-take-your-pick style and painted a dirty pink. A sex motel. A place for cheating spouses and young lovers, rather than snackered single *gringos*. The unlit plastic sign on a pole in the forecourt carried an ace of hearts design in front of the reception. Whether or not someone in town had had the idea of sending him there as a joke, Jake was beyond laughing.

He was finding that when he got tired his speech started to slur, his brain misplacing the adaptation it had made to the new shape of his mouth. It was a struggle to make himself understood, and the receptionist filled in the gaps by gamely listing the by-the-hour prices, the extra services and themed rooms. Jake was vaguely intrigued by The Space Station and The Underwater Love Suite, but what he really wanted was a shower and a lie down in the most basic room they had. He got one, but just had a number.

The decor in his room was lurid and shabby, but clean. The shower was good enough, and he had got used to the bare wires poking out of Brazilian shower heads for the heating element. They were just a passing worry now. He came out, dripping on the postage-stamp bathmat, rubbing some life back into his skin with the thin, sandpaper towel. He flopped on to the small double bed, the mattress like chewed marshmallow, pillows thin and lumpy. And he slept like a baby.

In the early morning he enjoyed half an hour of lolling in the frigid air rattling out from the air-con unit in the wall before wandering into town, getting some pastries and coffee at the bakery in the square. Fuelled up, he started working his way out from the square, speaking to every shopkeeper, shopper and passer-by he came across. He stuck to the shade as much as possible, moving at a speed that he hoped would generate the least amount of body heat, sticking so diligently to the task that he was in danger of getting overtaken by some of the town's more elderly residents.

By late morning, Jake was losing the will to live. He had almost got to the end of a residential street toward the edge of town, small shops and businesses strung along it. This was the last one before lunch. He wasn't sure he would manage to go for much longer after lunch.

He walked past a bungalow, a white metal fence fronting its garden. An old man was turning the dry soil of a flowerbed with a hoe. Slugging it out in the hottest part of the day in frayed clothes, it looked to Jake like he was doing paid work.

He stuck with his most polite Portuguese to get the old man's attention.

The old man pushed up his hat, wiped his forehead with a handkerchief and then blew his nose loudly. He shook his head. "Never heard of her. Maybe you should look in the other end of town," he said.

"Which other end, sir?"

"The wrong end," he said, rolling a lump of dirt with his tatty boot.

Jake hadn't come across anything that looked like a wrong end. He looked up the hill.

"The other way," the old man said, pointing downhill, "and turn left over the river."

Walking down and then back up the hill on the other side of the dried-out riverbed and taking the left turn, he noticed there were more cracks in the paving slabs, the surface more uneven. The shabbier part of town. The houses were much smaller, the build more homespun. A couple of open doors revealed rough concrete floors and the most basic of furnishings.

This was the place he would find Vilson's mother.

Sitting at a small, round table on a plastic chair with his head in his hands the next evening, Jake wasn't so sure. The bar, if it even qualified as one, was on a corner in the wrong end of town, with a lean-to beneath which were a few more tables and chairs, all empty. A handful of locals sat on a ragtag row of high stools at the bar.

The night had just settled in, the bar lit by two bare bulbs, each a miniature solar system, a mad host of insect planets careening around and crashing into their star. Jake spent a while staring at them, a place far from here.

He took a slug from his bottled beer. His third evening in Cruzeiro and already just about everyone in town knew him, and not in a good way. The scar-faced *gringo*, pestering everyone at least twice, had fast become the person to avoid. And all he had learned was that, if Vilson's mother had ever lived in this town, she didn't now.

He wanted to finish his beer, get a night's sleep and get the first bus back to Rio. It would not be the return of the conquering hero.

A guy strolled in and took a stool at the bar. Jake didn't recognise him.

He had already heard the other drinkers at the bar muttering dark things about *gringos* when he had bought his beer. He was getting pretty sick of the *gringo* thing. He prevaricated and stewed for twenty minutes before downing the warming dregs of his beer.

Hauling himself out of the chair, shoulders were tensing at the bar before he even cleared his throat.

"*Meu Deus*," one of the guys said in exasperation, whirling on him before he had even got his introductory patter out. "Why don't you just leave us in peace?" he said in a low growl. "You're driving everyone around here crazy."

A couple more turned on Jake, eyes swimming with drunken belligerence. He was an irritant, he was willing to admit to that, but this was definitely an overreaction. He stood his ground. "Goretti Lima lived in this town, someone must have known her. Her son is desperate to find her."

"No one knows this boy's mama, and no one cares," the growl was becoming a snarl, "so why don't you disappear before someone really loses their cool?"

The raw scars on Jake's cheek were beginning to throb. He rubbed the corner of his brow to distract from it.

"Maybe your friend's mother doesn't live in town." That came from the guy whose back had remained turned on Jake, the one he had wanted to question. The others stared at him.

The man turned slowly on his stool, took a drag on his cigarette and scratched at the greying bristles on his chin. "Could be that she works on one of the farms out of town."

"Yes," said Jake. His readiness to grasp at hope seemed like it was a sting to the other drinkers. "That would fit. She wanted a small farm to set up with her son."

"She wouldn't be running any place out there," said the helpful smoker.

"How would I get to these places?" Jake asked.

"I am driving out that way tomorrow. I can maybe drop you by one if you want."

The growling barfly shook his head and sucked his teeth. "Take him out there to stir that shit and we'll smell the stink for a week."

The smoker shrugged. "Who am I to stop a boy finding his future? Who are any of us?"

"You're as crazy as he is," the growler growled.

Chapter 19

Jake

The agreed time was eight in the morning, on a corner opposite the bus station. It hadn't come easy but the army had fixed his aversion to early mornings, and he was there for seven-thirty. He couldn't miss this opportunity.

There was a clock hanging from the flat concrete roof of the deserted bus station. Sitting on the kerb, he watched it mark the seconds, the low sun warming his skin.

The next two hours gave him plenty of time to regret missing breakfast and only bringing a small bottle of water. He had noticed that he was forgetting things, basic everyday stuff that he would never ordinarily miss.

His lift eventually drew up in the shape of a dusty old pickup, a cigarette hanging from the corner of the driver's mouth. He did no more than lift a couple of fingers from the steering wheel at Jake's greeting. Jake looked in the back of the pickup: it was a jumble of sacks and tools and empty buckets, with a mangy old dog sitting on a pile of plastic sacks.

"Up to you," the driver said. "Ride in the back if you want but it's more comfortable up here."

They drove in silence for a few kilometres, before turning off the main road that skirted Cruzeiro. The driver then bucketed along a smaller, broken road for ten kilometres, trying to avoid the worst of the potholes and cracks, until he finally slowed, came off the crumbling tarmac and pulled up by a turn-off to a dirt track. It ran down a hill between a field of sugar cane on one side and a field of coffee on the other, the little red berries beginning to ripen. There was a rocky plateau out in the milky distance, a slab sitting on the horizon. A bent metal sign hung off a wooden post. Whatever message it had once carried was long lost to peeled paint and rust, only a few faded letters surviving. Getting out of the pickup, Jake felt like he was stepping onto the set of a Western.

The driver spoke through the lighting of another cigarette, the tip twitching. "There are other farms along this road, but down there is your best bet."

He chunked the pickup into gear and started to roll forward in the dirt. And then braked. An afterthought, leaning out the window: "Watch out for yourself, understand?"

Jake nodded. "Always." If the driver got the irony of that, given his scars, he didn't show it. But then Jake didn't really know what he was supposed to be watching out for either.

"*Vai com Deus*," – Go with God – the driver said and stepped on the accelerator, rocking the creaky old pickup back onto the tarmac.

Jake watched it disappear up the road in a low haze of dust before he set off down the rutted track. The sun was cranking up to full power in a sky as hard as metal, and he had already drunk most of the water in his bottle.

The track was a downhill trudge, then a hot sweaty grind back uphill. And repeat. Every turn promised something but delivered more of the same. Rolling pasture with coarse tufts of grass was starting to fill in gaps in the sugar cane and coffee. The shade of the occasional tree at the edge of the track gave only fleeting respite. The first farm he came to was no more than a smallholding. He found the old farmer working at the back of the property in a grove of mango trees. Jake's heart was thumping. But the old man hadn't heard of Goretti Lima. And it was the same with the second and third places he came across. It seemed that inquisitive strangers were as popular out here as back in town.

He only had a few drops of water left in the bottle, and his throat was dry. The rolling fields were mostly pasture now with healthy, green copses and thickets of waving bamboo, twenty metres tall. The distant plateau he had seen from the road was slowly becoming the dominant feature of the landscape. Its sharp slopes rose from a tract of forest, the crown mottled grey and red, earthy rock and boulders, strangled vegetation sprouting here and there. It bent around the farmland, shepherding a giant corner.

He stepped over an old cattle grid, alongside a broken gate with rusted barbed wire dangling off ancient wooden posts. The track faded halfway across the next field, just cattle paths snaking away through the fields beyond. This was the last farm. He noticed a puff of smoke out in the distance, rolling upward in the still air. Another followed it.

The farmhouse was built in the same bungalow style as the others he had passed. It had an abandoned look, the whitewash grubby and the terracotta-tiled roof bowed. But there were vegetables growing in a watered square of tilled earth to the side of the house. Fruit trees and a banana plantation lay beyond. On the other side of the building there was a low cattle shed and a rough-timbered pen. Raggedy chickens were flipping over dead tree leaves and picking through the soft dirt between piles of fresh cow shit. There was an old, blue VW pickup parked under a tree alongside the pen.

"Hello?" he called out, slumping to the smooth, cool tiles of the shady veranda, no more than a low platform upon the rough concrete surround. His face was burning and his scars throbbed. Droplets of sweat fell from his drooping head onto the tiles. He rested for a couple of minutes and then checked out the yard at the back, calling out, his voice ringing off the hot walls of the outbuildings. Nothing.

"Follow the smoke, then," he muttered, surprised at talking to himself.

The smoke was still going up in irregular puffs somewhere out beyond a rise in the next field.

The earth around the farm was sandy, making for soft going as he laboured up the rise, draining more of his already depleted energy. Pushing up his body temperature. Over the rise the track dropped to a shallow ford in a stream, the banks around it eroded into deep ruts by the hooves of cattle. He splashed water over his face and head, resisting the urge to drink.

Cattle paths meandered up from the ford into dense scrub and low, scorched-looking trees. And the smoke.

Jake caught the *whack whack* rhythm of human labour. Someone was either cutting something or hitting it.

He weaved his way up a cattle path through thorny shrubs that pulled at his clothes.

The *whack* was getting louder, the rhythm sometimes broken, sometimes rapidly repeated. There was more than one person. His heart quickened.

The sharp tang of wood smoke caught in his nostrils. Lifting his arms to edge sideways through a gap in the thorns, he found himself at the lip of a shallow bowl that had been half cleared. Beyond it was the tract of forest and then the plateau, looming now.

There were two scrawny men wearily going at a wall of thick brush with machetes, intent to the task in ragged clothes, thorns tearing at the bare skin of their arms. There were piles of cut brush in the clearing behind them. It looked to Jake like they had been at it for days. Two bonfires coughed up thick gobs of smoke, another pair of men lobbing pitchforks of the green rubbish onto them.

Jake approached the nearest of the bonfire stokers. "Excuse me, sir, do you know if Geberti Lima works on this farm?"

The man broke away from his work, seemingly noticing him for the first time, out in this wilderness. There was no surprise in his eyes, no spark of interest. "No, there is no Goretti Lima," he mumbled.

"Are you sure?"

"Yes." He was about to turn back to his work when something seemed to occur to him. "There is a *Dona* Goretti."

Jake sank to a squat in the airless heat. "Is she here? On the farm?"

The man looked at him for a long time as if lost in some distant, unwelcome journey, before turning to the others. They had stopped work to stare at the stranger with the same detachment.

Prompted by nothing in particular, it seemed to Jake, the man lifted his chin to shout, "*O Dona Goretti.*" He stared at Jake for a while longer and then shouted again, summoning. "*O Dona, vem aqui.*"

"*Oi?*" A thin, quavering shout came from a woman somewhere out beyond the cutters.

She appeared through a gap in the brush, her skin burned dark and lined. A bleached-out scarf tied round her head framed her gaunt features. She was tiny, looking barely capable of swinging the heavy cane knife she carried with its broad, hooked blade.

Her slope-shouldered, shuffling gait was the unmistakable legacy she had passed to Vilson.

Jake had found her. He had found Vilson's mother. He rose, exhaustion forgotten. He almost laughed as her eyes flicked irritably between him and the labourers.

"*O que foi?*" – What's going on? – she asked, her voice matching her frame.

"Goretti Lima?" Jake asked.

She recoiled, as if stung.

"I know your son, Vilson," Jake said gently, unsure if it was his demeanour or appearance, or both, that was putting her on edge. "I came here from Rio to find you, to bring you back together."

Goretti's face screwed up. "Vilson? *Meu Deus.*" The cane knife dropped from her hand. She shook her head, hugging herself. Just like Vilson.

It wasn't the reaction Jake was expecting.

"And Gabriel? Where is Gabriel?" she asked.

"Gabriel? I – I don't understand."

"My elder son, Gabriel. Where is he?"

"You don't know?" Jake felt suddenly light-headed with confusion. She looked scared. "Know what? What's happened to him?"

"I'm so sorry, *Senhora*, Gabriel died years ago, when Vilson was young."

"No, no, not my poor Gabriel." Her head dropped to one side, her eyes staring at the ground.

"But that happened so many years ago. I was sure you knew."

Her jaw was working, but no words came.

There was a murmur amongst the men and they started shifting from foot to foot uneasily.

They heard it before Jake. The hollow beat of hooves on thin, dusty earth. A man on horseback came belting through the scrub on the other side of the bowl. Sweat was frothing on the neck of his small grey horse. The man gave it a good dig with his heels to make a show of bursting into the clearing, dominating the space and then wheeling past his men and around in front of Jake.

He reined in harshly, making the horse yaw at the green-frothed bridle, nearly sitting it back on its haunches. The worn saddle sat on top of old sacks. The skinny mare's ribs protruded beneath but her belly was distended, full of worms.

This was not a rich landowner. Beneath his sweat-stained straw hat there were deep lines scored at the corners of his eyes and a greying beard around his hard-set mouth.

"What are you doing trespassing here?" he demanded.

Jake looked expectantly to Vilson's mother. She would smooth this out.

But she just stepped closer to the mounted man, looking down at her rough, dusty feet pushed into ancient flip-flops.

"I came here to find *Dona* Goretti," Jake said.

She lifted her eyes to him, silently pleading, wringing her hands.

Whatever she did or didn't want him to say, Jake had to see it through. "I know *Dona* Goretti's son, Vilson, from Rio."

"Her son?" the man laughed bitterly. He turned on Goretti contemptuously. "Is this true?"

She hugged herself again, a faint keening coming from her. She was crying but no tears fell.

The man shook his head. He seemed used to disgust and disappointment. "So now you have found her you can get the hell off my property."

"*Dona* Goretti, please, what is this?" said Jake. "I came a long way. Vilson has waited for so many years."

"You shouldn't have come. You can never tell Vilson you found me." She couldn't meet his eyes.

"What is going on here?" Jake asked.

She nodded. She had made a decision. "Tell Vilson that I am dead.

That old life is gone now."

"You can't do that," Jake pleaded.

The man slammed his heels into the mare's ribs, ... at Jake, then hauled on the reins, the mare stamping her ... cking her head.

Jake felt hot breath and flecks of spittle on his face. His ... feet planted, looking the horseman dead in the eye.

"Get the hell out of here," the man shouted, stan... rups and shifting in the saddle. "And never come back."

The labourers with their machetes and pitc... on impassively. They were like zombies.

"I'm not leaving unless she tells me to leave," ... as all he had.

She moved closer to the man on the horse, la... his dusty trouser leg.

Shit. He should have realised. She was *Dona* Gore... this place. She and the horseman were a couple, she wasn't ... one of the zombie workers.

"I want you to go," Goretti said, her voice firm ... ime. "When I left Vilson behind in the city it was forever. ..."

Jake backed up a couple of paces. The din of ... sects around him rose and fell, as if someone was covering an... cring his ears. He was close to fainting. He fought it. Turn... bled away.

He had made nothing better. He had only gai... to destroy the dream that had held Vilson's fragile li... since childhood.

Chapter 20

Vilson

The lawyer hadn't locked the door to Jake's apartment on her last visit – Vilson guessed that she probably didn't want any rich-person guilt over making him a prisoner. It hadn't stopped her deadlocking the tall metal gate in the courtyard though. In spite of himself, he had taken the cop's advice and put on some of the *gringo's* clothes. They were baggy on him, but that worked okay. He only had to sit by the open lounge window for an hour before he heard a door open and shut across the courtyard. He grabbed the flimsy, rolled-up plastic bag that was carrying his own clothes and tucked it under his arm. Following the neighbour, he waited behind her as she unlocked the gate. She held it open and he walked past her, looking up and down the road, not paying attention to whatever she muttered under her breath. He was scared, half expecting to see a line of cop cars with lights flashing. Or maybe the black, glittering eyes of Anjo, and the barrel of his gun.

But traffic and regular city people were all he had to deal with. He watched how the people walked along the street and tried to copy them. He played different roles as he went – the guy going to the supermarket for his mother, the guy going to meet his friends to catch a movie, the guy going to start a shift at his job. He was just like everyone else. His fear was turning to amazement. People on the street walked straight past, some almost brushing him. No one gave him a wide berth. It felt like a superpower.

It was a three-hour walk to the bus station and he didn't get there until late morning.

"Only a couple of seats left on tonight's bus," the ticket-office man said. "You want one?"

"I'll come back," Vilson replied.

He had no money.

He scoped the place out and, finding that there were fewer station officials hanging around in the area by the bus bays, he moved along the queues, begging.

Two hours. Nothing. He noticed a bus driver holding his passenger checklist in the next bay watching him.

He went back to the main entrance. He couldn't beg here – still too many officials. He had an idea. Picking out a better-heeled young woman standing beneath a departures and arrivals screen, he sucked in some air to bolster himself and went up to her.

"Excuse me, I'm in a bit of a mess," he said. "I lost my wallet, all my money, everything, I think it was maybe stolen. I'm so embarrassed having to ask, but could you spare me a few *Reais* so I can get my bus home?"

She looked him over, doubt in her face.

"It's the only way I can get home," Vilson said. "Please."

"Sure, okay." She searched in her bag, pulling a note from her purse. "I can only spare five *Reais*, is that okay?"

Vilson was elated. Five *Reais*. She would never have handed over that sort of money if even for a second she had suspected he was a favela kid on the make. His transformation into a regular city person was complete. He felt a little rush of power, something entirely new to him. It felt good.

There were a couple of misfires but after three more hits he was over half way to the bus fare.

Someone gripped his shoulder. Instinctively jinking his body away, he caught sight of the cop uniform.

Horrendous pain in his wrist stopped him in his tracks. The cop twisted more, he had an iron grip, and pushed his arm up behind his back. It was agony. He was helpless. And scared stiff.

"Leave me alone, man," Vilson shouted, wanting to cause as big a scene as possible, "I haven't done anything." Maybe the regular city people would come to the aid of one of their own.

The cop leaned close into his ear. "Keep it down. It's me, idiot. Marinho."

Vilson was on tiptoes trying to escape the twisting pain in his arm. "Then what the hell are you doing? Let me go."

"You shut up and keep walking wherever I point you."

The regular city people stared, but that's all they did. A station official came over. "I saw this kid earlier, what did he do?"

"Suspected robbery," said Marinho.

"Yup," the official said, nodding, like he'd thought as much.

Marinho pushed Vilson forward, out of the bus station and across the road to his cop car.

"Where are we going?" Fear and suspicion were overwhelming Vilson.

Marinho opened the back door and shoved him in. "Just get in and keep your head down." He slammed the door and jumped in the front. "You're going back to the *gringo's* apartment."

"No, no way," Vilson pulled on the door handle in vain. "Let me out, I need to catch this bus tonight."

"Quit tugging on that thing, you're locked in." Marinho started the engine and pulled away.

"Just let me get on that bus and you'll never see me again, I promise."

"Trust me, when the time is right, no one will be happier than me to watch you go."

"Why can't you people leave me alone?"

Marinho stamped on the brake as they drew up to a red light, Vilson flying off the back seat and crashing into the metal grill dividing the car. "I wish to God we had left you up on that hill," Marinho said, turning on him. "I'm not doing this for you, you little asshole. I'm trying to keep myself alive, plus a few other people, while you're doing your best to do the opposite, wandering around with a giant target pinned to your own back."

Vilson got himself back on the seat, rubbing his forehead. He stared sullenly at the regular people walking by. Lives that were never touched by this kind of shit.

"I said keep your head down, or I'll put you off that seat again," Marinho said.

Vilson slid down in the seat, his eyes level with the door sill.

Marinho looked in the rear-view mirror as he pulled away from the lights. "Eliane's been chasing around Ipanema half the day looking for you. She is frantic. I guessed you might have headed here. You're lucky I got to you before another cop did. I mean, Christ, what was going through your head?"

"What do you care?" Vilson muttered.

Anjo

The metal window shutters were pulled shut against the mid-afternoon heat, the floor-standing fan swirling cooled air around the dimmed room. Anjo had just had an air-con unit put in the wall for his friend.

Franjinha lay on the couch, eyes closed, a near-empty bottle of Johnnie Walker Black Label on the tiled floor next to him. The boy had expensive tastes, Anjo mused. His arms, bandaged in the greased gauze, were outstretched by his sides, palms turned upward.

There was something spooky about the way he was laid out. Anjo shivered as he perched on a plastic chair and waited.

Franjinha's eyes eventually fluttered open. They began to focus and he winced with pain. It was a few moments before he noticed Anjo. He didn't move his head or his arms.

"Hey, man," Anjo said gently. "How's it going?"

"Hey. Huh. You know, I wake up and just for a second I don't feel anything, and then it comes, stinging like a bitch. So now I'm waking up and trying to tell myself that if I stay still the pain won't come."

"And that works?"

"Yeah," Franjinha said, "for about a second."

"Shit, man," Anjo laughed, "you're in a bad way."

Franjinha spread the fingers of his upturned hands. It was his only movement other than a vague grimace on his unreadable face.

"I got something to cheer you up," Anjo said, waving a small plastic bag of white powder. "Another special delivery."

"Man, I can't take any more of that stuff right now. I need to sleep properly, it's driving me crazy. I've got those pills the doctor gave me but they do nothing."

"Ah, he's an idiot. I know proper medicine. I'll get you some heavy-duty downers, they'll straighten you out."

"Thanks, brother. I'll be back soon, good and strong again."

"Don't sweat it, just get there in your own time," said Anjo.

Franjinha gave the faintest of nods and closed his eyes.

Anjo let the silence drift for a while but his eyebrows were knitted. Something was scratching away at the back of his narcotic-fuddled brain. He needed to know. "You think we're playing this thing out the right way?"

Franjinha's eyes stayed closed. "Sure we are, brother, just like we planned – we play along with Nogueira but we keep chipping bits off him, break him down nice and slow."

"But he's in a corner now. We don't want him starting a war before we're ready."

"It's all cool. You got it right in that shop. You didn't let him push you around and you didn't make him lose face."

Anjo thought for a moment. "Yeah, I did get it right, didn't I?" He twisted the plastic bag around his finger. "You know, one of the kids told me a real head-fuck thing today."

"Oh yeah?" Franjinha's eyes remained closed. "Who?"

"Tôca. He says he thought he recognised that young cop that Nogueira brought with him to the shop. He thinks it was him who came to meet Vilson when he tried to escape."

Franjinha laughed and then winced. "Ah shit, that hurts. Come on, brother. Why would a cop want to do that?"

"I don't know, it doesn't make sense." Anjo frowned, his black eyes dull.

"Nah," said Franjinha. "My guess is that it was one of those charity do-gooders who tried to help him, or the church people. They need a reminder of who runs this place."

"Maybe you're right."

"Sure I'm right, brother."

Chapter 21

Jake

His legs gave way and he collapsed on the hot, dusty track back up to the road. He crawled to the shade of a mango tree. The grassy verge and the track were littered with the fat fruit, some of them crushed in the tyre tracks. Picking a good one, he tore the skin from it with his teeth.

Energy trickled back into him from the sweet flesh. Enough to get him back to the road. It took more than an hour of walking along the shimmering length of cracked tarmac before a truck wobbled out of the haze and stopped for his outstretched thumb.

He should go back to Rio. There was nothing more he could do in this place. There was nothing more he could do for Vilson. But the next afternoon he was in a bar down the hill from Cruzeiro's central church square. Drunk.

He had outstayed his welcome in Cruzeiro, that was for sure, but washing through his veins along with the alcohol was a good dose of belligerence. He would move on when he was good and ready.

They could mutter to themselves and avoid his eyes all they wanted. He was used to that.

It was market day, stalls lining the church square a few streets away, lots of people milling around up there. He could do without the lots of people. He sat at one of the plastic tables by the pavement, the only customer. The bar was next door to a butcher, both places opening onto the street, metal shutters closing them down at night. The butcher's was popular with flies and, with its smells of overheating meat and blood, Jake's beer wasn't tasting so good.

He rubbed his eyebrow, trying to distract from his itching scars. The system was a brick wall. He doubted that Eliane could ever bring Nogueira to justice, but at least she still had something to dig away at. Jake had looked for the back route to beating the system by fixing Vilson's life, and now all he could take back to Rio was something that would break the kid. Could he let him just stumble on through his miserable life living a lie? Bitter experience had made Jake a truth fanatic. No cover-ups, no shirking. But now that he was the one holding the power, where keeping a clear conscience wasn't the most important thing, the resolve to do the right thing wasn't coming easily.

He stared out at the thick, black clouds that had started to fill in the sky around lunchtime. Around the time he had started drinking, immediately after emerging from his motel bedroom. The atmosphere was close and uncomfortable. It suited him.

Lowering his gaze from the sky, he noticed a flyer pasted to the lamp post outside. It was advertising a rodeo that was coming to the big town nearby. He had seen others pasted all around town – the rodeo seemed like the only half-intriguing thing he had come across here. The few good memories Jake had of his father mostly involved watching old cowboy movies with him as a kid. His father had been crazy about them, and it was a Saturday-afternoon ritual between his lunchtime and evening sessions in the pub. His father's all-time favourite was the one with Dean Martin playing the town drunk who finds redemption. If Jake's father had possessed half the charm of a drunken Dean Martin maybe it would have worked out differently with his mother. Probably not though. Jake smiled grimly. It felt to him that for the last couple of days he had been blundering through the set of some low-rent Brazilian version of a Western that was falling a long way short of the simple code of good beats evil.

The sky darkened more and, when the rain came, it was sudden and hard, hammering the thin roof. The downpour was so intense Jake could scarcely see the other side of the street. The raindrops bounced and danced off the concrete and tarmac in an angry mist.

A tremendous crack directly overhead. The white glare of a lightning strike. The lights in the bar winked and wavered, the overhead wires in the street crackling and fizzing with static. The woman behind the bar cursed.

Cold air rushed in around Jake's bare legs and he could feel the splashes from raindrops against his skin.

A giant fork of lightning burned up the sky somewhere outside the town, the deep roll of thunder following it. Within minutes there were torrents running down the gutters on either side of the road.

Jake was beginning to enjoy himself. This was breaking up the day.

A pickup drove past, up the hill into town, the tyres slashing rainwater aside.

Jake was about to take another lug, the beer bottle hovering at his lips. It was the same old, blue VW pickup he'd seen out at the farm. He was sure of it.

He put the bottle down and followed.

"Are you crazy?" the woman behind the bar called out. "You can't walk out into that."

THE BURNING HILL

The rain drummed into his skull, stinging his bare skin. His hair and clothes were plastered to his skin in seconds. The rain felt like it had blown in from somewhere colder than Brazil. He was shivering within a minute.

The market on the church square now looked deserted on the lower side, just the stall holders and a few strays sheltering beneath the stall tarpaulins.

The rain eased and visibility instantly went from twenty metres to fifty. He thought he could see the pickup parked at the end of a line of cars on a side street. Then the rain came back just as hard and the road disappeared.

He hugged his arms around him and walked toward the side street. He saw the pickup, battered, with soaked litter and old feed sacks in the back. It was just houses on this street. Empty of people.

He went back to the square, checking the stalls along the upper side. At the end was a makeshift bar, a long, low marquee. Scaffolding poles draped with a heavy green tarpaulin, water pouring off the sides in tearing sheets. There were older men, drinking and smoking, and mixed groups of young people crowding in away from the open front of the marquee where the rain splashed in.

Jake pushed through the bodies and smoke, ignoring the looks and comments.

He found the farmer in a far corner, sitting with a couple of older men in plastic chairs. He was slouching, outstretched legs crossed at the ankles, a cigarette between his fingers, beer bottle hanging from the same hand. The sleeves of his checked shirt were rolled up to show strong forearms. A dripping stockman's coat hung off one of the scaffolding poles behind him. His straw cowboy hat was pushed back on his head, water droplets clinging to the rim. He looked like a bit-part baddie from one of those Westerns Jake's father had loved so much.

Jake stood in front of him. The farmer let his head drop to one side, staring past, chewing at the inside of his cheek.

"I can stand here for as long as it takes," Jake said. He couldn't stop himself shivering.

The farmer took a drag on his cigarette and his eyes rolled onto Jake. "Get out of my face, *gringo*," he said thickly. "Go on, beat it, I'm relaxing."

"Yeah, well, get those people out on your farm aren't. Do your friends here know what's going on out there?"

"Shut your mouth." The control disappeared.

Jake had touched a nerve. Now he was getting somewhere. "You've got a hold on those people, haven't you? And it's not just your natural charm, is it?"

"You dare come in here? You've no idea what you're talking about." The farmer rose from his plastic chair and jabbed a finger at Jake. "You get out of here before I have to teach you a lesson in front of all these people."

Jake smelled the beer and tobacco on his breath.

The chatter in the marquee had petered out, just the hollow drumming of rain on the tarpaulin remaining. Everyone had turned to stare.

The anger was boiling up. He had to keep control. Let the farmer go first and then unleash the dogs. He looked around at his audience, raising his voice. "I'm guessing your workers don't get much in the way of afternoons off, or wages, do they? I don't know the Portuguese word for what they are, but maybe you can tell us all."

The farmer was quicker than he looked. Flipping the beer bottle up, he caught it by the neck, upside down, the dregs splashing out, and whipped it into the side of Jake's head.

Chapter 22

Vilson

He didn't resist as the cop pushed him ahead into the courtyard of the *gringo's* apartment. He hunched his shoulders and dropped his head, playing his part.

It was dusk and fairy lights were strung around one of the little trees. It was a warped fantasy world here. He would let the cop give his lecture and he would nod along. It was the cop routine, Babão had always said that. They did it to make themselves feel more important.

He would need to plan better, get all the money he needed before he went for it again. There was no time for mooching around the streets, chatting people up with the sob story he had used at the bus station. He would have to take.

He had buried Babão's old revolver in a plastic bag in the undergrowth up behind their shack. There was no way he could go back for that. He would have to knock over an easy target, maybe some old tourists. They would hand over with the threat of one of the *gringo's* kitchen knives. Or maybe he could snatch a purse or rip a gold necklace from a neck.

Just thinking about it made Vilson feel cold and hot at the same time. But there was no choice. He had been given the sign. This was his time. It had to be.

The cop unlocked the front door, checking around the courtyard as he did so. He shoved Vilson through. "You stay here and you stay quiet. One of us will come by tomorrow with food and to check up on you, okay?"

He shut the door.

No lecture?

Vilson heard the set of heavy mortice bolts clunk home down the length of the reinforced door frame, and the key turned in the lock. And then silence.

He heard the faint creak of the exterior gate opening over the hum of traffic and the clang as it swung home.

The bastard cop had locked him in. He raced around the apartment, turning on all the lights, but he already knew he was trapped. All the windows in the apartment had a lattice of wrought-iron bars set into the exterior walls. He was in jail.

He paced back and forth, checking and rechecking the on the windows, checking the doors, hoping there might be ose, something to prise. He cursed them all. What the h oing to do? Keep him in this place forever? What did th him?

Pacing around, he tried to figure out his escape. think of anything. He hadn't had any water since he'd left and finally he gave in. He couldn't concentrate on than making himself a squash using the tin of *Suco de* sion-fruit syrup. He flopped on the couch. The TV screen was dark outside now.

Uga Uga would be starting soon. The frustration hing weight. He cursed himself.

Chapter 23

Jake

He woke up on a hard bed, plain white tiles close to his face. The temple on the good side of his head was throbbing and he had a killer headache. He was in a small cubicle. Dread snaked around his insides and gripped tight. He ran through his mental index, trying to find a match. But there was no hospital smell, just the tang of unwashed bodies. He rubbed the bleariness from his eyes and focused. His stomach lurched. It was a jail cell.

Tiles on three sides, iron bars made the fourth, a pocked, whitewashed wall across the corridor. The bed was just a wooden slab with a rough blanket covering it. A cracked plastic bucket in the corner the only other feature.

He dabbed his fingers at the sore points around his head and face. There was a tender lump over his temple. A thin bandage tied round his head had blackened scabs of dried blood flaking from it. His hair was matted.

His tee shirt was ripped and had rust-red bloodstains. Lower lip split, nose swollen and his body felt scraped and bruised. His injured jaw seemed intact. That was a plus.

He was soaked in sweat and had a raging thirst. Swinging his legs slowly to the floor, everything stiff and hurting, he hobbled to the bars, pressing the less painful side of his face between a gap. Swivelling his eyes, he could see another cell diagonally across the corridor. Three pairs of arms were hanging through the bars. Part of a face appeared, pushing between the bars, eyes straining in his direction.

"Wow, Sleeping Beauty finally woke up," the prisoner announced over his shoulder. He spoke to Jake with a harsher note. "Hey, *gringo*, how come you get the special attention?"

"I've stayed in better."

"You know, they cleared us scumbags out of your place and shoved us in with a whole load of other scumbags here. You're in the presidential suite compared to us, fucker."

Jake couldn't muster the bile for another row. His headache was cranking up to piledriver level and there was a dark flicker at the periphery of his vision. He went back to the wooden bed.

"Hey, *gringo*, I'm not done with you yet."

Leaning back against the tiles, Jake closed his eyes, the flickering becoming an invasive red pulse.

"I don't like rudeness, *gringo*, it's disrespectful. You might find yourself taking a long holiday here, and they might decide you're not so special after all, and we might end up as roomies. You won't like that."

There was a lazy roar of approval and laughter from his cellmates, and something hard was rattled over the bars.

"Glad I could break up the boredom," Jake said to himself. He was just a novelty. He hoped he wouldn't be sticking around long enough to become something else.

A voice shouted from the other end of the corridor. "Hey, keep it down back there."

Jake went to the bars again, but he couldn't see to the end. "Excuse me, sir, please can you tell me what's going on?"

His friend across the way chimed in: "I think our *gringo* guest isn't happy with his upgrade, sir."

His cellmates guffawed and whistled.

"Shut the hell up, all of you," the guard shouted. A door slammed.

Jake's friend across the way wasn't put off. "Disappointed with room service, *gringo*? I've got a number you can call."

More guffaws and insults and whistles.

There were no lights inside the cell, and no windows. No night and day, just the bled-out glow from the corridor lights. He lay back on the wooden bed. Even with the pain and the buzzing in his head it wasn't long before he fell asleep.

When he woke up he had no idea whether he had slept for minutes or hours. The lights were still on and he could hear the odd cough and shuffle from the neighbours over an electrical hum coming from somewhere. He was still sweating, hair plastered to his head, tee shirt clinging to his skin. His face was close to the wall tiles. They would be good and cool, but he didn't touch them. There was a chill deep in his chest, a damp shiver penetrating his lungs that the deadening, stinking heat could not burn away. It was what he was left with sometimes when the anger faded.

The two trays of brown slop with a congealed lump of rice that were pushed under the bars with a mug of water might have been any one of breakfast, lunch or dinner. The guard serving the food was not much interested in his existence, let alone his questions.

Some hours later the same guard unlocked his cell and wordlessly ushered him out, pushing him on through the gauntlet of the shouting and spitting neighbours.

"You're out," the officer at the main desk said. He looked disillusioned, elbow on the desk, chin resting on his hand. "I'm glad to be rid of you – we'd have probably had a riot on our hands if you were here much longer. Seems to be a thing with you, huh?"

"How long have I been here?"

"Since the night before last."

"Two days?" It didn't make sense to Jake.

"We had to dick you with a tranquiliser – you were still causing a scene when we got you in here."

"I was just arguing with a guy."

The desk officer looked at his notes. "Yes, *Senhor* Torquato was the guy, I believe. Must have been quite an argument."

"He swung a bottle at me and knocked me out – I don't know why I'm here."

"Oh, you weren't knocked out then, for sure. A couple of local cops got there pretty quick, but they called us for backup straight off. The party was still in full swing when we arrived."

"He smashed a bottle over my head and I blacked out." Jake repeated the less worst version, the one that made some kind of sense.

"You caught the bottle all right, there was blood everywhere. They said you went down and they expected you to stay there. But you? No. You jumped right up, smashing everything and throwing chairs around – crazier than a house rat – screaming and foaming at the mouth."

Jake could see that person, he could see that it was him, but it seemed like he was on the other side of a thick wall of glass. When the dogs were loose and anger became fury and everything seemed to stop. Impossible to communicate with, impossible to understand.

The officer was looking at Jake's scars. "Seems like this stuff is getting out of hand with you, huh? You scared the shit out of a lot of people. They had you on the ground when we arrived but it still took five of us to get you in the patrol truck. You're just lucky you're a *gringo* and you got the nice treatment with the tranquiliser. Only one time I've seen anyone put on a show like that before, and that was a guy who was so high he didn't even know which way was up for three days."

"I wasn't high."

"So what the hell is wrong with you?"

Jake stared at the counter, trying to think about something other than what was wrong with him. "Do you realise that guy is probably using forced labour out on his farm?"

He had put the pieces together as he had lain in the motel bed, unable to sleep, after returning from the farm. He had remembered seeing a TV news report in his apartment in Rio about migrant labourers who were often lured thousands of miles from home with the promise of good work and then trapped. Their documents taken from them, no money to get home.

The officer shrugged. "That's a pretty serious accusation to be levelling at someone."

"So you'll go after him?"

"Not our department. There's a whole government agency that deals with that."

"How do I get in touch with them?"

"I think you'd do better to concentrate on looking after yourself for a while," the officer said. "I'm letting you go, but you go galloping back into Cruzeiro like the Lone Ranger and your next stay here will be longer and less pleasant. I should charge you now, but with you a *gringo*, it's more trouble than it's worth. And besides, you got bailed."

"Bailed?"

"That's right, *gringo*, your lawyer bailed you."

"I don't have a lawyer."

"Her card was in your wallet."

"Oh, shit."

When they brought Eliane in to sign the papers she barely glanced at Jake.

She marched to her VW Polo parked outside the station and unlocked it. They weren't in Cruzeiro, this town was bigger. Jake hovered by the station entrance, unsure.

"Get in, before I change my mind," she said.

"Can we stop by the motel so I can get my things?"

"You need to take a shower too."

"Thanks for getting me out."

"I drove fourteen hours to get here and only because they said you were injured. I'm going to get a couple of hours sleep before driving back. Don't say another word to me until I've calmed down. That could be a long time from now."

Marinho

Nogueira's wife led Marinho through to the dining room where Nogueira's granddaughter had her schoolbooks spread over the dining table in front of her. Nogueira was in uniform, sitting beside Ana Lucia. It was just after midday and Marinho was a little early to pick up his boss to take him in to the station.

"A moment, *cabo*," Nogueira said, "we are just finishing off here." He sucked on a pencil, making a face at Ana Lucia.

"Come on, Grandpa, you don't know how to do this stuff, do you?"

"I think the problem is that they make the questions too easy these days. I would understand if it was more difficult, eh *cabo*?" he said, glancing up at Marinho.

Marinho nodded, playing his part. "True enough, Chief."

"We haven't even started on the difficult stuff," Ana Lucia said. "I have algebra to do next."

"My God, algebra." Nogueira looked at her, crossing his eyes.

She slapped him playfully on his arm. "Ah, Grandpa, you said you could help."

He picked his head up and sat straight, pushing his shoulders back. "And I can. I will."

His mobile phone rang.

"Hold on a second, child, let me just take this."

"Nogueira," he said and then listened. "Yes, that is my precinct." He listened some more. "Yes, I know that name. Where was it you said you were calling from?"

His face turned to stone and Marinho could see that his granddaughter was wary, pretending to concentrate on her homework now. Marinho guessed that she must have seen this before – her grandfather turning into a different person. A scarier person.

"No, I don't understand," Nogueira said. "Why all that trouble from going to tell the mother her son is dead?"

His face grew darker as he listened, harsher lines drawn in it. "I see," he said. "And you're absolutely certain?"

After the call he held the phone in the palm of his hand, as if weighing it. "Okay, *cabo*, let's go," he said.

It was only as he stood that he seemed to remember his granddaughter. "Sorry, child, Grandpa's duty calls," he said, smiling and bending to kiss the top of her head.

Her grandpa was back, and Marinho saw her shoulders relax.

Chapter 24

Vilson

He heard the front door open and close from the kitchen. The *gringo* was standing with his back to the door, the deadbolts clunking home from outside. What the hell was this? Was he now a prisoner too?

The *gringo* looked even worse than before. And he looked beaten. That angry, crazy flicker in his eyes had gone. Vilson's heart was thundering in his chest. He needed a weapon to go at him. There was nothing to hand. The cop had removed everything sharp from the kitchen. He had even taken the heavy glass ashtray that had sat on the coffee table. Vilson bunched his muscles to attack. Willing himself on. But the *gringo* was bigger than him, stronger. Bide his time. That's what he would have to do. He had been given another chance to rebalance fate, but he had to take the opportunity at the right time. The moment would come. He tried to ignore the voice in his head that was saying something else.

The *gringo* went through his bedroom door and closed it.

Not even a word? Vilson heard the sound of a latch on the other side of the door. He strode up to it and tried the handle, even though he knew it was pointless. He hammered his fist on the thin wood. "What's going on? I can't be kept prisoner."

"I'm sorry," came the muffled reply.

"What does sorry do?" Vilson shouted. "I just want out of here."

He pressed his ear to the door. Nothing. "Is that it?" He thumped the door, swearing. "*Porra.*"

The courtyard was filled with early-afternoon sunshine, the brief period each day when it escaped the shadows cast by the surrounding buildings.

Vilson was on the couch, legs pulled beneath him. Watching the run of afternoon *novelas* on the TV.

The *gringo* hadn't reappeared.

The gate buzzer went. Vilson didn't even look away from the TV. It buzzed again.

The *gringo* emerged from his room and went through the process of unlocking the door. He had a key. The son of a bitch wasn't a prisoner after all. He left the door ajar.

Vilson reached down for the plastic carrier bag of clothes he had kept next to the couch, ready for a quick escape.

He held his breath. The *gringo* hadn't returned.

He left the TV on and went to the front door. Peeping out, he could see the courtyard was clear, the gate half open.

He crept up to it. No sign of the *gringo*. Stepping through, he was on the street. Free. There was a car pulled up at the kerb, an old Japanese saloon with tinted windows. Something drew his attention to it. The dappled light coming through the trees lining the road made it difficult to see through the car's back window. He squinted. There was movement inside.

An enormous weight slammed into him from behind, taking him off his feet.

Chapter 25

Jake

Jake opened the door cautiously. He didn't recognise the two men. One of them had a piece of paper. "*Bom dia, Senhor*," he said, sounding bored, "you must sign for your delivery."

"What delivery?"

"Don't ask me, man, I just bring the stuff. Look, I've got your address right here," he said, holding the piece of paper up.

Jake opened the gate more, leaning forward to take a closer look. The other man grabbed his wrist, twisting it behind his back. He got his other arm around Jake's neck in a choke, kneeing him in the back of his legs to move him toward the waiting car. Jake tried a couple of digs with his elbows, tried to twist and drop. The guy was big and solid. Incredibly strong. Jake couldn't get any purchase or leverage. Couldn't hurt him. Then the paper-toting fake deliveryman sprayed something in his eyes. Jake managed to turn his head and only caught it fully in one eye. Pepper spray. He tried to concentrate on working an escape but his eyes were burning like crazy. Even the good one was closing up, tears blurring his vision.

An ageing street cleaner in his baggy orange uniform was pushing his dustcart toward them, the handle of his broom sticking out.

The arm tightened around Jake's neck. He could barely get any sound out. "Please help me."

"Just go on about your business, man," the fake deliveryman instructed the street cleaner. "Nothing to see here, right?"

The street cleaner did as he was told and went on past with his dustcart.

The fake deliveryman rushed ahead to open the back door of the old Nissan parked a few metres away. Jake was bundled into the back, his captor following him in and stuffing him facedown into the footwell. The door slammed shut. Some kind of hood was dragged over his head. Boots and fists thumped into his spine and ribs as he fought. They got his arms behind his back. He heard a zipping noise and felt a sharp pain in his wrists as a plastic cable tie was pulled tight. The car door opened and a heavy weight landed on the back of his legs.

There were thumps on another body and gasps of pain.

The car pulled away. Jake heard the zip of another cable tie and the weight on the back of his legs was still. He was furious with himself. Cold-cocked like an amateur. He'd let his guard down because he'd allowed Eliane to whip him into submission on that long drive back to the city. But straight on the back of that thought was the acknowledgement that he only had himself to blame. He would have had to go a long way to find a pair that looked less like deliverymen than those two.

Pressed down in his confined space he started to feel nauseous as the car rolled along the city streets. His eyes were still burning. He badly wanted to rub them. And then the note of the engine rose. It felt like they were going uphill. There was no point in thinking about where they might be going or what might be about to happen. He had to blink the pain from his eyes and concentrate on the moment. Right now, they had him trussed up like a chicken at the bottom of a bag of groceries. He just had to stay alert for any opportunity.

The car finally slowed and started to lurch and bump. They were off-road now. He felt a bang and scrape on the metal beneath him as the car bottomed out. When it stopped and the engine died, there was nothing for a few moments, just the sound of Jake's own breathing inside the hood and the ticking of the hot engine.

Another car drew up nearby. Doors opening.

Rough hands hauled Jake from the car and dumped him in the dirt. He could hear footsteps near his face. Tiny pinpricks of sunlight shone through the dark cloth of the hood. He curled up protectively.

The hood was torn from his head and he tried to blink the tears away from his stinging eyes in the harsh light of a small clearing in a forest. He was lying on a patch of red dirt at the end of a track surrounded by lush green. The glare of the sun and the pepper spray kept him squinting.

"On your feet," the guy holding the hood commanded. With his hands tied behind his back, Jake had to roll in the dirt to get his feet beneath him. He saw Vilson struggling to do the same at the rear of the car. And he could see that Vilson understood just as quickly where this was going.

Perched on the bonnet of the other car was Nogueira. A heel propped on the bumper, resting his arms on his raised knee. He didn't have his amiable-cop face on. It was set hard. The jeans and tee shirt he was wearing seemed to be the dress code of the day. A bunch of uniformed cops out of uniform. Not good.

Three of them were standing with handguns close by Jake and Vilson. Another stood at the edge of the clearing holding a carbine, covering them. And there was one more cop inside Nogueira's car.

He got out. Jake hoped the shock didn't register in his face.

It was Marinho.

He looked from Vilson to Jake, giving each a casual once-over.

Now Jake wasn't sure about anything.

"Thank you for joining us at such short notice," said Nogueira. "I appreciate you must be busy people."

He just couldn't leave it with the lame jokes, thought Jake. But there was no smile from Nogueira.

"The *gringo* who didn't learn a lesson," Nogueira went on, "and the favela boy who wouldn't die. An odd pair. Your little game – did you cook that up with your crazy favela boss?"

Vilson shook his head, stumbling over his words. "No, sir. I've got nothing to do with him. He believes I'm dead."

"He does, uh? It might have worked on a strung-out hoodlum but you really thought you could fool me? They'll never find you two, you know. A *gringo* that got into one too many fights and was never seen again, and a favela kid that was already dead. Neat, I think. No paperwork."

"You can't do anything to us." Jake was brazening it out, even if he didn't believe his own words.

Nogueira tutted amiably. "Oh, *gringo*, you really should have listened to me in that hospital. You're in a different country, my friend. You won't get your moment on TV, not even as a fried corpse, and if it's not on TV no one cares. You got one thing right, though, I'm not going to kill you."

He swapped legs on the bumper, leaning on his other knee. He looked at Marinho, flicking his head toward Jake and Vilson. "I get other people to do that for me," he said.

Marinho went to the car and pulled a wooden pick handle from the back.

The blood turned to ice in Jake's veins. Everything seemed to slow down around him.

The cop on the edge of the clearing brought his carbine to bear. The cops near to Vilson and Jake moved out of the firing line.

Marinho was looking at Jake, holding his gaze. There was nothing there. Nothing at all.

Jake took two deep breaths, refocusing on what he could do to stay alive. "You honestly think no one will notice we've gone?"

"You think someone will miss you?" said Nogueira. "Oh wait, I know, you're talking about your lawyer friend, yes? Don't worry, I'll be paying her a visit."

Jake lunged for him, fury exploding. The nearest [...] and caught one of his tied arms, checking his progress as [...] pped up to block him. He jabbed out the pick handle, ca[...] the solar plexus and folding him.

Jake writhed in the dirt, winded.

Marinho held the thick head of the pick handle [...] face. Clean, blond timber ready to stove in his skull. Ma[...] re as the inside man, ready to turn on Nogueira to s[...] had obviously decided things had got too sticky and ha[...] his boss.

Gasping for air, Jake realised he only had one [...] betray him, as Marinho had betrayed him and Vilson. H[...] isn't going to keep them alive, it was just an act of venge[...] ance for Eliane. For all the good it would do her.

Nogueira sucked his teeth. "This taste you h[...] ging authority, *gringo*," he said. "I don't know. Even j[...] zeiro didn't put you off, uh?"

Nogueira looked from Jake to Vilson, screwing [...] the sunlight. "Oh, wait a minute, our young favela fr[...] looks very confused," he said. "I suspect that someone d[...] one else about their little escapade to Cruzeiro. Am I r[...]

Nogueira slid off the bonnet of the car and pace[...] Jake stared straight ahead. He couldn't look at Vilson.

"Maybe I should give you a little time so you c[...] your friend about his mama?" Nogueira marked his rou[...] the clearing and back, ambling now. "You two made [...] , as you know, *gringo*, anger clouds the judgement. No[...] ore clearly, and I'm thinking that I can make you two [...] little better. Ha. Yes. I have an idea."

Retrieving a newspaper from the dashboard o[...] ueira went to Vilson. "Cut him loose," he said to the n[...] ing a lock-knife from his pocket, the cop unfolded it a[...] tie binding Vilson's wrists. Nogueira then presented [...] to Vilson. "Hold it against your chest while I take th[...]

Vilson just rubbed his wrists. He looked like he[...]

Nogueira thumped it into his chest. "I said hol[...] my temper."

Vilson took it.

Nogueira pulled his mobile from the pocke[...] and snapped a couple of photos. He shaded the scre[...] to check the results. "Perfect. Now I can start playing my own game." He gestured to the other cops. "Okay, let's go."

Marinho followed Nogueira to the car without a backward glance. The cop with the lock-knife cut Jake free. Jake tried to rub away the pain in his hands and wrists as the circulation came back.

Nogueira leaned on his open door, watching the other cops get into their car. "You keep an eye on him, *gringo*, that's your job now. That's why you're still alive. I will have need of him. If he disappears or you think about running back to England, then I'll be calling on the lawyer, and if she's not there I'll go after her family. There's a thread running all the way through to our favela friend here. I just tug on one end and he comes running. You understand?"

Jake had no smart answers, no angry retort. He was still struggling to get enough breath into his lungs.

Nogueira got in the car and the driver made the turn to get back down the track, stopping level with Jake. Nogueira leaned out the window. "So long, *gringo*. You need to head that way for the city," he said, pointing down the track. The driver chuckled.

The tyres spun, kicking up dirt, the other car following. The cop in the back tossed Vilson's plastic carrier bag of clothes out as it passed. The billowing dust swallowed up the cars.

Chapter 26

Vilson

The *gringo* lay curled in the dirt, coughing. Still trying to get his breath. Searching around him, Vilson prised a chunk of rock from the hard earth with his fingers and went to stand over him. He could tell that the *gringo* knew he was there a good few moments before looking up.

Vilson raised his arm and the *gringo* shrank back, flinging his hands up protectively.

"Did you go to Cruzeiro? Was he telling the truth?"

"Put the rock down, for fuck's sake."

Vilson raised it higher. "Tell me."

"Yes, I went there."

"Did you find my mother?"

"Yes."

"Alive?"

"Yes, of course. She's okay."

"*Graças a Deus.*" The relief was overwhelming. His arm was starting to shake and he lowered the rock to shoulder level. And then the anger came back. "You thought it was okay to keep this from me?"

"I didn't know how to tell you. I found her, out on a farm. I think she's with the Family. There's something bad going on there, but she didn't want to be found, she didn't want to go back to the past."

"You're not making any sense."

"Look, I know it's hard, but that's what she said."

"You know nothing," Vilson said. He knew the truth. It was in all those letters his mother had written. "You don't know her mind."

"Vilson, she asked me to tell you she was dead."

"You're lying!" Vilson shouted, raising the rock with both arms. Something had snapped inside him. He could do it.

The *gringo* scrabbled backward in the dirt. Vilson could see the fear he had felt so many times himself.

"Tell me where I find her," he demanded.

And then the *gringo* took a breath and lifted his chin. "No."

Vilson loaded his arms to strike, but the *gringo* didn't budge.

"Kill me and you'll never find her," he said.

Chapter 27

Jake

Vilson walked ahead of Jake on the dusty track, deceptively fast with his shuffling, slope-shouldered gait. They were in an area of thick forest just above the north-western side of the city. Reaching a tarmac road that ran down a steep hill, Jake could see the ocean below them through a gap in the trees.

He trudged on down the road. Simple thoughts were like pieces of furniture that wouldn't fit through a door. Vilson wasn't the same kid. Something had shifted or broken inside him. Wavering out on the beach with a revolver. The shaking hand brandishing a knife in his kitchen. Vilson hadn't had it in him then. Holding that rock above his head, ready to smash it into Jake's skull, his eyes had changed for a few moments. Jake recognised where that change could take a person.

Maybe something else would change. Maybe Vilson's mother would have a change of heart when she saw him. Could be, that with Jake's low expectations of people, he had misjudged her. Whatever was happening out on that farm with the zombie workers and his mother, Vilson needed to find out for himself. The way Jake saw it, he was the only one who could get him there in any kind of a hurry.

The sun was setting by the time they reached the larger roads and signs for areas of the city that Jake recognised. Pavements were few and far between, and a lot of the time they were stumbling along scrubby banks, trying not to fall into the traffic that was screaming past.

"Hey, I need to stop for a bit," he shouted ahead to Vilson when they reached a major junction. The straps of his flip-flops had rubbed his skin raw. He was dehydrated and even the green sludge in the storm drains was starting to look tempting.

Vilson didn't break stride.

"Ipanema's the other way," he shouted. The traffic was noisy but not that noisy. "You shit."

He loped painfully up to Vilson, catching him by the shoulder. "I know you heard me. You're heading in the wrong direction."

Vilson slapped his hand away. "I'm going to the bus station."

"Look, unless you've got money for a bus ticket, you're stuck with me for now, so we might as well do it the right way. We go back to my place, get something to eat, get some money and then we can go to the bus station."

Vilson stared at the pavement, weighing it up, an[d] [walked] [o]ff in the direction of Ipanema without a word.

It was evening when they finally reached a section [of street] [that] Jake recognised as home. He could see the grey metal ga[tes] [of his apartm]ent. He picked up the pace to draw level with Vilson.

A few metres down from the apartment there [was a car] [pull]ed up by one of the trees lining the kerb. Its headlights flas[hed] [but Vilson] didn't seem to notice. Jake was trying not to notice.

The headlights flashed again.

"You've got to be kidding me," Jake said to hi[mself.] [He cou]ldn't do any more of this gangster crap today. They'd ju[st have to kno]ck him and he'd deal with it in the morning.

The driver's door opened. It was Eliane.

"Thank Christ for that," Jake mumbled.

He could see that it wasn't just the unhealthy [glare of the] street lights that was making her look drained. Her eye[s were] [set in] [t]he dark circles beneath them.

"Get in," she said.

"I really need to rest – come into the apartment."

"You haven't got one any more. Your landlad[y dumped your] stuff outside in a plastic sack. She's thrown you out."

"She can't do that."

"Nogueira must have told her she could," she sa[id.]

Jake sighed, beaten. "Man, he's been busy toda[y."]

"Yeah, tell me about it," she said bitterly. "He'[s be]en [stirring t]hings up with my boss – there's a good chance I'm going [to be sacked] over this. And to top it all, he paid a visit to my dad this [morning. My pa]rents are furious with me."

Eliane had rescued his bin-liner of belongings a[nd put it] [i]n her boot. There were some clothes in it and his cards [were] [st]ill in his wallet. But his mobile and passport were go[ne.] [Going ba]ck to England wasn't an option now, even if he'd wante[d to.]

Eliane pointed Vilson to the passenger seat an[d] [han]d[ed] out bottles of water. Jake drained his. It was the first g[ood th]i[ng all] day. And he was so grateful for the comfort of the po[oled back of] her VW Polo that it didn't even occur to him to ask wh[ere] [they were g]oing.

He nodded off with the warm night breeze bl[owing in] [throug]h the window, only coming to when she pulled up and to[oted her horn.] They were in some low-rise residential area he didn't recognise.

"Where are we?" Jake asked, peering across the dimly lit street.

"Jardim Botânico," she answered.

The door on the other side of the car opened and Marinho got in. He was wearing running gear. "Go," he told Eliane.

Vilson spun around in the passenger seat as the car pulled away. Back pressed up to the dashboard, like a frightened animal.

Jake shot out his hand to grab Marinho's throat.

"Calm down," Marinho gasped, his hands raised, placating, but ready to defend himself.

"Calm down? You're joking, right?"

"Shut up, Jake," Eliane said. "Let him speak."

Jake released his grip but kept his hand on Marinho's throat. "You don't know where he was a few hours ago."

"Yes I do," she said.

"I bet he didn't tell you he was about a second away from beating us to death with a pick handle."

"And you'd have been the glorious hero, right?" Marinho asked. "Three dead idiots in the forest instead of two. Sound better to you?"

"I wouldn't have sold someone out, that's for sure," Jake said.

"You think I told Nogueira about you going to Cruzeiro? No, *gringo*, you made that happen all by yourself. The cops who arrested you out there called him up."

That shut Jake up. He took his hand away from Marinho's throat. He felt like the token twat in the car now. And he resented it, given the company.

Marinho handed him a cheap mobile phone. "There's a number on here for Eliane and one for me," he showed Jake the screen, "but not with our names obviously. Don't make calls to anyone else on it and don't pick up calls from anyone else. Understand?"

"Yes. Thank you."

"You can drop me off just up here," Marinho said to Eliane, pointing ahead. "I can run home."

"And then to the bus station," Vilson instructed.

"You can't go anywhere near the bus station," Marinho said. "Nogueira has cops staked out there."

"*Meu Deus*," Vilson murmured, head dropping, "what do I have to do?"

Eliane pulled the car over. "I'll drive you to Cruzeiro," she said.

"Now?" asked Vilson.

She nodded.

"Why not start out tomorrow?" Jake asked. "You look done in."

"It has to be this weekend. I've made arrangements, and I must be back here on Monday," she replied. It was Friday night.

Marinho got out, limbering up as he walked away.

"Hold on, I just remembered something," Jake said. He needed to speak with Marinho alone.

Getting out of the car, he caught up. "Back up in the hills this afternoon, I was so pissed off that I was going to tell Vilson that it was you who shot his friend. I'm glad I didn't. He still has no idea and it has to stay that way."

"It will until Nogueira needs to play that card."

Chapter 28

Vilson

At one of the bus stops Vilson swapped with the *gringo*, taking the back seat.

He lay down, resting his head on his arm, pretending to sleep every time the *gringo* turned around to check on him.

The *gringo* read out the road signs and kept switching on the reading light to check the map. If he was trying to get onside with the lawyer, it wasn't working.

When he was very small, before his mother had left, Vilson had a neighbour in the favela, a little girl. He had a memory of her walking around with a small doll trailing from her hand. She was never without it. And then something terrible had happened to her family. Vilson's mother wouldn't say exactly what. And then more stuff happened. Everyone knew that it was more than just bad luck, and the family had gone to the old women in the favela who knew about these things. The women arranged one of their evenings for the family, dressing in their flowing white clothes, lighting their candles, burning their incense. They sang and they danced and they shook as they went into trances and spoke with the spirit world. They were told that the doll held a curse. They took it from the little girl and burned it.

Vilson's mother had told him that the little girl had wailed and cried for her doll. He remembered seeing her around the favela afterwards, always with a sullen look on her face. But things got better for her family. The curse had gone.

Something bad had latched onto that little girl's doll, and there was something with the *gringo* that was bad. And he probably didn't even know it. How it had become so knotted up that he had become the key to finding his mother, Vilson couldn't figure. But once he was back with his mother they could free themselves of the *gringo* and all the bad stuff wrapped up in him. Vilson didn't know if that still meant killing him. He tried not to think about it.

Chapter 29

Jake

There were orange flashes behind his eyes and he could feel his breath getting rapid and panicky. One of the flashes picked out a silhouette. A faceless man. He didn't see it, but Jake knew he had a gun. Another flash and a crack and he flinched.

The car jerked and his head slipped from the windowsill, waking him. Dropping off the jagged edge of the tarmac, the nearside wheels rumbled and shuddered on the gritty surface of the verge. What was she playing at?

He looked over at Eliane. Her head was lolling forward. Her eyes closed.

"Whoa," he called out, making a grab for the wheel.

She gasped, head snapping up.

She pulled on the wheel, the car swerving back into the lip of the tarmac. The tyres bumped and rubbed against it before jumping back onto the relative smoothness of the road.

"Goddamn," she said. "Goddamn it."

"I meant to stay awake with you to stop that happening."

She shrugged her shoulders and shook her head.

"Look," he continued, "why don't you let me drive for a bit so you can get some sleep?"

"You can't drive this car," she said.

"I don't think you're up to it either right now."

But she was wide awake, stoked with adrenaline. She drove on into the dead hours before dawn, the road empty. Jake stared out into the darkness. The state of Goiás and the capital, Brasilia, were out there somewhere to the north-west of them, out in the vastness, halfway between the coast and Bolivia. And then she started rubbing her eyes, drinking water, shaking her head. The tiredness wrapping her up once again.

"Is there no way you can convince your dad that you're doing the right thing?" Jake asked her. He wanted to get her talking, distract her from the inner battle to stay awake that she was losing.

She was immediately more alert, shaking her head. "No. And if you came to our apartment you would see that it's stuck in time. Still the same things in it that I grew up with. My dad is still in that place. The fancy cars have gone now, though – he used to dri[...] BMW and I used to love going on trips with him to the fac[...]

She described the smell of the leather, the air-c[...] cool to the touch. Her father's successful printing bus[...]rant, noisy place, the workers nodding in respect when th[...]ther, and smiling at Eliane. She loved the clatter of the [...] the giant blocks of paper, moved around by the fork[...] And another smell. Hot ink on paper.

When Eliane was at home she used to watch th[...] wall in the evening, hoping that her father would be h[...] read her a story. He was working late on his own one nig[...] floor silent, when the robbers came. His only sliver of goo[...] that it was the little VW saloon that Eliane's mother c[...] the car park – his BMW was in for a service. He had ju[...] ne to set off the alarm. He then managed to convince th[...] he was not the boss, that he couldn't be the boss dri[...] like that. Just an office worker, with no ability to turn [...] no access to the safe. There was a lot of money in[...] The business was successful but, like many, it was balance[...]dge, always at the mercy of cash flow. If he opened the [...]ined. The business would have sunk long before any insu[...]t. In her father's head, the business was everything for [...]

The robbers smashed everything heavy they co[...] the immovable lump of metal. They barely chipped th[...] They beat him and beat him but he stuck with his stor[...] in. They went crazy with anger, and panicked in the [...]sant alarm. Eventually, they dragged him to the little V[...] him into the boot, driving him out to the city dump.

"The robbers said stuff to my dad about a rans[...] d as she drove, "but they knew they weren't going to ge[...] him by then. They were just angry and frustrated, so [...] wrist against the door frame of the car and slammed t[...] They kept doing that until he passed out, and then the[...] the boot and left him. He wasn't found until the next d[...]tion and dehydration almost killed him. His wrist wasn'[...] the hospital and we couldn't afford to get it reset later o[...]ked, even now. He went through all that for the bus[...] he found it hard to go back to the factory. He went fro[...]ever in the apartment to always being there. Fortunate[...] least aware enough to sell up before the business compl[...], but he never worked properly again."

THE BURNING HILL

She had told Jake her story without emotion. "I'm pulling in at the next place, I need some sleep," was all she said afterwards. The next place was a service station and they hunkered down in their seats at the dark end of the car park and got snatches of restless sleep.

The sun was coming up when she started the engine to drive over to the fuel pumps.

Jake was yawning non-stop as he went to the shop counter, putting the fuel on his card along with coffee, cans of Coke and pastries. They had breakfast standing around a tall table in the service station, no conversation as Jake chewed at his pastry, trying to avoid looking at Vilson. His mouth was a gaping cement mixer of churning dough as he poured Coke in, his blank stare focused anywhere but this place. Eliane was looking over the tops of their heads, swaying with exhaustion.

"Fuck me, this is depressing," Jake mumbled in English.

"What?" Eliane asked.

He shook his head. "Nothing."

"Okay then, let's go," she said, handing him her car key. "You can drive."

The country rolled away along the endless, chipped-up roads, scorched by the sun. He was seeing more of the distinctive white cattle in fields, with their fleshy humps over the shoulder and heavy dewlaps. Standing there, chewing and enduring the heat and all the biting insects and parasitic worms and disease, whether with admirable stoicism or bovine stupidity, he couldn't decide. And he wasn't sure at which end of the spectrum he was either.

He flicked through the radio stations, keeping the volume low while Eliane slept in the passenger seat. There were a lot of shouty DJs playing salsa and grating pop and he didn't last long on the stations playing Brazilian hip hop and heavy metal either. He kept flicking. It was something to do.

"You need to come off at the next town," Eliane said quietly. She must have been awake for a while, but she was still curled in the seat, head resting on a rolled-up tee shirt against the door.

It was the last town before Cruzeiro, and much bigger. This was a proper town. He slowed at a roundabout coming into the outskirts.

Vilson popped upright on the back seat. "Is this Cruzeiro?"

"No, we're about fifty kilometres away," Jake replied.

"Why are you coming off here?" Vilson asked.

"I told him to," said Eliane. "There's an ILO office in town."

"A what?" Jake asked.

"The agency that investigates human trafficking and forced labour. I called them yesterday."

"But it's Saturday," Jake said.

"They said someone would be in the office."

Vilson leaned forward. "Why are we doing this? We just need to go to the farm and get my mother."

"Whatever is happening out there, we need to do it the right way, with the right backup," Eliane said.

"This farmer must be holding my mother against her will, like the workers," Vilson said, more for himself than for anyone else.

"Which makes it all the more important we use the ILO."

"They will go to the farm for my mother today, yes?"

"They'd better. I have to drive back to Rio tomorrow."

Vilson sank back in his seat and tutted and shifted about and leaned forward and sank back all over again. He was going through the wringer. Jake gave him that.

They passed a pristine shopping mall with a giant car park of fresh black tarmac that was shimmering like a non-stick frying pan on high heat. The streets through the town were lined with trees and parked cars. There were boutiques and businesses and banks, everything broiling beneath the midday sun.

"Looks like the rodeo is in town," said Jake.

There was a billboard featuring a mean-looking bull and a cowboy on a bucking horse.

The other two paid no attention.

It was the same rodeo that Jake had seen advertised on his previous visit to Cruzeiro, and it was on this weekend – it was on now. He imagined himself having a lot more fun at the rodeo than the gig he was lined up for.

It took a while but they found their way to the ILO office near the centre of town. Jake bagged a patch of shade beneath a clump of trees and parked up. Eliane was back within a couple of minutes.

"There is no one in the office at the moment," she said, both resignation and irritation in her voice.

"When will they be here?" Vilson asked.

"I don't know. We'll just have to wait it out."

Vilson put his hands to his head, like his team had just missed a goal. "We can't hang around here waiting for something and nothing. We must go to the farm."

"We have to do this the right way, Vilson," she said. "Otherwise we could all end up in jail, or worse."

She opened the driver door and sat down with her feet sticking out. Vilson paced around at the back of the car.

"We could be hanging around here for hours, couldn't we?" Jake asked Eliane.

Eliane shrugged. "Maybe. But I'm going to make use of the time by getting a bit more sleep."

"I might have a wander, maybe check out the rodeo."

She was looking at him like he was mad. "What for?"

"I don't know. I've never seen one." Jake had half hoped that his suggestion might have piqued her interest, but now he was going to go out of belligerence. And something else. He felt like he needed to go there. It was an odd feeling.

"Keep your phone handy and don't go far," Eliane said.

Chapter 30

Jake

The rodeo was on a chunk of scrubby land near the town's football stadium. Most of it was temporary rig. Metal livestock pens, trucks and trailers with horses and cattle, stalls selling food and cowboy gear. A travelling show moving around cattle country. The arena looked a permanent fixture, with a fence of thick iron bars hung with advertising hoarding, and a simple tiered stand of bare concrete on one side. There was a marquee set up at one end of the arena with a PA. The holding pens for the bulls and the horse paddocks were at the other.

Jake was wearing a baseball cap and sunglasses as a nod to keeping a low profile. Farmers from all over would come to this thing, he guessed, including some from around Cruzeiro. He bought a ticket and pushed his way up the side of the crowded concrete stand closest to the end with the holding pens. With no safety rail along the edge and heights not on his favourites list, he ducked into a space halfway up.

If he had imagined some sort of lame Country and Western knockoff, he was way off the mark. They had the gear, for sure, and they followed the format, but there was a thick streak of Brazil all the way through. Man and horse roping cattle, tipping them over in the dirt and hog-tying their legs in the quickest possible time. The skill and horsemanship required to rope the young and skittish cattle were off the chart. When they started the bull-riding competition, a completely different animal was wheeled in.

The bulls were monsters, malevolent blocks of muscle, hoof and horn. Eyes rolling with incomprehension, fear and fury. Kindred spirits with Jake, Eliane would probably have said.

The riders didn't last more than a few seconds before they were flicked off. And it was down in the dirt where the real danger lay, trying to scrabble away from the thrashing hooves and horns. Three rodeo clowns tripped and cavorted around the arena, but they were serious professionals, distracting the bulls to allow the thrown rider to escape.

It was only when the adult competition was over that Jake realised how much his backside was aching from the concrete bench. It was compelling stuff. The PA announced that a junior national championship was up next.

The afternoon had wound the sun across the sky and Jake texted

Eliane, asking her if there was any sign of life at the [...]. No.

He was going to hang around a bit longer there. [...] seemed like a better bet than the car park.

The first few junior competitors were healthy s[...] boys who were near enough men. Strong and confiden[...].

Something caught his ear in the white noise of [...] the PA announcement. He looked over to the electron[...] the marquee end and saw T. TORQUATO as the rider [...] looked to the holding pen and spotted the farmer standing [...] bars, looking down on the bull. It was *the* farmer. T[...] ding dickhead farmer. Jake hunched down on his c[...] even though the farmer's attention was anywhere but on [...]

A boy of maybe thirteen or so climbed over th[...] the farmer to mount the bull. He was smaller th[...] vious competitors, but he was lithe and he carried hims[...] same confidence.

T. TORQUATO was the boy's name. He shared [...] name as the farmer. His father, most likely. Jake had a si[...] oped to fuck that he was wrong.

A man in front of Jake nudged his wife [...] inho Torquato. That's the kid, the one I was talking ab[...] e's a future champion. He's got it all, I'm telling you. H[...] oday and he's on the way to the big league, sponsorship [...] ney, all the stuff."

Jake saw the bull raking a hoof in the soft dirt, [...] pen, the heavy bars clanging a deep tone of alarm. Toninh[...] self, sliding onto the huge expanse of back.

"Look how he handles the bull," the man in f[...] tle — see, he goes with the animal, not against it like mos[...] do."

Jake watched, fascinated now, as Toninho push[...] ough the loop in the coarse braided rope that was tied aro[...] ody, grabbed the slack in the rope and wound it around [...] uled at it and thumped his fist with the other, making s[...] tight. Glancing up at the metallic blue of the sky, he cro[...] Then he pulled his cowboy hat down tight on his h[...] his shoulders and curled his legs into the enormous bull [...].

The buzzer went, a low, flat sound, and the gate [...] with a clank. The bull knew his cues and burst thro[...] and thrashing, his massive head dipping and swinging, hi[...] king high in the air.

THE BURNING HILL

Toninho was flicked around on the bull's back, his hand anchored by the rope. His other arm and his legs were flailing counterweights as the bull bucked and thrashed. But it was clear, even to Jake, that he was somehow tuned into its rhythm of madness and fury and he stayed on as the seconds rolled. The man in front and people around were shouting excitedly. It was a good ride.

And then one of the bull's great forelegs gave way, a momentary weakness in the beast. It stumbled and lurched.

It broke the rhythm and Toninho was off, both legs coming down on one side of the bull. He was coming down to land on both feet, with grace, carrying it off like it was the intended dismount of some circus acrobat. Amongst the gasps of horror in the crowd, those in the know were gasping in admiration. An image flashed through Jake's mind – a bronze sculpture from ancient Greece or somewhere that he had seen on a school trip to a museum. Toninho touched down in the dirt, looking like he would saunter away from the giant wrecking machine.

But he was torn forward with the bull, his cowboy hat fluttering away. His hand was caught fast in the rope. The three rodeo clowns were quick. Two racing in to distract the bull, one waving his arms, the other flapping his joke matador's cape. The third tried to get to Toninho. Crazed by the human activity dancing around it, goading it, and by the rope pulled tight around its body, the bull launched its hindquarters up and around, swatting Toninho into the air. He was upside down, his cowboy boots pointing skywards for a moment, and then the bull whipped him back on his arm. Everyone heard his scream as all that force went through his shoulder and elbow. He careened off the granite of the bull's ribcage and then the beast lurched again, threatening to trample Toninho as his legs were swept beneath him.

The third rodeo clown managed to grab on, pulling at the rope binding Toninho's wrist. The bull was trying to turn its head to gore him. With the bull distracted, the other two rodeo clowns were also able to dart in and grab hold. Tiring and confused, the bull's legs buckled. The huge body tipped to one side with its untidy pile of human cargo.

The rodeo clowns had less than a second to work on the rope before the bull came to its senses and relit the fury. It kicked out its hooves, rolled and tucked them back beneath its body, got purchase in the dirt and staggered back to its feet. It whipped around again, flinging the rodeo clowns and Toninho away. They had freed his hand and Toninho landed out in the dirt, his body limp.

The bull twisted its head, fixing a mean, pink-rimmed eye on the slight strip of motionless human. Its horns were shaved to blunted stumps but the instinct to use them was undimmed. It came around like a great sailing ship, tossing in a storm.

The stocky rodeo clown who had freed Toninho's hand was quick and he didn't hesitate, jumping in front of him, square onto the animal as it bore down. The bull dipped its head and shoulders, bringing all its strength back up to smash into his torso. Flicking its horns as it struck.

Jake heard the slap of flesh and the crack of breaking ribs over the gasps of the crowd. The rodeo clown somehow held on as the bull tossed him around, veering away from Toninho and plunging down the length of the arena.

The other two rodeo clowns gave chase and Jake saw Torquato darting through the bars of the holding area to get to the boy.

The bull finally rid itself of the rodeo clown, flinging him away. It was on him in a second. He curled up as it gored at him with its stunted weapons, flipping him this way and that in the dirt. The other two tag-teamed, one dashing in to flap his cape in the bull's face, drawing it away. The other went to their injured comrade. The bull made a half-hearted lunge at the cape and stopped, exhausted. It shook itself, blinking its malevolent eyes, ropes of saliva hanging from its open mouth.

Torquato gathered up Toninho, the boy limp in his arms. Something drew Jake back to the bull. He could see that it was now ignoring the noisy human buzzing around it like a stinging fly, instead focusing on Torquato and the boy. It stamped and raked the dirt with its hoof, just once, and charged.

Jake could feel the beat of the hooves in the dirt beneath the screams of the crowd. Torquato was running now, trying to get the boy to the safety of the holding area. The bull bellowed. It was almost on them.

The heavy metal gate was swung ajar. Hands reached out to grab Toninho, dragging him and Torquato in. The gate clanked shut, shuddering with a thunderous clang as nearly a tonne of bull cannoned into it.

The bull wobbled away, stunned. The two rodeo clowns picked up their injured comrade and got him out. The bull had the arena all to itself now. Breathing heavily, tongue lolling out, it kicked out its back hooves and cast an irritable eye around. It stood for a while, waiting, challenging. And then when nothing more came at it the fury began to subside. It trotted off down a run that was opened in the side of the arena, giving the odd cantankerous buck and flick as it went. It was done with them in for the day. The crowd seemed unsure whether to cheer or applaud or voice dismay.

Jake made his way down the steep concrete stand as quickly as he could.

Vilson

He had hardly moved all afternoon. There wasn't any point. He mostly sat, leaning against a tree in the car park, knees up, elbows resting on them, hands covering his face. He had packed away his frustration to wait it out. It was a trick he had learned long ago. He had spent a whole chunk of his life waiting for things.

The lawyer had slept for periods on the back seat. The rest of the time she had spent pacing around, or looking through the windows of the closed ILO office, then cursing, and trying to call people who didn't answer. Right now she was in the driver's seat, tapping her phone on the dashboard and doing some more cursing.

Vilson's backside was beginning to ache again. He got up, stretched and walked beyond the car park to the main drag for a change of scenery. Cars and trucks flew past, buffeting him with the warm air of late afternoon. Each of the lamp posts lining the road was plastered with paper flyers, the freshest of them connected with the rodeo, stallholders and horsemen who followed it from town to town.

Vilson recognised a flyer. He had seen one very similar in Rio. He couldn't read the words but he recognised the layout and the girl pictured. She was around fourteen, dressed in white, wearing strings of beads with a long white scarf wrapped round her head like a turban. It was the traditional dress of Bahia, up in the north. The same garb that the spiritual women in the favela wore. Those women had spoken about this girl and the word had spread around the favela. Yara was her name. He remembered. She was from a family with a powerful spiritual history. The girl was a seer and a healer. Just looking at her smudgy image on the flyer gave him a superstitious shiver. They said she was the most powerful of them all.

Vilson had tried to get to one of her shows in Rio the previous year – anyone could go as long as they had the money to get past the door. But the ticket price had been way beyond his means. He remembered how much that had hurt. She would have seen everything. She could have guided him to an easier path to his mother. In the end, though, he had found his own way to his mother. He was so close now. Just a little more waiting.

He saw the *gringo* before Eliane did. He came running. Sweating and red in the face.

"Any sign?" the *gringo* asked.

"Nothing," the lawyer said with bitterness. "*Desordem e Regresso.*"

The *gringo* didn't get it, but Vilson knew it as a sarcastic flip on the country's motto, *Ordem e Progresso* – Order and Progress.

"We need to go to the farm," Jake said.

Vilson jumped up. It was the first sensible thing he had heard all day.

"You know we have to wait," the lawyer said.

"It's nearly five," the *gringo* said, looking at his phone. "These ILO people aren't coming. And, trust me, we have to go right now."

Chapter 31

Vilson

The *gringo* used the map to get them to Cruzeiro, directing the lawyer to the bus station in town.

"Okay, I can get my bearings from here," the *gringo* said.

"You don't know where the farm is on the map?" the lawyer asked.

"I'll get us there, don't worry."

It didn't bother Vilson. He had never looked at a map in his life and he could find his way around, no problem. He assumed it was the same for everyone.

Dusk was passing quickly into night as he peered out at the quiet streets that his mother must have walked. The town was different to the one that had grown in his imagination, but he pushed that to one side. He moved his mind to the farm, the place she had always promised for them. He didn't understand why she hadn't told him in her letters. Maybe it had only been a recent move. She probably had her reasons. It was all history now anyway. He was going to her.

They drove along the dark, broken roads, the *gringo* pushing his face up to the windscreen to see the coming turns and then twisting round to see the turns they passed.

"Okay, this isn't it," the *gringo* said. "It wasn't this far out."

The lawyer turned the car around and drove back the way they had come. There were more stops and more wrong turns, eating up hours, the *gringo* getting more and more agitated, going through all his Brazilian curses and shaking his head each time. "We really need to find this place soon," he said.

Vilson felt for the small screwdriver in his pocket. He had found it in the passenger door pocket. With every wrong turn the *gringo* made, he wanted to ram the screwdriver into his neck. But he sat back and kept quiet. He needed the *gringo*. For now.

"Stop, stop," the *gringo* called out. "Back it up a bit."

The rear lights gave the empty road behind a red glow as the lawyer reversed. The *gringo* looked out his window at a turn onto a track. There was an old metal sign, the words rusted off.

"This is it," the *gringo* said.

The lawyer had to take it slowly down the dirt track, the bumps and ruts casting long shadows in the headlights. It was a good twenty minutes of driving before the car clattered over the ⟨…⟩ into a grass field that overlooked the unlit farmhouse. The ⟨…⟩ to an area of worn, sandy turf at the bottom of the field ⟨…⟩ cattle shed for the lawyer to park up.

"He stays in the car," Vilson instructed.

The *gringo* kept quiet for once, as Vilson and the ⟨…⟩ it.

They could hear the air blowing from the nostril ⟨…⟩ tle in the shed. There was no wind and the sky was clear. ⟨…⟩ never looked up at the night sky outside a city. The st⟨…⟩ lliant. Countless, dizzying in their depth. At ground level ⟨…⟩ tiny green flashes everywhere as fireflies zigzagged ar⟨…⟩ This was a magical place. It was *the* place.

"*Mãe?*" Vilson called out for his mother. The ⟨…⟩ total darkness, the windows covered with louvred woo⟨…⟩.

They moved around the side of the farmhouse, ⟨…⟩ooth tiles of the veranda. Rounding a corner, they were in ⟨…⟩ low windowless building opposite. Vilson stepped of⟨…⟩ here was a doorway, the overhung eave making it imp⟨…⟩ and there was another shuttered window. Flickering ⟨…⟩ was coming through the slats. A television, the tinny v⟨…⟩ ut.

Vilson peered through a slat. The television was ⟨…⟩ce of light in the small room. He could make out a slight ⟨…⟩ in a chair, illuminated only because it was so close to the ⟨…⟩

"*Mãe?*" Vilson called out again, more quietly, ⟨…⟩ The television went off and the sounds of the night in⟨…⟩ the darkness was complete.

Vilson heard a movement in the room. And the⟨…⟩

A dull, bare bulb flicked on in the recessed cor⟨…⟩ of hallway – and Vilson's mother appeared. She h⟨…⟩ arms hugging her body. There was shock as well as el⟨…⟩ He knew she was his mother, but she was so shrivelled ⟨…⟩ was not the mother of his memory.

He could see the uncertainty in her face but he c⟨…⟩ that she knew who he was. There was no mistaking the f⟨…⟩ ance.

"I've come to take you away, *Mãe*," he said, walki⟨…⟩ding his hand out.

She shrank back, shaking her head. "No. No, no, ⟨…⟩ *Sen* Torquato angry. This is bad."

"Then we must go now, before he comes back." ⟨…⟩ his hand still outstretched.

"I cannot leave. My place is here."

"No, *Mãe*, you are not tied to him any more," Vilson said. "This woman is a lawyer, she can help."

His mother stared at the lawyer. She didn't seem to understand. "Why did you have to come?" she said to Vilson. "Why bring this unhappiness to me?"

Vilson was stunned. Confused. His thoughts were trying to swim against a torrent that was flooding his brain. This wasn't how it was meant to be. "There was a sign," he finally managed to say. "I received a sign, and I knew it was my time to find you."

"I cannot go with you. I don't want to."

Vilson swayed and stepped back to steady himself, like a boxer wobbled by a punch. "But the sign, *Mãe*. It came from God. Even Padre Francisco believed this."

"Padre who?"

"Francisco. He looked after all the letters you wrote. He helped me write replies."

"What are you talking about?"

Chapter 32

Jake

He had gone along with what Vilson had said. He didn't want to be a spectator in that conversation anyway. But he didn't have to *stay* in the car. He wasn't a ten-year-old. He leaned against the boot, watching the fireflies. The sky was quite something too.

He caught a wisp of light against a distant hill out in the darkness. Shit.

Then there was nothing. He kept looking.

Several minutes passed before another slice of light cut across the gentler slope of the field. It could be one of the neighbouring farmers. There was no need to get overexcited just yet.

The headlights silhouetted a line of trees on the hillside opposite the farm, sweeping one way and then bouncing the other. He heard the engine for the first time.

He found his way along the dark veranda and rounded the corner to see the small group in the doorway. "We need to leave," he said, breaking the awkward silence.

The headlights bore long shadows along the grubby whitewashed walls of the outbuilding on the other side of the yard. Vilson's mother looked terrified. "*Ai meu Deus*," she cried, her feet pattering from side to side. "You have to go. For my sake, go," she pleaded with Vilson.

"*Mãe*, I will not leave without you."

They heard the vehicle hit the cattle grid and rumble over it.

Jake drew Eliane to one side. "Talk to him, for Chrissakes," he whispered to her. "I can't stick around for another showdown with this guy and he's not going to take kindly to seeing you two either. I saw him at the rodeo – I couldn't tell you in front of Vilson."

She looked at him sharply, uncertainty in her eyes.

Jake had no idea how badly Torquato's son had been injured, or whether he had even survived. He had hoped that they would be able to get Vilson's mother away from the clutches of Torquato and then tell her what had happened to her younger son. He whispered to Eliane, "Something bad happened at the rodeo – he will be a very upset man. Please trust me."

She looked Jake in the eye for a moment, and then nodded before turning to Vilson. "Today is not the day, Vilson," she said, her voice calm and soothing. "Let's do this right. Come on."

Vilson wasn't listening. He was still looking at his mother. She was staring at her feet.

The vehicle pulled up somewhere on the other side of the farmhouse, a door groaning and creaking open, before it was slammed shut.

Jake turned to the sound and took a couple of steps toward it, back toward Eliane's car. Eliane put her arm on Vilson's shoulder and gently tugged him.

The dark veranda, and that whole side of the farmhouse, was suddenly flooded in harsh white light. Jake squinted at the two floodlights on top of the cattle shed.

The light finally seemed to rouse Vilson and he allowed Eliane to lead him away. Torquato had parked his pickup in the corner of the field by the cattle shed, ahead of Eliane's car. He appeared from the side of the cattle shed and came toward them.

Jake had to walk on by. He had to do that. Get in the car with Eliane and Vilson and drive away. He was going to keep a lid on his temper and his mouth shut.

Torquato's eyes looked puffy and bloodshot, sweat shining on his neck and chest, his straw cowboy hat pushed back on his head. He almost staggered back in surprise when he recognised Jake. "You?" he said. Jake could see fear and anger fighting for control in the farmer's eyes.

"You're trespassing, *gringo*. Again," Torquato said.

"You're breaking an awful lot more laws than that," Eliane bounced straight back at him.

"Oh yeah? And who the hell are you?"

"I'm a lawyer."

"A lawyer? Ha." Torquato forced a laugh, and then looked at Vilson. "And, let me guess, this must be the prodigal son. So you got yourself a lawyer to try to get your sticky hands on my farm, huh?"

"I came for my mother, nothing more," Vilson said thickly.

Eliane said, "And I just want to find out what the hell you're up to out here. Which is why I've arranged for the ILO to meet us here."

"Really? The thing is I smell bullshit, because I don't see any ILO." Torquato forced a smile but there was suppressed panic in his face.

"They're coming." Eliane was locked in professional mode and she sounded unshakeable, but Jake just wanted to get in the car and get them out of there. He could see that Torquato was on a knife-edge. There was nothing to be gained from a stand-off.

"Let's go," he said, putting a hand on her back and gently pushing her toward the car. She started walking.

Torquato caught sight of Vilson's mother hovering back at the corner to the rear of the house. "You planned this, didn't you?" he shouted angrily. "And tonight of all nights." He started toward her and she shrank away. He strode past and went inside the house, and she meekly followed.

Eliane went to the driver's side when they got to the car.

"You okay to drive?" Jake asked.

She nodded.

Vilson hesitated a few metres from the car, looking back at the house.

"Not today, Vilson," Eliane said to him. "Your mother is frightened of this guy, and we can't get around him without the ILO."

Vilson's head dropped for a moment and then he walked to the car and got in the back.

Eliane started the engine, found reverse with the gearstick and turned to look behind.

"Okay, nice and calm," Jake said. "But we need to go, fast."

Torquato was coming back from the rear of the house. He was carrying a pump-action shotgun.

Eliane turned to Jake quizzically and then saw Torquato. She stamped on the accelerator and snapped the clutch. Engine howling, the little Polo scudded and bounced across the soft, uneven turf as she turned the wheel and then braked. Torquato broke into a lumbering run, bringing up the shotgun to bear. Eliane wrenched the gearstick into first and put the revs into the red. The car lurched and then rocked back, the wheels spinning uselessly in a patch of soft sand. She didn't let up, the tyres whining as they slashed sand into the wheel arches and across the turf.

"Out of the car. All of you," Torquato shouted. He was less than twenty metres away now.

The blind fury that Torquato had worked himself into somehow stilled the anger in Jake. And his head was clear. "Lower revs – do it gently," he said to Eliane.

She followed his instruction and the car moved forward a few centimetres and then rocked back again. It was useless. They were stuck.

Torquato stopped five metres short of the car. He aimed and fired from the hip. Muzzle flash and report and punch of pellets into the front tyre and wheel arch. A scream from Eliane and then silence.

THE BURNING HILL

Stunned silence amongst them all. Torquato had ma... ... sure the car was going nowhere.

Jake and Eliane and Vilson stared at Torquato a... ... back. Torquato finally stirred himself, pumping the spe... ... ith a wisp of smoke and locking another into the cham... ... g the barrel on to Jake and Eliane. "Turn the engine of... ... ." His voice was shaky.

Jake could see that the enormity of what wa... ... was catching up with Torquato. He didn't look ready f... ... was guessing he had decided he had to do. "Let's get out," ... ... tly. "It'll be fine." It didn't feel like it. It felt like as ba... ... had ever been in. He was scared, and he was scared ... ... for Vilson, he didn't know how he felt about Vilson.

Eliane killed the engine and they got out and mo... ... the car. Jake put his hands up, palms turned slightly ... ... the antagonism. Be ready.

Torquato gestured at them with the shotgun, ... stop in the loose sandy dirt between the farmhouse and ... ... No-man's-land.

He brought the shotgun to bear somewhere ar... ... belly. "You mad, crazy son of a bitch, why did you have t... ... here? Why did you have to do this?" He shook his head, ... ir.

Jake dragged his eyes away from the pitted ... ... old shotgun. He needed to concentrate on Torquato. I... ... that it didn't seem like he wanted to pull the trigger, ... he would. And from where Jake was standing it lo... ... had convinced himself that he had to.

Torquato glanced at Eliane. "Toss me your car k... ... ded. It was in Eliane's hand. She didn't move.

"I'll shoot him," Torquato said, his eyes fixed ... ... w.

It was another second or so before she flung the ... ... Head height. He blocked it with a hand, fumbling it, be... ... up. Cursing.

Jake darted forward, kicking at the soft ground, ... spray of dusty, sandy dirt in Torquato's face. He stagger... ... and flying to his eyes.

"Run," Eliane shouted. She and Vilson bolted.

Torquato still had the wherewithal to keep the sh... ... and he brought it up, instinctively, to take Jake's head off. ...

The deafening spit of white–orange stopped J... ... , the lead shot whipping the terracotta tiles of the bo... ... roof above his head.

Torquato pumped the spent shell out, even as he was still blinking the grit from his eyes. Torquato would have another one pumped back in and fired before Jake could make the three strides between them. Jake went for him anyway.

The shotgun jammed on the return action. But Torquato was quick enough. Stepping to one side, he flicked the butt up at Jake's jaw. It was only a glancing blow but it clicked Jake's teeth, the raw injured nerves lighting up right through his head. He was still slow, off the pace. His legs went and he dropped in the sandy dirt. He shook his head, trying to clear the stars, and staggered back to his feet.

Torquato backed off a few paces, blowing at the grit in the breach of the shotgun and wrenching at the mechanism. Jake lurched toward him unsteadily. Still holding the shotgun in one hand, Torquato stepped back and drew a heavy knife from a sheath tucked into the back of his waistband, the blade polished and keen.

Jake just didn't have the speed of thought or action. He knew it. He couldn't trust his reflexes.

For once, reckless compulsion didn't propel him forward. He turned and ran unsteadily for the deep slab of shadow on the other side of the farmhouse. He had heard Eliane running that way. Ducking into a patch of tall maize, he thrashed his way through and into the banana plantation beyond. He stopped for a moment. He couldn't see any trace of Eliane. The floodlights on the cattle shed went off.

Jake squinted to pick out shapes in the murk and strained his ears, but there were cicadas everywhere in the surrounding trees, their noise filling the air.

A flash silhouetted the broad leaves in the plantation, the sharp report coming with it, shot peppering the leaves way off to his right. Torquato had got his shotgun working again.

Torquato was shouting hoarsely, "You brought this on yourselves. No one is going to take my farm from me."

Jake's heart was going like a runaway train and he was hyperventilating. The feeling panicked him more and he felt light-headed. He had to tap into his training. Deep breaths, slowing it all down.

He didn't hear anything more from Torquato for a long minute, and then he saw a long slash of light cutting through the trees away to his left. Torquato had got himself a torch.

Jake's head was clearing. He had to flank him, get up behind him and jump him before he found either Eliane or Vilson. He moved off through the darkness of the plantation, away from the torch at first, wincing each time one of the big, dead leaves cracked beneath his feet. When he was beyond where the torchlight was flashing back and forth, he jinked left, groping his way along, hands outstretched, flinching each time a waxy frond brushed his face.

The crunchy ground beneath his feet gave way. He tumbled down a bank into a stream, cracking his shins and knees on rocks. He sat on his haunches in the cool water, still. The banana plantation extended to the other side of the stream and looked just as dense.

He could hear Torquato bludgeoning his way through the plantation now, the crackle of dead leaves and the tearing of live fronds. The torchlight momentarily flashed across Jake's face. Torquato had changed direction. He was coming at Jake. The torchlight flickered, dimmed and then died. Torquato cursed and bashed the torch on something. It came back, but now Torquato was crashing off in the other direction again.

Jake clambered back up the bank and crept through the plantation in the direction of the farmhouse, following Torquato. He came to the edge, a sagging barbed-wire fence separating the plantation from a thicket of dense bush and trees. He was disoriented. He wasn't anywhere near the farmhouse. He had no idea where it was. But he could see the sweep of the torch ahead of him, and the occasional flicker, and hear the cursing and bashing from Torquato to get it working again.

When he reached the other side of the thicket there was no fence this time, just patchy scrub and stands of bamboo, stems as thick as his thigh, as tall as trees.

Tripping over coarse tufts of grass was infinitely better than the racket of dead leaves. He could move faster.

The scrub gave way to a copse of stunted trees. He was closer to Torquato now, who was no more than twenty metres ahead through the trees.

Torquato shouted, "I see where you are. Come out now and I swear I won't shoot. You just get off my property and you never come back. Deal?" There was a waver in his voice. Being jumpy and fearful didn't make him any less dangerous. Jake couldn't know whether he was bluffing or whether he really had found Eliane or Vilson.

Torquato slowed and Jake came up on him as silently as he could. He could smell the stale tobacco smoke and sweat. Torquato's torch was shining on a big woodpile of thin logs in a small clearing, the barrel of the shotgun propped on his torch hand. The torchlight was his line of fire. He edged closer to the woodpile. "Come out now." He was almost cajoling, almost kindly.

Eliane's trembling hands appeared over the other side of the woodpile, followed by her head and pale, frightened face.

Jake was within five metres of Torquato. *Crack*, he stepped on a branch. And then go. He went low, Torquato only having time to half turn before Jake's shoulder connected with his lower ribs. They both went sprawling into the woodpile. The torch spun away from Torquato's hand as the logs tumbled. Something else moved next to Jake. Not the slide of a log, nor the scuttle of an animal. He had no idea what it was but the bolt of fear was primaeval.

Amid the cascade of logs, Jake tried to wrench the shotgun from Torquato's grasp. A yelp of pain and fear came from Torquato and suddenly the fight was gone from him. A branch moved near Jake's feet, short and thick. But it wasn't a branch. It slid away in a fluid, rippling motion. A snake.

Jake ripped the shotgun from Torquato, jumped to his feet and stepped back to cover him. Torquato hardly seemed aware of him. He was sitting up in the broken pile of logs, nursing his calf, pulling up his trouser leg, looking around. Looking at the area where the snake had been. Looking at his leg.

"Find the bastard," he pleaded. "You have to find it and kill it or I will be dead."

"You've got to be kidding?" Jake said.

"I'm bit. It's burning and swelling already – that means it's a bad one. Without knowing which kind they won't know which serum to give me. You've got to help. Please."

"You were going to shoot her a second ago," he said. Rage was flooding out the narrow. It was the response he was familiar with, but it felt out of place, unwelcome.

"I wasn't going to shoot. I don't want to kill anyone."

"You shot at me back there."

"You went for me. Scared the crap out of me. What the hell else was I going to do? I just want to protect my family and my place. This is all I have. I am nothing without this farm." He gasped. "*Meu Deus*, it hurts. Please."

He undid his own leather belt, took it off and looped it around his thigh, tying it as tightly as he could. A tourniquet.

Eliane returned Torquato's torch and shone it around in the undergrowth, poking tentatively with a long stick. She had obviously already made up her mind.

The rage was sucked down a plughole inside Jake and he was just left with the shakes again. Finding himself a stick, he knew it was a waste of time well before his minute of searching was up. The snake was long gone. "Can you hold this?" he said, handing the shotgun to Eliane.

He squatted to get one of Torquato's arms around his neck and got him up on his good leg. "Which way to the house?" he asked.

Torquato pointed about ninety degrees away from where Jake thought the farmhouse lay.

Chapter 33

Jake

Using Jake as his crutch, the farmer hobbled through the trees and then the banana plantation, and then through a sparse orchard pocked with old machinery and sheds and sties. The unlit farmhouse was hunched in the darkness.

"Woman," Torquato called out, his voice hollow as they entered the yard, "come and help. I'm bit – a snake."

The dim bulb in the doorway came on a moment later, Vilson's mother beneath it. She beckoned them toward the house.

"No," Torquato said, "my pickup. We need to go straight to hospital."

"We need to call an ambulance," Eliane said, pulling her mobile from the pocket of her trousers.

"That's a waste of time," Torquato said. "You won't get a signal out here."

"You don't have a phone inside?" Eliane asked Vilson's mother. Goretti shook her head.

Vilson appeared from the shadows of the trees by the cattle shed and followed them cautiously. The floodlights came on as they passed between the house and cattle shed, illuminating the corner of the field where Torquato had parked his pickup.

Vilson hung back as Jake dropped the tailgate of the pickup and Eliane and Goretti helped heave Torquato into the back. His jaw was clenched and he was soaked in sweat, his leg blowing up, the trouser leg already too tight to roll up.

Jake climbed into the back of the pickup, making a pillow for Torquato with a sack of animal feed. "Give me your knife," he said.

Torquato tipped up his hip, allowing Jake to pull the knife from the sheath tucked into his waistband. Jake slit his faded jeans to the knee. Torquato's lower leg was distended, a mottled, purple–black balloon, the skin shiny and tight around the two puncture wounds. It looked like it was about to burst. Watery blood and pus dribbled from the punctures. Torquato looked down at his leg and gasped, his head thumping back on a feed sack. He put Jake's hand on the belt tourniquet. "You've got to keep this tight. If I pass out you have to remember to undo it for a few seconds every ten minutes, but then tighten it again. Understand?"

"Sure," Jake said, undoing it and pulling it tight... ...ing it. Torquato cursed with the pain, his eyes wild an... ...he nodded. "That's good, it has to be like that."

"Okay, let's get going," Jake said to Goretti.

"I can't drive," Goretti said.

"You don't have to help him now anyway," Vilson s...

"You don't get it," the farmer gasped. "You ...d... ... stand what's going on here at all."

"I understand plenty," said Vilson, but his de... ... ...tting it. He could see his mother wrapping her skinny a... ... ...rself, her shoulders hunched, staring at her feet.

Torquato's body stiffened, agony wracking him, ...ng in and out of his chest. He took a moment to gather him... ... ...on't tell you, I'll put you out of your misery. Your mother ... ... you elbowing your way in to stake a claim here. She alrea... ... ...o do that."

Vilson's eyes widened in disbelief.

"That's right, a son. My son. And right now he's l... ... ...pital bed."

"What happened?" Goretti cried out. "Is he ok...?"

"He's fine, all things considered. He fell in the ro... ... ...d his arm. He will probably never ride again. I came to t... ... ..."

Goretti's hands went to her face.

"You had a child with him?" Vilson whispered, h... ... ...g his jaw down. Jake could see that she wasn't listening. S... ... ...ck at the farmhouse and then at the fields and the cattle sh... ... ...ying to think. Trying to calculate.

"For the love of God," Torquato gasped, the pa... ... ...him. "Let's go. The *gringo* will have to drive."

"Where's your car key?" Jake asked, clambering f... ... ...ck of the pickup.

"Under the passenger mat."

Jake searched beneath the dusty rubber mat. It... ... ... He searched the driver's side. He searched the dark re... ... ...dim interior light couldn't reach with Torquato's torch a... ... ...nds.

"I can't find it."

"In the ignition?"

"Not there."

"It's got to be there somewhere." Torquato's vo... ... ...king, panicked. "*Meu Deus*, my eyes. My sight is going. I...

THE BURNING HILL

"I'll have to change the tyre on the Polo and we can go in that," Jake said.

Goretti was ahead of him, reaching to take Eliane's car key as Torquato pulled it from his jeans pocket. She backed away as Jake held his hand out for it.

"Where are the papers?" she asked Torquato.

His breaths were coming in painful sobs now. "What the hell – are you – talking about?"

"The papers for the farm. I should know, in case…"

"Not even a corpse – ah – and the vultures – are already circling."

"Tell me where they are."

"In my cabinet – third drawer down."

"Those are just the old papers."

"You went through my stuff?" He gasped. "That cabinet is locked."

"Where are the new papers?"

"With the lawyer, woman – ah – they are doing their stuff."

She was a different person now. "*Are* doing?" she said, her head going still like the snake before it strikes. "You said it was all done. Done a good while back."

"It's lawyers – they hold stuff up with their bullshit – but it will be done. Ah – I swear."

Goretti shook her head slowly. "You would cheat your own blood?"

"He'll be taken care of." He was panting now with the pain, his eyes screwed shut.

"He will? Even though he has no value now that he can't ride?"

"Don't be stupid, woman – he's my son."

She looked at him and then at the car key, holding it out in her open palm. Her fingers closed over it and she flung it off into the darkness of the thick scrub bordering the field.

"No," Eliane yelled.

The insects filled the silence that followed.

"What's happening?" Torquato rasped.

No one answered immediately.

"She threw away the key," Jake said after a few moments.

Torquato sighed and his breathing evened out, his head dropping back, body relaxing. "Then she has killed me."

Chapter 34

Jake

The floodlights went off on the timer. Vilson's mother didn't move.

"Please can you turn them back on and keep them on?" Jake asked her.

She didn't move for a long moment, before shuffling off to the cattle shed and lighting the place up again. She returned and perched on the shiny tiles of the veranda, head in hands. Jake watched as Vilson went to her, but he stopped short. Unsure. He shuffled from foot to foot and paced around in the dusty sand.

Jake took the shotgun from Eliane, pumped the remaining shells from it and pocketed them. He thought for a moment about the safest place for it, before swinging it by the barrel and flinging it off into the brush.

"I'm going to change the tyre on your car," he said to Eliane. He left Vilson standing by his mother as Eliane went off to start searching with Torquato's torch amongst the thick, tall grass and fireflies out where Goretti had flung the key for the pickup.

Eliane's Polo had a jack but Jake had to search around in the cattle shed before he found some planks of wood to support it on the soft sand beneath the car.

When he got the wheel clear of the sand he undid the bolts and then broke off to check on Torquato. He climbed into the back of the pickup, loosening the tourniquet, counting out the seconds and then retying it. Torquato moaned with the pain, his breathing rapid and laboured. The moans dropped away to become a faint whimper every few breaths, eyes staring blankly.

Jake got the damaged wheel off and put the spare on. He put a plank of wood beneath the tyre before lowering it, to give it purchase. It wasn't fully inflated but it would have to do.

Checking on Torquato again, the sweat had dried up on his skin but his shirt was still soaked and he was beginning to shiver. Jake went to the farmhouse and found a cheap, gaudy blanket on the worn sofa in the TV room.

Torquato smiled as Jake laid it over him, his face filled with fear, eyes blank and confused. He reached out, searching for Jake. When he touched his forearm he gripped it, pulling Jake closer. "My Toninho is a good son," he said in a whisper. "He really could have made it. The doctors say he might recover but I've seen injuries like that before – his shoulder will never be the same again. Life is cruel."

He broke off with a series of painful, gasping breaths. Jake tried to quieten him but Torquato shook his head, insistent on continuing. "I have another son, older than Toninho, full of big ideas that his mother stuffed into his empty head before she died." He told Jake that the son had left home at nineteen, travelling from farm to farm providing a service branding and castrating bulls. The son had said he would show them all, expand his business, become a big shot. "I know that beneath all the boasting, he is just a son trying to impress his father," Torquato said. "It breaks my heart because it is never too long before he is back with his head down and his hand held out for another loan. And now there is another who is coming with his hand out."

"Vilson only wants to know his mother," Jake said gently. "He wants nothing else. I promise you that."

Torquato seemed not to hear. "Anyone who is not a son of mine will get not a scrap. There are no scraps to spare, *gringo*. Do you understand?"

Jake felt no desire to add to the farmer's pain. The man was dying. "Sure," he said.

Torquato's grip relaxed a little and he let out a sigh. Relief.

"I've got to help Eliane search for the car key," Jake said to him.

"You'll come back, yes?"

"I will."

He joined the search with Eliane, breaking off every ten minutes to attend to the tourniquet.

"This is useless," he said to Eliane after an hour. "We're never going to find the key without daylight."

When he went back to Torquato the next time, the leg had swelled even more, purple veins streaking away from the blackened flesh, the skin shiny and grotesque. Torquato's breathing was shallow and rapid. His unseeing eyes opened for a moment. "Is that you, *gringo*?"

"Yeah."

"Don't go this time," he said, his hand moving weakly.

"Okay, I won't leave you."

Jake laid a hand on Torquato's shoulder and his eyes closed and his breathing evened out. Jake thought about trying to look for the car key again with Eliane, futile as it was. But every time he moved, Torquato stirred and put his hand out, and was only quiet again when Jake laid his hand back on his shoulder.

THE BURNING HILL

Another hour passed, probably more, and Eliane kept on searching the undergrowth. Jake was staring out at the stars in the eastern corner of the sky, trying to decide whether it might be turning a shade lighter than the deep black that was splashed with brilliant constellations. Torquato's breathing started to catch in his throat.

His fingers curled and reached out in turns. He no longer seemed to have the strength to move his arms. His shallow breaths were rattling in and out now. Eyes open. Fearful.

He struggled over several breaths to get words out, choking and gasping. He groped around with a hand, managing to find Jake's wrist. "Please."

Jake held his hand with its thick calluses. Torquato squeezed with surprising strength and then relaxed his grip. The tension went from his face, eyes closing. His breathing was quieter now. But it was becoming shallower and shallower until, finally, it faded away to nothing. His chest was still. His suffering was over.

Jake let go of his hand, laying it back down, and pulled the blanket over his face.

Goretti was still perched on the veranda, clutching herself, Vilson still hovering awkwardly nearby. It seemed to Jake that the few metres separating mother and son were impossible to bridge. He got out of the pickup and called out to Goretti, "You can turn those lights off now, he's gone."

She stood and crossed herself and went to the cattle shed. Vilson didn't move until the floodlights went out. As Jake's eyes struggled to adjust, he could only just make out the murky shape of Goretti coming back and going into the house. A few moments later he saw Vilson follow her. And then it was just the stars again, the fireflies and the torchlight as Eliane made her way back.

Jake waited for some emotion to hit. Any emotion. But nothing came. Instead, the space filled with a tiredness that dragged on his limbs.

Chapter 35

Vilson

In all that time while the farmer lay in the pickup, with so much he wanted to ask his mother, Vilson had not managed to ask anything. And his mother hadn't had the look of someone who wanted to talk.

This son that the farmer had spoken of, it was like a punch in the stomach. His mother's son. He could not even make a picture of the boy in his mind. He would not. The boy did not exist.

The dream that had kept him living and breathing since he was a child was unravelling. He had to put it back together. He had to be the man.

When he followed her inside the house from the darkness, he found her sitting at the small kitchen table, staring blankly at the cheap plastic tablecloth. A wash of low, white light was coming from a fluorescent tube beneath a kitchen unit. Insects blatted into the light and the walls were mottled with the squished bodies of others, along with the dusty marks from the shoe that had swatted them.

Vilson pulled out a chair to sit, the metal legs scraping on the tiled floor.

His mother put her head in her hands. A tear splashed on the plastic tablecloth. He didn't understand. She had killed the farmer by throwing away the car key. And now she was crying?

"You are free of him."

"Free?" she said, looking at him directly for the first time. "I made this my home. This should be the home for my Toninho."

"I am your son too."

"And there is another son, Toninho's half-brother. He will try to throw us off the farm. Others in the family will help him. They will all want to put a hand on this place."

"We can go to Toninho. I will help you bring him back here," Vilson said. He had difficulty even saying the kid's name. But he would do this thing for his mother. She would see that he was only there to make things right.

"I cannot leave here," his mother said. "Not for anything. You ask your lawyer friend – if I am here in the house I at least have some rights."

"Then I will go get him and I will bring him back. We can face this thing all together." He would have to do it. Rework his dream. Make room for this kid. This parasite.

"Yes, you must get him – you are a good boy. But you cannot stay. It would only make things worse. There is nothing for you here, do you understand?" She was looking away now, her eyes unfocused. Looking into the future, to a place that Vilson was scared he didn't inhabit.

"No, *Mãe*," Vilson said. "All those letters – you promised me that we would be together one day." He couldn't let himself believe that the letters were the last real part of his mother, he couldn't let himself believe that she had been twisted into the woman in front of him. "You said we would be together on a farm. It has to be this farm."

"Letters, letters, I don't know what you mean when you talk about these letters."

"The letters you wrote, *Mãe*. I kept every single one since you went away."

"How could I write you letters? I cannot read or write."

"You – you got someone else to write them." Vilson was reeling. "You told them what to write and they wrote them for you."

She shook her head. "There were no letters. Someone has lied to you."

Vilson stood. He didn't hear the legs of the chair scraping this time. The blood was singing in his ears. He felt as if he was about to faint.

Someone had lied. It was all a lie.

Chapter 36

Jake

The day was coming in quickly. The sun hadn't yet risen but they could see across the field now to a low, shabby building on the other side. A ragged line of workers was emerging to stand by the stained whitewash of the wall, looking in their direction.

Jake followed Eliane across the coarse grass, cropped close by cattle. The workers shifted from foot to foot. They would have heard the commotion the previous evening. They would have heard the shots. And yet this place had stayed dark all night. The faces of the men were drawn, their bodies too lean. They were hungry. And overworked.

"*Senhor* Torres died last night," Eliane told them. "He was bitten by a snake. If you don't want to stay here any more you can go."

There was no celebration. The men took sideways glances at one another, confused, as if they suspected a trick. They did not look like men just freed.

"He didn't pay you any wages, did he?" Eliane asked.

A couple of them shook their heads.

"He gave us food and lodging," one of the others piped up. "He looked after us when we got sick."

"He was treating you as little more than slaves," Jake said. "But he has gone. There is no one to hold you here now."

"But this is where we live," the same one said, "where we work. We have no place else to go."

"You can go home," Eliane said. "Back to your families."

"I am from Pará," said another. "I don't have the money to get back there." Pará was a state way up in the north, days away. "I haven't seen my family for years," he said. It seemed as though the thought had only just come to him.

"Just sit tight," said Eliane. "The ILO will come, and they will get you home."

They seemed far from reassured by that, murmuring and whispering to each other, shaking heads.

"You haven't done anything wrong," Eliane said. "The ILO only want to help. They will protect you."

There was nothing else she could do. She was flustered as they walked back toward the field by the farmhouse to look for her car key again. "I don't really know what I was expecting," she said, "but it definitely wasn't that."

"Looks like they've been here so long that it's all they know. That probably makes even good change scary."

"Maybe they'd have been better off if we'd just left them alone."

"You don't mean that?"

"I don't know. It doesn't feel like we did a good thing right now. It's such a mess. But I'm so tired I'm maybe not thinking straight."

In the daylight it only took fifteen minutes of poking around before Jake saw the key lodged in a muddy rut gouged by a cow's hoof, deep in the long grass.

When he handed it to Eliane he noticed her hand was shaking. "Are you going to be okay?" he asked.

"I came here thinking I knew what I was doing and a man ended up dead."

"He was going to kill us."

"He was scared of you – he said so."

"That's not the only reason, and you know it." Jake could feel the anger uncoiling in his gut.

"I know, I know," she said, lowering her eyes, "but you're getting angry now and it makes me scared of you. All this, it's too dangerous, too crazy. I'm not used to this kind of stuff. It's all out of control."

She walked away from him back to the farmhouse. The anger went still inside him and he followed her in silence.

They found Vilson slumped at the kitchen table, asleep, head resting on his arms. "Vilson," Eliane said, shaking him gently.

He awoke with a start, but he was groggy, eyes puffed and bloodshot.

Goretti appeared from the hallway. Holding herself.

No one was saying anything, so Jake prompted Eliane. "You need to get back to Rio, right?"

She nodded. "I might not have a job to go back to," Eliane said. "But if I don't go now, I definitely won't."

"Okay, but we need to get the body to a hospital."

"Why?" Vilson asked flatly.

"Because things will be difficult enough as it is for those guys out there when the ILO come." He turned to Eliane. "We'll have to move the body to your car."

"You don't need to," said Vilson, producing a key with a mangled leather fob from his pocket.

"You had his key all the time?" Jake asked, incredulous.

Vilson shook his head. "I found it this morning."

Jake didn't believe him but he was too tired to enter into another pointless row. "I'll call the ILO as soon as I get a signal and direct them here," he said to Eliane.

"They have my details and I'll leave you a card," she said to Goretti. "I can come back once things have settled down in Rio, if I can help in any way."

Goretti looked at her blankly.

Jake couldn't see much beyond what needed to happen in the next hour. It was a sketchy plan to pick a way through the catastrophic wreckage of a naive one that it was now clear was doomed from the outset. Jake hadn't yet decided whether he was going to come back to the farm and stick around when the ILO descended. Even with Torquato's body transported to the hospital, it was likely that the cops would find their way to the farm at some point. If that happened, he and Vilson needed to get themselves very far from this place.

"Will you bring my son from the hospital?" Goretti asked Jake.

"Sure," he replied wearily.

"I will go with him," Vilson said to his mother.

"You are a good boy," Goretti said to him.

The words seemed to sting Vilson.

Chapter 37

Jake

Jake found his way back to the outskirts of the big rodeo town. It didn't feel like a brilliant option to take Torquato's body to the same hospital that his kid was in, but he couldn't risk going to Cruzeiro. He'd never seen any sign of a hospital there anyway.

"*Porra*," Vilson suddenly swore, and slammed a fist into the door panel. "This is not right, none of it."

The harder edge that Jake had seen in Vilson after Nogueira had dumped them in the forest outside Rio was hardening further.

Just before they got to the hospital, Jake pulled over. "You need to get in the back with him. We need to make it look convincing, like we were rushing him here, trying to save him."

Vilson looked at him for a long moment. Jake couldn't read anything from him other than deep animosity. "You'll see this thing through with the kid for my mother, yes?" Vilson said finally.

"Of course, but I need your help to do it."

Vilson nodded and climbed in the back. Jake took the blanket from the body, and then drove the pickup into the hospital car park. He rushed in and grabbed a passing orderly, telling him that his friend had been bitten. It wasn't hard to make a show of it, to give a sense of urgency. There was still plenty of emotion boiling around.

A nurse came out with the orderly, checking the corpse and confirming the obvious before they got it on the gurney, Jake and Vilson following them inside. The nurse started going through her list of questions and Jake gave his filtered answers. She pushed a collection of forms held on a clipboard with a biro at him, saying, "I'll be back shortly. If you can start filling these in, please. Where did your friend go?"

Vilson had been on Jake's shoulder as they walked in. He hadn't noticed him slip away in the melee of people drifting about and waiting for attention. He was nowhere to be seen. There was no time to hang around for him or go looking for him. As soon as the nurse had gone, Jake went to reception and asked for directions to Toninho's ward. He kept the clipboard with him and walked with purpose. Whether it was the hint of officialdom that the clipboard gave, or his own scars that suggested he was a patient, or some kind of confused mash-up of both, or just a total lack of interest, no one questioned him. He walked straight into the small ward and found Toninho sitting up in bed at the end, his injured arm in a sling.

"My name is Jake. Your mother asked me to take you back to the farm."

Toninho didn't look surprised or fazed. He just studied Jake for a few moments, sizing him up. "You're the *gringo*, right? I heard my parents arguing about you."

"Yes."

"Is the half-brother with you?"

Jake shook his head. "He was earlier, but I don't know where he's got to."

"Why would I come with you?"

"I'll explain as we go. You can shout the place down if you think I'm doing anything other than trying to get you back to the farm – there are plenty of people about."

"What happened to your face?"

"I was robbed and the bad guy shot me."

"Does it hurt?"

"Yeah, but less and less."

"Mine hurts," Toninho said, as he pushed back the bedsheet with his good hand and got out of bed. "Where's my dad?"

Chapter 38

Vilson

Painted in fading blue and white, the place was a small cinema that had once been a church. It was in a line of shops in the old part of town. The double wooden doors were set in an archway with a stone crucifix above. Vilson saw the poster on the noticeboard to one side of the entrance. This was the place.

He bought a seat, even though the old man in the foyer told him the afternoon show was nearly over. Every one of the wooden chairs, set out in neat rows in the auditorium, was taken. Vilson joined the group of people in the standing area at the rear. He felt the atmosphere the moment he walked in. There was a charge in the hot, still air.

A middle-aged woman with a flushed neck and face stood on a dais at the front of the hall, the white cinema screen hung behind her. There was an old man beside her, a look somewhere between hope and fear in his face. A young girl was sitting on a chair behind them, looking down at the hands folded in her lap. This was Yara.

Vilson had heard that the woman was Yara's aunt. Having had the gift as a child, the story went that her powers had faded as she had grown older. Yara was now the channel to the spirit world and the aunt used her experience to guide that power.

The aunt closed her eyes and raised her hands, palms up, her bare underarms sagging. She stayed like that for nearly a minute, her lips moving in silent prayer. Then she turned to the old man, placing a hand over his stomach. The prayers continued until she finally nodded her head, satisfied.

"Amen," she said.

"Amen," the man once repeated.

"The pain will fade away," she said to the old man, "and the growth in your stomach will shrink and disappear."

She gestured for him to return to his seat.

"*Graças a Deus*," the old man said, crossing himself. Placing a hand on the aunt's shoulder, he said, "Thank you."

Yara continued looking down at her hands as the man turned to her and bowed his head before making his way back down the aisle. The audience murmured and turned to carry on looking at him as he passed. This man had been touched by something special.

179

The aunt checked her tiny wristwatch. "We might be able to call upon the spirit world one more time."

Yara's head turned slightly, as if she had heard something, and she looked up for the first time. Straight at Vilson. She smiled. It seemed to Vilson that it came only very gradually, like a flower opening to the sun. It was a slight, weary kind of a smile. Sadness in her eyes. It wasn't the smile of a child.

Vilson's heart skipped, people in the audience turning to look at him.

Yara's eyes dropped as the aunt went to her, bending to hear the girl whisper. The aunt whispered something sharp back to her.

And then she straightened and looked around the audience, taking in Vilson for the briefest of moments as she did so. "A man in a blue suit and tie has come forward," she said after a few moments.

Vilson was confused. He had been sure that the aunt was going to say something about his mother. Or about him. Or both of them. He didn't know anyone that wore any kind of suit. Unless she meant a cop?

The girl sank in her chair, her head dropping a little lower.

The aunt looked around the room again, this time avoiding Vilson's eyes. He racked his brain for a connection. There had to be one.

"The suit is pale, a bluish–grey," the aunt said. "He likes to dress smartly. He is looking for someone. He needs to say something."

A middle-aged woman in the audience raised her hand. "My grandfather wore suits," she said. "I think he had a blue one."

"Yes, he is nodding and smiling now," the aunt said. The grandfather wanted to help the woman with a problem. The woman's eyes went down to the floor. She said that she suspected her husband was cheating on her. The aunt asked if the husband had had health problems and the woman said yes, he'd had a heart attack the year before. The aunt cocked her head for a few moments and then nodded. It was his health that the husband must concentrate on. The woman's grandfather was warning that he needed to see a doctor and keep away from other women or the next heart attack might prove fatal. She should tell him that and all would be fine. The grandfather had passed on a message that could keep her husband alive. He said he was proud of his granddaughter before he withdrew to the spirit world again.

There were amens as the aunt brought the show to a close, awe amongst the audience at what they had experienced.

The place began to empty, people speaking quietly and intently. Vilson didn't move. He couldn't understand what had just taken place. He had to speak with Yara. She had noticed him. She had seen something.

As the last members of the audience filed out, Vilson made his way down the aisle between the chairs.

The aunt flapped her arms, shooing him away. "No, no, that's it for this afternoon," she said. "There will be more this evening – eight o'clock – come back then."

"Please," said Vilson. "I have come a long way. I must talk with her now."

"We have to rest," the aunt said. "The healing is hard on us."

"There is no illness here, Aunty," Yara said. Her voice was unhurried. "He just wants to speak."

"Yes," said Vilson. "That's all I need."

"It'll cost," the aunt said, her mouth hardening.

Yara looked down.

"How much?" Vilson asked.

"Two hundred and fifty for a personal reading."

Vilson had never handed over that much for anything. It was a crazy amount. "Okay," he said. The girl was his last chance.

He made to go around the aunt, but she blocked him. "Money first," she said, holding her hand out.

He pulled out the *gringo's* wallet and counted the notes. There would only be a few left now.

The aunt took the money and pulled out one of the wooden chairs from the front row, placing it opposite Yara on the dais. Motioning for Vilson to sit, she moved away to straighten chairs and pick up rubbish. Vilson could see that she had lost interest now.

Vilson sat on the edge of the chair, leaning forward, shoulders hunched, fists balled up on his knees. Yara closed her eyes and reached out a hand, placing it lightly over one of his fists.

She was so calm. It spread to Vilson, the tension going from his shoulders. She went quite still, her eyes closed. She was like that for a minute or more. It felt to Vilson like many more minutes had passed before she opened her eyes.

She kept them lowered. "I see you with your friend, cooking over your stove on the floor," she said. "He is looking up, smiling at you."

"What does he say?" Vilson asked in a whisper.

"He is not speaking, but he does see you."

Yara's eyes came up and they were filled with tears. And then her brow furrowed. "There is a small woman," she said. "She works and works. She seems sad and angry at the same time, and doesn't seem to know what to do."

"My mother," Vilson said, his voice catching.

"Yes," Yara nodded. "But she is turning her b__d. _ _ is _ _ving away."

"We have been apart for many years, but peopl_ _ _ _ _ _her, lying to me. She is confused." Vilson was wrestlin_ _ _ _ _ _ _rds, saying what he needed to believe rather than what h_ _ _

"She doesn't want you to follow."

"How can I make her see?"

Yara's shoulders hunched over. She was hugging _ _ _ _ _ there was an ache there. "Whenever you follow she is unl_ _ _ _ _ not change. It is always like this."

"There must be something I can do?" Vilson _ _ _ _ _ _ nust know."

"You cannot reach her," Yara said. She concen__ _ _ _ _ g for something. "She always turns her back."

"I got letters from her all my life, but she told m_ _ _ _ _ _ ome from her."

Yara frowned. "I see the letters, they made yo_ _ _ _ _ _ your mother is not with them."

Vilson blinked, his mouth open. Washed fro_r _ _ _ _ _ _orm with no lifeline, the ship disappearing in the wave_. _ _ _ _ _

"I don't know. I see someone, but I can't see the_ _ _ _ _ y are walking away. It's growing too dark to see them."

"You have to tell me," Vilson said. He shifted _ _ _ _ _ _ n his chair, gasping for air.

"They have gone." Yara searched and searched. _ _ _ _ _ ow. There is a young man – a policeman," she said. "H_ _ _ _ _

"That dumb cop is nothing to me," Vilson said.

"But he wants to help." She put a hand to he_ _ _ _ _ _ _, _meu Deus. He shot your friend."

"What?" Vilson's head jerked up. "You see tha_ _

"You didn't know," she whispered.

Vilson hammered his fists against his thighs. "_ _ _ _ _ _ lied. Liars and murderers and cheats. All of them."

"No, not all of them," Yara said. "Someone else _ _ _ _ _ _ He speaks in a strange way. With anger. He is difficul_ _ _ _ _

"No." Vilson jumped up from his chair, _ _ _ _ _ _ lling backwards.

Yara didn't seem to notice.

And then she recoiled. She had seen something _

Chapter 39

Jake

Toninho was staring out at the rush of green as they flew past the cane fields, tyres thrumming on the lumpy road. His head was lolling on an arm propped on the windowsill, the hot wind blasting his thick hair. If he was crying he wasn't going to show it to Jake.

A police car came up behind them and overtook at speed, lights flashing, no siren. There was only one place it was likely to be going to along this road. That made up Jake's mind for him – he couldn't go back to the farm now.

A few kilometres further on, he pulled to the side of the road by the turning for the farm track, leaving the engine running. "Are you sure you're okay from here?"

Toninho was still looking away from him. "I've been driving this thing for years, one-handed, two-handed, whatever."

"I didn't just mean the driving."

"What does it matter to you?"

"I'm sorry, I really am. For all of this. I was just trying to do what I thought was a good thing for Vilson."

"Doesn't look like you've helped anybody to me."

Jake had given him a potted version of what had happened. He hadn't skipped the confrontation with Toninho's father and how he had got bitten by the snake, but he had left out the part that his mother had played in his father's death. It seemed a better option to Jake to take all the blame rather than to wreck the relationship between Toninho and his mother. His mother was all he had. It was up to Goretti to decide when or if she would tell him everything. This wasn't how Jake worked. He'd always chosen the truth in the past, however brutal. Take responsibility, take the pain. But it just wasn't fair to hit this kid with everything right now. She might choose never to tell him and he would grow up as another living with lies. The thought of that was bad enough; what was worse was that things as toxic as this had a way of seeping out eventually. It was knotting Jake's insides.

He grabbed the plastic sack of belongings that was lying on the floor of the pickup and got out. Toninho shuffled over to the driver's side. His eyes were puffy from crying, but they were dry now, and they met Jake's with a steady gaze. He was made of sterner stuff than the rest of his family. Jake reached inside the plastic sack to get his wallet. He was going to give the kid as much as he could spare.

He could only feel clothes inside the sack. He looked in, ripping around inside the thin plastic, already jumping to the obvious conclusion. Nothing. Not even his phone. He tipped his clothes out onto the dirt and sifted through. All he found was confirmation.

"He took your money?" Toninho asked.

Jake kicked at the ground, sending a spray of dirt onto the sticky black tarmac of the road. "Yep."

He checked his pockets. He had enough cash to cover a light lunch for one. And he was stuck out here again. On another bitching hot day.

"What are you going to do?" Toninho asked.

"Not sure, but I'll be fine."

The kid had to perch himself on the edge of the driver's seat to reach the pedals, his good forearm flat against the steering wheel. He looked at Jake for a moment, reached across with his good left hand to put it in gear and he was away, the pickup creaking and knocking down the farm track.

It took half the day and two hitches before he got back to the big rodeo town. He had a reasonable amount of thinking time on the way. He remembered Vilson chattering excitedly on the drive to the farm before it had all gone so badly south. He had mentioned the girl he had seen on the poster, the one that he said did the clairvoyant healing show. Jake didn't believe that Vilson would want to go back to Rio. There was nothing good for him there. It didn't look like there was anything back on that farm for him either, but maybe he would stick around, hoping that the wind might change. Whichever way he was going, Jake hoped that he might have made the stop to see this girl beforehand. It was all he had to go on.

Finding the place wasn't a problem; it seemed most people in town knew about the show. But he had already clocked up some mileage on foot between his hitches, and the last one, in the back of a stinky chicken-shit truck, had dropped him on the wrong side of town. The final stretch in the late afternoon was a slog, walking on baked potatoes for feet.

He hammered on the wooden doors of the old cinema. The rattling of the doors on rusty hinges and iron bolts was the only response. But he was going to keep on hammering until something happened.

An old man eventually poked his head out of the barber's shop next door. "If they were dead in there they'd be awake by now," he scolded. "You might have better luck if you try the *pousada* where they're actually staying."

The old man directed him to the guesthouse a couple of blocks away.

"See?" Jake said to himself. Belligerence wasn't always the wrong tactic.

The guesthouse was in the oldest part of town, a colonial-style place in a terraced row of bleached-out yellow-painted houses. He rapped on the door, toning it down a little, but ready to wind it right back up. He needed to catch up to Vilson and his money in a hurry.

It was the girl who answered the door. For Jake, all that spiritual guff that infected Vilson, and seemingly pretty much every other Brazilian he had met, was just that. Guff. But there was no mistaking that this was The Girl. Standing there in the doorway with her head cocked to one side. Serene.

"I'm trying to find someone," Jake said.

She stepped back to welcome him in. "I know. I have spoken with him. I hoped that you would come."

It was more than just her serenity that gave her a look that separated her from anyone else her age. Tell someone enough times that they are something and they'll probably start believing it, he supposed. And he could see that she most definitely believed. It was no self-conscious act.

She led him down the dark hallway. Despite himself, Jake was relaxing more with every moment in her presence. He had an image of himself lying on the grassy bank of a beautiful river in England on a summer's day. He was trying to remember if he'd ever done that. He half smiled his cracked smile and shook his head. Stupid. But any grain of anger was dissolved.

"You came at the right time," she said over her shoulder, "my aunt is out shopping."

They went through a large reception room and kitchen, and out to a yard surrounded by high whitewashed walls. A couple of mango trees were throwing loose shadows over the balding dusty lawn. Beneath the covered barbecue area there was a long table with a bench on one side and chairs on the other.

On the table there was a tall jug and two glasses.

"It's lemonade. I made it this morning," she said, reaching over to pour. "I'm Yara, by the way."

She gulped hers down and wiped the back of her hand across her mouth. The only childlike gesture she had made. "Maybe you already knew my name?" she asked.

"I was told who you were."

"But you don't believe what you've been told." She said it lightly, her grey eyes deep and clear.

There was no need to offend her. "What do I know?" he said, shrugging and looking at his glass.

"I knew you were coming. That's why I put the lemonade out."

"You saw me coming?"

"I saw you both, walking down a dusty road, going in the same direction but not together. I see stuff and hear stuff – it happens all the time. I don't always know whether it is something that has already happened, or is happening now, or whether it is something that is going to happen," she said. "It doesn't always make sense. My aunt says that only she has the experience to guide the spirits that come through me. She says I don't have the maturity to handle them on my own – spirits can be cunning, they don't always reveal themselves truly or exactly as they are. She says messages have to be interpreted. People want certainty. They want to be told what to do."

Yara's eyes were fixed on her glass of lemonade. It didn't look like she believed her aunt and it seemed the lack of belief wasn't giving her a good feeling. Then the guilty look went and her grey eyes came back up to Jake, steady. "I see your anger. I can see places where it has exploded and done you harm, but I can't see where it comes from."

That scraped at the inside of him. Vilson must have really spouted some crap. And just as quickly, it went away. "The boy that came to see you, he took all my money. I really need to find him."

"The distance between you is less than he thinks," she said, as if it had just occurred to her. And then her brow furrowed. "But I don't know if he will ever understand that."

"Do you know where he went?"

She looked distracted now. "Home."

"Home where?"

"The city. Rio," she said, staring at the lemonade jug.

"He told you that?"

"He has nowhere else, but I saw something terrible for him there." Her words were almost a whisper as she wrapped her arms protectively, fearfully. "I saw a darkness around him. I've never seen anything like that before. A terrible darkness. And he was falling. Hands were grabbing at him to save him, but they couldn't hold on and he kept dropping away in the darkness. His body was limp, his eyes unseeing. Like the dead. I was trying to get him to reach out. He had to do it. But he kept on falling, and as he fell his eyes turned to me. And somewhere in the blankness there something shifted."

She shivered and dropped her head to blink away tears. "It scared me. There is a poison seeping in, but you can help him draw that poison if he lets you. The future isn't always set – he can take a different path."

She stood then. Coming round to Jake's side of the table, she reached out, touching her palm to the scarred side of his face. "I see shadows in people sometimes," she said. "That's how I know they are ill. But my aunt only likes to pick out the ones who already know they are ill. They come looking for a cure. They come with hope, and faith. My aunt says that miracles make for a steep road if hope and faith are not already at work."

She traced gentle lines around his scars with her fingers as she spoke. "There is no shadow in you, by the way. How does it feel?"

Almost without noticing, he realised that something had passed from him. There was a lightness. "Uh, better," he said, surprised.

She nodded. "Your policeman friend will be in a fight in a ring. You must stop him if you can."

"I don't think I can."

"You must try."

He nodded.

She looked at him for a few moments. "That anger in you, it is part of you, but you can only cheat death so many times."

Chapter 40

Vilson

Climbing the hill up to his shack, the journey to get there was almost forgotten. There was just one thing filling his head. There was no room for anything else.

Not even fear. The thing that had stalked him all his life had gone, just disappeared. And he had scarcely noticed.

It was the sleepy time of the hot afternoon, few people about. He hadn't seen any of Anjo's sentries, but he hadn't gone out of his way to avoid them. He didn't care.

Kids had pulled the door away from the shack, everything useful inside gone. At least they hadn't taken the time to kick the whole thing down yet. Only the old sacks that he and Babão had slept on were left. Babão, his only friend. He looked around in the undergrowth and trash at the back of the shack, hoping to find some of his things that might have been discarded when whichever kid had taken them had got bored. But he found none of his stuff.

He followed a skinny trail up the forested hill behind the shacks, turning off the track when he got to a tree that had the thick, muscular limbs of a strangler fig twisted around it. He pushed through tangled brush, having to zigzag a few times, until he found a sapling with a knife mark on the spindly stem.

Beneath a nearby shrub there was an area of disturbed earth. He used a fallen branch to dig. He uncovered the edges of a polythene sheet. He pulled it from the loose, soft earth and it came up with a heavy lump wrapped inside. Shaking the dirt off, he looked around. Nothing but the insects, lizards and birds. He unwrapped the old revolver and checked it over. It had stayed dry and didn't look any more grimy or pitted than he remembered. He pulled the extractor rod beneath the barrel and pushed the cylinder out – one empty chamber, five loaded. It was all he had. It would be enough.

He tucked the revolver in the back of his shorts and made his way back down the hill. Emerging from the rear of his shack he heard a sharp intake of breath, "*Meu Deus.*" It was a woman's voice. Shaky.

It was a neighbour, with her daily food shopping in a thin plastic carrier bag. The old lady lived in a shack little better than his. She had lost her sons to the gangs and her husband to alcohol. She didn't have much to live for but she had kept on living. She stumbled back and crossed herself. And then she fled, the carrier bag of groceries flapping. Even in her terror she kept an instinctive grip on the little that she had.

It wasn't until she was out of sight that Vilson understood. He was dead.

He had died that night on the Burning Hill when Anjo had fired at him. Anjo had missed, but everyone in the favela believed he was dead. His corpse had been on the TV news.

He was a ghost.

Chapter 41

Jake

In the state he was in, with his filthy shirt and torn-up face, he wouldn't have picked himself up. Luckily for him, there was the odd trucker out on the endless highways of Brazil who was less fussy. But in the grand scheme of things, with the vastness of the country, each hitch didn't really move him very far along the road.

When he had said goodbye to Yara, she had reached into a little purse covered in brightly coloured plastic beads and emptied it for him. It was her pocket money, only a few *Reais*, but it almost doubled what he already had. Whether or not she could tap into any higher power, or whether she just had an uncanny ability to read people and get them to volunteer information outside awareness, she was certainly a better kid than he had ever been. He managed to eke the money out on food and water rations to the end of the second day.

Four days in and he was outside a roadside café, waving the heaving layer of flies off a half-eaten pastry sitting amongst paper cups, cans and wrappers in a waste bin. He was amazed at how quickly his groaning belly had overwhelmed shame and revulsion. Retrieving the pastry, he gave a wipe with his fingers, even though, with blackened fingernails, they were probably dirtier than the litter on which it had been sitting. Give him another day and he reckoned he would be reduced to rooting right through the bins down to cockroach-and-rat level. After the first day no one would let him into the café or garage toilets to wash.

At night, trying to sleep in lit car parks or outside roadside restaurants and garages, the only people who had bothered him were those telling him to move on. He looked like a vagrant, and apparently a crazy one at that. Not worth robbing.

He had no chance of hitching a lift from passing traffic. He had to buttonhole truck drivers in garage and café car parks and give them a potted version of who he was and why he needed to get to Rio. And he had to do it quick before they had a chance to back away. Most of the drivers were willing to accept that he wasn't just some stinky hobo, but his hit rate was still only about one in every ten that he approached. And there was no way that the ten percent would let someone as stinky as him in their cab. He was travelling freight-only. And only then if he wasn't dirtying up the produce.

Finishing off the pastry, he looked at his dirty fingers, giving their infectious potential only half a thought before he started licking them. The greasy sugar was mixed up with all sorts of other tastes. He had stopped retching at those kinds of thoughts the day before.

He saw a driver walk out of the café, an older guy, stretching his legs as he went round his fruit truck, kicking at the tyres to check them. The truck was a flatbed with wooden slats running around it to hold in the stacked plastic crates of mangos and papaya. Jake had learned that fruit trucks were usually headed for towns or cities. He had finally got to a point where at least some of the goods trucks were Rio-bound.

He got the guy up against the side of the truck and launched. With practice, he had scrubbed it down to a thirty-second assault with the choicest elements, a smidge of desperate pleading and a dollop of spirituality. It seemed that no one could get too much of the spirituality but pouring on too much pleading or, worse, veering toward sentimentality, could easily tip them from workable Catholic guilt to running-for-the-hills discomfort.

The driver was backing away from Jake now, pulling a face. But he wasn't breaking eye contact. Jake was okay, it was just the smell putting him off. "I see there's a gap in the crates back there, I'd fit in that. *Senhor*, I am trying to save a life here. Please."

The driver looked at him for a long moment, and then nodded and gestured to the tailgate of the truck. "You can eat one piece of fruit. No more. Understand?"

Jake was in.

And it turned out this guy was going to Rio, and to near enough the centre of the city. It was just a long, hot walk from there to Ipanema.

Jake wedged himself between the rattling stacks of crates as the truck rolled out onto the road, belching oily diesel fumes, the engine and gearbox sounding like they weren't the best of friends. For just a moment he felt something close to joy. Begging for lifts and scavenging for food was a leveller that he had never known, and travelling in the back of a fruit truck that would take him almost to the doorstep was cause for celebration. He picked himself a nice soft papaya from a crate, flaying strips of skin with his furred teeth and dirty nails, and letting the rich flesh soak into him. Living like a king. He couldn't remember many moments in his life when he had felt better.

He wasn't even angry with Vilson any more. The kid had nicked his wallet and phone and left him up shit creek, but the place that Vilson was in was far worse, Jake was sure of that. He was enveloped by a sense of calm that he hadn't felt for a very long time. Maybe he'd never felt it. Maybe hunger did that, concentrated the mind on the task ahead without burning unnecessary energy. He was on the way back to the city to do a job. The kid had been done wrong. A lot of wrong. And Jake hadn't given up on him yet.

When the truck got to its final stop at a warehouse in Rio, Jake had trouble getting down off the back. It was painful straightening a body that had spent the previous five hours scrunched up and bounced between crates and the splintered plywood bed of the truck.

He walked off the stiffness inside thirty minutes, but he had to keep going for another hour and a half to get to Ipanema. The name of Eliane's street had stuck when she had mentioned it in one of their less tense conversations because he had viewed two apartments on the same street when first looking to rent one. He knew at which end of the street she lived but not the apartment number, nor which side of the street. He was going to have to ask at every apartment block.

He got through the insults and threats of nine security guards before he leaned on the button on a high, spiked gate. He could hear the buzzer going inside the lobby. The security guy eventually came a few steps out of the lobby, every bit as reluctantly as all the others on the street had.

"Get lost, *vagabundo*," he said, waving Jake away.

Jake gave him a machine-gun spiel, including Eliane's part in the story.

The security guard eyed him suspiciously, but Jake could see that he recognised her name.

Jake gripped the spikes on the gate and pressed his face up to it. "Please, *Senhor*, can you buzz up to them for me? I'm a friend of hers – the *gringo*, tell her."

"No, I can't do that."

For maybe the first time in Jake's life, the buzz of anger felt alien. The surprise of it knocked him and he just let silence fill in.

The security guy shifted on his feet, uncomfortable. "She doesn't live here any more. The family moved out yesterday."

"Do you have a forwarding address?"

The security guard shook his head.

Chapter 42

Vilson

He was hungry. Even ghosts had to eat. Vilson had hidden out in the forest behind his shack all day. He made his way down the hill in the early evening through the maze of narrow alleyways. There was a kiosk outside the bottom of the favela that sold meat *pastels* and chicken *coxinhas*. He could afford something fancy: he still had a little of the *gringo's* money left.

Lights were on inside homes in the favela. He didn't hesitate at the junctions – the places where sentries might be posted. He was no longer fearful of the demons that might be lurking around a corner. He was the demon now.

In a small clearing amongst the dense greenery up behind his shack he had found a washed-out fire that some kids must have lit. Heavy rain had tamped down the ash into a crumbly grey paste and he had rubbed it into his skin and hair until he was streaked whitish–grey all over.

"Hey," a young voice called out behind him. "Hey, you, I'm talking to you."

Vilson hadn't noticed the boy standing in the doorway of the rough, hollow-brick house. He had walked right past him. Vilson stopped and turned slowly. He felt nothing, no fear, and he stood his ground. It was one of Anjo's kids, Tôca, the sentry kid who had raised the alarm the night Vilson had tried to escape the favela.

There was only a dim bulb in a rusty bracket over the doorway throwing a weak glow across the alley, but it made the ash on Vilson's skin glow. Deathly white.

The kid frowned for an instant and then came recognition, and with that his knees wobbled and he crossed himself. "You. Oh my god." He banged a small fist on the closed door behind him without taking his eyes from Vilson. "Hey, Franjinha, you need to get out here, man." His voice quavered, so frightened that he hadn't even pulled his gun.

A muffled shout came from inside. "Are you kidding me? I'm busy with a woman in here."

"You have to see this."

"You little prick. You wouldn't be bothering me if your balls had dropped."

"It's – it's Vilson." He lowered his voice at Vilson's name, seemingly fearful that saying it might somehow cause him harm.

"Who?"

The kid couldn't even bring himself to say Vilson's name this time. He was barely able to get any words out. "It's – it's the ghost, he's out here."

"You really think I'm gonna fall for that crap?"

"I'm not kidding. The old woman wasn't lying." The whisper had spread through the favela like an airborne disease, infecting people.

Vilson could hear Franjinha cursing and banging around inside. "You'll find your joke less funny when I'm beating the living shit out of you." He hauled the door open, Tôca falling inwards onto him, pushing him backwards. Franjinha was bare chested, his erection pressing against his hastily pulled-up shorts. A bandana hid his burned scalp and there were still expanses of angry, raw flesh across his arms and chest. He slapped Tôca around the head until he realised that the kid was taking no notice of the blows. His attention was elsewhere.

Franjinha looked up.

And Vilson saw fear in his eyes. For the first time in his life, Vilson was in control. He held the power.

Franjinha was rooted to the spot for several seconds. He finally jolted himself into action. "Give me your gun," he commanded.

The kid handed it over, looking glad to be rid. Everyone knew that Franjinha liked the powder, but it wasn't drugs making his hands shake as he fumbled and dropped the pistol with a clatter. He bent awkwardly to pick it up, scrabbling, unable to take his eyes from Vilson.

Vilson stepped forward and Franjinha yelped in terror, staggering back, forgetting the pistol. Vilson lifted his hand level with his shoulder and mimicked a pistol, his index finger the barrel, raising his thumb as the hammer. He dropped his thumb back down with a little kick of his hand as he mimed a shot.

Then he let his hand return slowly to his side and walked away.

Anjo

Anjo ordered his soldiers to leave their guns on a table just inside the reinforced-steel door before filing into the living room. They weren't acting like soldiers. They were like frightened old women, gabbling and praying to God and to Our Lady and to the saints for protection.

They quietened to anxious whispers when they noticed the Beretta dangling from his hand. He took a small glass vial from the pocket of his shiny, baggy shorts and popped the plastic lid. Just a small hit to keep him sharp. He tapped a shaky line of white powder onto the back of his gun hand and snorted. He was trying to remember how many small hits he had done today. He had to stay in control of the powder. He had to stay in control of this. Of everything.

He was keeping the windows and metal shutters closed at all times these days, and with his soldiers all squeezed in the temperature was beginning to climb, even with the rattling air-con unit and the big floor fan.

Get it done and get them out.

He sniffed and rubbed his nose. "Shut up, all of you." They went silent immediately. That was good. They still respected him.

He waved the Beretta at Tôca. "You. Tell me what you saw."

Tôca was a confident kid, a leader amongst his age group, maybe even a future boss. But Anjo had seen that he was scared stiff even before he had lifted the Beretta to him. Tôca was trying to find some sense in his scrambled head, mumbling, trying to find the right words. The kid wasn't playing a game, but someone was definitely fucking with him. And Anjo didn't let anyone fuck with him. He kept the Beretta loosely trained around the kid's belly, finger resting on the trigger.

A space appeared around Tôca. Anjo's soldiers knew from bitter experience that he didn't always bother with the safety catch.

Franjinha pushed through the crowd and lay on the sofa by Anjo, trying to show he was relaxed. "Come on, boss," he said, "he told you already. I told you."

Anjo nodded, weighing up what Franjinha had said, and then waved the Beretta at Tôca again. "Speak."

"I don't know what to say." Tôca finally got some halting words out. "His skin was grey, like a dead body, except it kind of shone, you have to believe me. I'm sure it was him, he looked the same, he walked the same, and he had that old Flamengo shirt on."

Soldiers were crossing themselves.

Anjo snorted. He wanted to show derision, that he didn't believe. "And he would be the only one on the hill wearing a Flamengo shirt?"

"I'm sure it was him too," Franjinha said quietly. "Listen, we've known that kid our whole life, it couldn't be anyone else. But something was different, apart from his skin. His eyes. They were dead. There was nothing there, not from this world anyway. I swear it. And he wasn't scared of us, that kid was always scared of his own shadow. It was creepy as hell."

More soldiers crossed themselves and mumbled prayers.

"I put bullets in him. I saw his burned body," Anjo said, trying to keep a hard edge, swallowing down the panic.

Franjinha shook his head. "I know it sounds crazy but I know what I saw and then he was gone. In a second. Just disappeared."

"Too quick for you two gangsters to shoot him?" Anjo asked.

"Come on, man, are you forgetting that I was on the job when he turned up? He was gone before I had a chance to even pull up my shorts."

Anjo turned back on the kid. "And what about you, soldier? Didn't think to see if a bullet might stop this ghost?"

Tears were beginning to well up in Tôca's eyes. He clasped and unclasped his hands in front of him wretchedly. He looked like what he was. A child. "You had to see him, boss, it was so scary."

Anjo shivered involuntarily. He didn't know whether it was the powder or tiredness or this crazy ghost shit making it happen, but he had to keep a lid on it. He couldn't show any sign of weakness.

He pointed the Beretta at the kid's chest. "You failed me."

Tôca's knees buckled slightly and he held his hands out in front of his chest protectively. "It won't happen again, I swear it."

"You swear it?" Anjo cocked his head. He could be a merciful boss. Sometimes that was the way to play it.

Tôca put a hand over his heart. "On my mother's life."

Anjo strung his performance out, pursing his lips, showing that he was mulling it over. Finally, he nodded, satisfied. The kid dropped his hands and giggled with nervous relief.

"That's the right thing to do, man. Tôca's cool," Franjinha said from the sofa, the tension going from his body. "It'd take more than a ghost to take down the Ants – you get me?"

The shot was deafening in the confined space. It made the soldiers jump, mouths open in an O of shock.

Tôca's eyes went wide and he grabbed at his neck, staggering back before his legs folded beneath him. Blood squirted through his fingers in vigorous pulses. He stared at the soldiers around him in terror, reaching out for help with his other hand. They shrank away as the blood sprayed across the floor and up the wall.

It took a few moments for Franjinha to blink away the disbelief before he dived from the sofa and went to Tôca, cradling his head. The boy was already on his last choking breaths. The blood subsided and he made a final gasp, eyes rolling. He was dead.

On the other side of the room one of Tôca's friends, probably even a year or two younger, doubled over and threw up.

"You call yourself a soldier?" Anjo yelled at him. "A Red Ant? Pathetic."

Franjinha laid Tôca's head gently on the floor and got to his feet. He was covered in his blood. "Jesus Christ. You didn't need to do that, you crazy fuck. He was just a kid."

Anjo let the Beretta hang at his side, but his black eyes were glittering. Ready.

Not even Franjinha was safe when Anjo had that look. It pleased Anjo to see him forcing his expression back to its customary blankness and dialling his voice down. "He was just a kid, man."

Anjo looked around at his soldiers. "And I will avenge his death." Hit by an emotional rush of parental protectiveness, he welled up, a single tear rolling down a shiny cheek. "I will rid us of this ghost."

Chapter 43

Vilson

He rinsed the ash from his hair and skin, and came down through the favela while it was still dark. The favela was deserted now at night, people shuttered in their homes, terrified of the ghost.

There was no stirring of the spirits as he approached the Candelária church, and the shot of religious awe that had always hit him on entering didn't come. Not this time; he was finally immune. Even though he was a ghost in the favela, it felt like he was as far from the spirit world as it was possible to be. He was inhabiting some strange in-between world, but he knew what he had to do there. He walked past the rows of empty pews, the only other movement the flickering of the votive candles beside the altar. There was scarcely one row lit; it was still early in the morning.

He went to the door of Padre Francisco's office, tucked away behind the stone column, and knocked.

"Enter."

Padre Francisco was sitting behind the scratched-up desk in his tiny office, wearing his plain black shirt and dog collar. It seemed as if he was expecting the visit. He looked very tired.

"Vilson. Please sit down," he said, his voice heavy.

Vilson stayed on his feet. "It was you who wrote those letters, wasn't it?"

Padre Francisco leaned back in his chair and closed his eyes for a moment. "Yes, it was me. I made a terrible mistake, with the best intentions, but a mistake that has caused you terrible pain and I am so very sorry. I have such a clear picture of you in my mind as a small child, playing with Gabriel, happy, but after your mother left a light seemed to go out. I remember it like it was yesterday. It was Gabriel in his innocence who asked me to write a letter from your mother. I should never have agreed, I should have known better, but it made you so happy, you kept asking when the next one was coming. I should have told you. And I should never have let you go off to find your mother without telling you."

"And you knew that it was the young cop who shot Babão?"

Padre Francisco bowed his head. "Yes."

"Why would you keep that from me?"

"Because I knew you wouldn't have let Marinho help you, and you needed his help."

"You were the only one left that I trusted. The only one. And you lied about everything."

"Did you come here to kill me?" Padre Francisco was looking him in the eye now.

There was a time when a question like that would have shamed Vilson, his shoulders would have hunched and he would have hugged himself. But now he stood straight, holding the priest's gaze, the old revolver tucked in the back of his shorts.

The priest was calm; he seemed resigned to his fate. "I won't beg for my life, but I will beg your forgiveness."

There was nothing in Vilson. He felt nothing.

"Something changed in you as a child," Padre Francisco said, "and I see that something has changed again. Life has been hard for you, people have taken advantage of your nature, but always remember that Christ said the meek shall inherit the earth."

"The meek die, and the powerful," Vilson searched his mind for a moment, "well, the powerful are just dead inside. That's all there is."

"No, my son, you mustn't believe that, it's not true."

"When bad things keep on happening you can't just pretend you can make a fresh start every time and put an end to the bad things. Sometimes it's just the end."

"We must always have hope. If we have hope we are never lost."

"You honestly believe that for someone like me, Father?"

"Of course. Absolutely," said Padre Francisco, but his eyes gave him away.

Chapter 44

Jake

It was a plate of rice and beans with a few strips of curled-up, reheated beef. There were two big pots on the stove. The meal was probably either leftovers from the night before or it would be making a leftovers dinner later. Lunch and dinner, dinner and lunch. He had gone off the Brazilian staples of boiled rice and black beans after his first few weeks in the country. Even chilli sauce hadn't been enough to break the monotony. But now, at Padre Francisco's tiny kitchen table, he closed his eyes with every mouthful, in ecstasy. He hoped the memory of eating this meal would stay with him a long time.

Padre Francisco came to sit opposite him, watching him eat. Padre Francisco's place setting was empty.

"Good?" asked Padre Francisco.

Jake nodded vigorously. "You not eating, Father?"

"Perhaps later."

Jake suspected it was the reason for the priest's lack of appetite.

The shower that followed lunch also felt like one of life's great experiences. In the tiled cubicle with a cracked plastic curtain, he watched the soapy brown swirl going down the plughole start to turn into something more acceptable by the third soaping. He had one more go with the soap after that just for the feel of the suds, to see them sliding off clean skin and to feel the squeak of rinsed, clean hair under his fingers.

Without Ed's new address, not knowing exactly where Marinho lived, and with no place of his own and no money, going to the Candelária church to find Padre Francisco had been his only option.

Jake would never have squeezed into any of the priest's clothes, so Padre Francisco had dug out a few things from the church's charity pile for him. He checked himself in the small hallway mirror. It wasn't a great selection and he looked like a double-glazing salesman going on holiday.

Padre Francisco looked at the mouldering heap of dirty clothes. "Would you like me to put them in the trash?"

Jake shook his head. "I'll take them with me, Father, if you have a bag?"

Padre Francisco dug a plastic carrier bag from a kitchen drawer stuffed with them, and watched as Jake dropped his dirty clothes into the bag. "If you want to keep them I can at least have them washed."

"It might be better to keep them like this."

"If you are thinking of going into the favela, I urge you to reconsider. I'm sure you don't need me to tell you how dangerous it would be for you in there. And, as for Vilson, he is not himself at the moment. I am praying for him, but I don't know that he'll ever be himself again. I believe he came to the church intent on killing me, I'm not sure why he didn't – maybe shooting a priest is a step he can't quite yet take. I don't think he would have so much difficulty shooting an English tourist."

In early evening, at the far end of Leblon Beach, the sun was dropping toward the dog's tooth and shark's fin that made the twin peaks of *Morro Dois Irmãos* – the Two Brothers Hill, part of Rio's famous skyline. The sunset was starting to fire up behind knots of cloud, and lights would soon be twinkling along the strip from Leblon to Ipanema and Arpoador.

Apart from food and shelter, Padre Francisco was a man in possession of phone numbers, and Jake was strolling along the wide mosaic pavement by the beach with Eliane. They were moving with the main flow of people, joggers weaving through them, skateboarders and cyclists rolling along the cycle path beside them.

"How does a lowlife corrupt cop have that much pull?" she wondered aloud. She had just told Jake that she had driven back from Cruzeiro in a fog of exhaustion, going straight into work to save her job. She was too late. Nogueira hadn't made direct contact, but he had somehow found a way to turn the screw with her CEO tight enough for her to go from annoyance to outright liability.

"I went home from getting fired to find my dad packing up the apartment," she said. "I thought it was going to be one of the worst conversations of my life. But he had already made the decision that we should move out to find a cheaper place."

"That must have been bad though?"

She shook her head. "The funny thing is that he said he was glad to move out. He said he finally realised that he had let that place become a prison to him. He said he had realised a lot of things, and he's adamant that he wants me to take the fight to Nogueira."

"Ah. I thought you were pretty upbeat for someone who just lost their job and apartment."

THE BURNING HILL

"With my family behind me, I know I can do this thing. Not for revenge on Nogueira but to bring him to justice." She took a sideways look at Jake's borrowed clothes. "By the way, what's with the disguise?"

Jake laughed. It felt like a stranger to him. "What do you mean? This is the pick of Padre Francisco's summer collection."

"You know, you seem better."

The stares bounced off Jake now, but he was still aware that he looked like what he was – a young man broken apart and put back together. "Yeah. I'm still getting a bit of pain but definitely on the mend."

"I didn't mean better that way."

As they walked toward the sunset along Ipanema, seeing the best of Rio, he was aware that there was something still lodged down in the base of his brain. It was like a strobe light, but dulled, pulsing away somewhere over the horizon. He wondered how long it would stay out of sight. "I don't know," he said. "Maybe."

"If it sounded like I was blaming you for what happened back out on that farm, I wasn't. Everything felt like it was out of control and I was just scared. I did at least get confirmation that the ILO is working with those people. What I don't know is if anything will really be better for them in the end."

A man's voice behind them, breathing hard. "Don't look round. Walk."

It was Marinho. He stayed behind them as they walked, in his running gear. "What the hell did you do to that kid out in the sticks for him to come back with a bigger death wish than you?" he asked, trying to catch his breath as he pulled up his knees, stretching his hamstrings.

"I need to know when's the best time to go in there to get him and what's the best way," Jake asked.

"You won't get that lucky a second time. You need to understand the hornets' nest the kid has stirred up on the hill. The whole place is convinced he's returned as a ghost – it's the only reason he hasn't been killed yet. They're too scared. Anjo is going nuts, they're all going nuts up there, and there are some very itchy trigger fingers. Other gangs are starting to look in, wondering if territory might be there for the taking. The whole place is on the brink of a turf war."

Eliane said, "Listen, I've made contact with a reporter at Globo interested in blowing this thing up – the story of the tourist and the ghost kid who shot him. It'll put Vilson in the spotlight too so we need to have him safe before it breaks. I think it's all we've got left to get Nogueira – if they make enough of it, that he knew Vilson was alive but was making out otherwise, then maybe people chain will let him burn rather than take the heat themselves before they even get to what happened with Babão."

"Your only chance of getting Vilson is at night all cowering inside their homes. As for how, let me hat," Marinho said. "But I didn't think you liked the after what happened to you in the army?"

"I changed my mind." He had let Eliane talk him oing it the right way a last chance, at least part of the way.

"But this reporter is in a hurry," Eliane said to M world has a short span of attention. Globo means big expo you know that."

Marinho puffed. "What's the timescale?"

"Monday," she replied.

"Goddamn. My fight is this weekend, that's be concentrating on. Not this shit."

"Then maybe you shouldn't take the fight," hout conviction.

"Are you crazy?"

In that scrubby garden back in the rodeo town Yara, had left a big impression on Jake. But out there rent place. "Look, I know how crazy this might sound out in the sticks – a medium. She did shows and stuff was maybe the real deal—"

Marinho cut across him: "No. I don't want to he kind of crap – I can't hear it. You don't understand w on me. And I know him well enough to know what don't fight."

Jake wasn't going to get any further. He rec f in Marinho's look. "Just think about it. And one last thi ows that it was you who shot Babão."

"I can handle the kid if he comes for me. I've be my shoulder long enough. Has it struck you that if he he might be more likely to shoot you than throw his ?"

Chapter 45

Marinho

Taking a slug of water from his water bottle, Marinho waited with a knot of people on the beach side of a pedestrian crossing on the main Leblon drag. The little green man lit up and everyone drifted across. Marinho started jogging ahead. It was seven kilometres home from here. A slow, relaxing run. Enjoyable. But his legs were twitchy and he kicked his heels up behind him to stretch his quads a little. The twitch was going all the way through him. It seemed to happen every time he had contact with the crazy *gringo* and the lawyer. The most unsettling thing was the medium stuff. Marinho was no more or less religious than the next man, but there were unseen things that were not part of the everyday world.

He shook it off and carried on down a road that ran away from the beach, into the deepening shade of a tall apartment block on the corner.

Up ahead of him, a guy stepped out from between the line of parked cars, past the line of trees on the pavement and stopped, looking down at his phone, blocking Marinho's way. Marinho swerved to run on the narrow part of the pavement between the parked cars and trees. The guy moved that way too, without looking up, and Marinho slowed. Wary now.

The guy had a bandana tied on his head with a loud baseball cap sitting on top, and big, mirrored aviator shades. Wearing a huge sweatshirt and shorts that hung almost to his ankles, he looked like a wannabe hip-hop star. But there was something familiar about him.

He looked up from his phone. It was Franjinha, Anjo's right-hand man, out of his favela-gangster uniform.

Marinho recoiled, sweeping a foot back to take a defensive stance, coming onto the balls of his feet. With the iron rails of the apartment block's security fence at his back, he whipped his head around to check that no one was racing up to blindside him. The pavement was clear and he whipped straight back to Franjinha.

"Whoa, man, chill out," Franjinha smiled. He lifted up his tee shirt, showing his torso and clean waistband. "I'm not carrying, see? Walk with me a little."

"I'm okay right here."

"A little wired, aren't you?"

Marinho came down from the balls of his feet but kept his feet apart, ready to fight.

"Wow," Franjinha said, "you need to work through your trust issues, brother. You like my disguise? It's good, no?" Franjinha was as poker-faced as ever, but he was clearly getting a kick out of his showboating.

"Looks like you've been rehearsing this," Marinho said. "It probably went better in front of the mirror, huh?"

"And how did your chat down on the beach go with that dude and the hot girl?"

"Not that it's anything to do with you but it was no one, just some guy asking about training."

Franjinha made a game-show buzzing sound. "Nope, sorry, wrong answer, friend. I'm guessing that dude is the *gringo* who got shot. Am I right? Yeah. Sure I'm right. See, I know things. Lots of things. Like that night when you tried to grab Vilson from the favela I had this feeling that I'd seen you someplace before. And then it all clicked when you came with Nogueira to meet us in the shop. But I said nothing, bided my time. Smart guys hold onto their cards."

"You're sure about that, are you?"

Franjinha made as if he hadn't heard, moving his head to one side, making a show of looking at Marinho from another angle. "You know, when I saw the ghost back in the favela, I was scared, man. Really spooked. And then I took some time to think, and I thought about you again, and then I started to add it all up. You had me going, man, it was a good scam."

"And let me guess, you haven't told your boss yet?"

"Hey, you're not as dumb as you look." Franjinha's attempted smile was more a grimace. "Your boss wants me as his inside man. He knows Anjo's losing it, and he knows I'm a guy on the up. One day I'll be one of the famous bosses. Everyone will know me, down here in the city, maybe across the world. Who knows, they might even make a movie about me."

"Good luck with that," Marinho said, making to move past him.

"I'm not done with you yet," Franjinha said, his voice hardening. "You know, your boss doesn't trust you."

Marinho stopped and turned.

"Yeah, that's right," said Franjinha, "I thought that might get your attention. He's ready to throw you under the bus whenever it suits him – if Vilson doesn't get to you first. But I'll look out for you."

"You will, huh?"

"Sure. And you just give me eyes in return. See, I don't trust your boss. I need to have one a man on the inside." Franjinha flapped a hand, like a bored emperor conferring some honour.

Marinho shot his right hand out, gripping the back of Franjinha's and twisting hard on his wrist. With the lock coming on, he moved to Franjinha's side, pulling his arm back. As it bent at the elbow he drew Franjinha closer, pushing the wrist up toward his armpit. The lock was on. Tight.

Franjinha's scream of pain was cut short as Marinho grabbed his throat with his other hand, a powerful claw, crushing the arteries either side of his windpipe.

Franjinha tried to break away, hitting out with his free hand. Marinho ratcheted up the torque in the wrist, the agony stripping the fight from Franjinha. He was up on his tiptoes, trying to release the pressure. And then he sagged, the restricted blood supply starving his brain of oxygen.

Marinho eased off on his throat a little. "Don't you ever assume I'm one of yours. And you mention what you saw today to my boss and I'll finish wringing your worthless neck. Is that clear?"

Across the road, a couple of young men on the way back from the ocean with surfboards under their arms had stopped. Marinho could see that they were debating whether to come over.

"I said, is that clear?" Marinho repeated, and then turned an ear to Franjinha to catch his reply.

"Yes," Franjinha managed to croak.

"Then we're all good." Marinho released Franjinha and he dropped to his knees on the pavement, coughing and retching. He nursed his wrist and rubbed gingerly at the livid marks Marinho's fingers had left on the sore, bruised skin of his throat.

The two surfers were crossing the road now. Marinho waved a peaceful gesture but they eyed him suspiciously and kept coming.

Franjinha saw them too and was emboldened. "You're an asshole, man," he shouted at Marinho, coughing some more. "A complete fucking asshole, you know that? All I did was come down here to offer you a way out. Well, fuck you. You just better hope the other guy tears your head off in that fight because if you do manage to crawl out of the cage you'll be taking a slow, painful ride to hell."

"What's going on?" the lead surfer asked as they filed between parked cars.

Marinho backed away. "Everything is cool, just a disagreement between friends." He held his palms out, non-threatening.

The other surfer stooped to help Franjinha up. "You okay, man?"

Franjinha got to his feet and slapped the help away. "Get your fucking hands off me," he said. He stood for a moment, glowering at Marinho, before lurching off toward the beach.

Whatever was coming, Marinho had to stay with the programme. Act normal and keep training. The next morning he was hard at it in his local fight gym. The wooden parquet flooring was the best bit of the place; the rest was all cracked walls and stained ceilings. It smelled of stale sweat and floor polish. There were no fancy machines, just weights, scuffed kick pads and lumpy, taped-up punchbags. But the sparring mats were new and the place was spotless. Only Marinho and his trainer were in the place.

The skipping rope whirred around Marinho, the tendons in his neck standing up as he wound it faster and faster.

"Last thirty seconds," his trainer called out. "I want every last drop."

Marinho jumped, pulling his knees high, the rope making two revolutions before his feet hit the ground again. He kept on jumping, the rope whipping the parquet floor, even with the energy bleeding away from him.

His trainer called time, Marinho doing a couple more jumps – higher than ever – before taking both handles in one hand and letting the rope wind itself down. Dropping it to the floor, he hunched over, hands on his knees, taking in gulps of air. Sweat ran in tickling rivulets through the close-cropped hair of his scalp and onto the wooden floor.

"Okay, that's enough rest. Onto the bags now," his trainer said, "then mat drills."

"Let my boy have a drink."

Marinho hadn't seen Nogueira come in. He was in uniform, proffering a cold bottle of water, frosted droplets running down it.

Marinho nodded thanks and took a slug.

Nogueira spoke to the trainer. "Give us a couple of minutes of privacy, uh?"

"This session is high intensity – he can't stop," the trainer protested.

Nogueira turned his face to stone.

The trainer huffed before instructing Marinho, "Make sure you keep moving, you need to stay warm." He shuffled off, swearing under his breath.

Marinho whirled his arms around, shook them out and started rolling his head across his chest to stretch his neck, all the while keeping his feet moving on the spot. He didn't want to look Nogueira in the eye.

"How's it going?" Nogueira asked.

"Good."

"Ready to fight?"

"On track."

"That's good," Nogueira said. And then he chuckled. "That dumbass kid and his ghost thing – who saw that coming, uh?"

The good humour wasn't fooling Marinho. He could feel Nogueira's eyes boring into him as he dropped to the floor for push-ups. "He up to something, or just crazy you think?" Marinho said.

It was a while before Nogueira spoke again. He was rubbing his belly. "My doctor says I've got an ulcer. That's what these fools have done to me, and it burns like hell when I hear of crap like this. But then I got to thinking that maybe this kid becoming a ghost is a stroke of genius. I had my hunch that it was better to keep him alive a bit longer, and now he might just turn out to be the ace in the pack."

Chapter 46

Anjo

It went straight to voicemail again. Anjo paced around his lounge. Why wasn't he answering?

A handful of his soldiers were hovering near the reinforced front door, nervy.

"Fuck this," Anjo shouted, hurling his mobile against the wall. It burst apart, components skittering across the tiled floor. The nearest soldier flinched as a shard hit him.

The minor act of violence calmed Anjo a little. He had found things to do in the last couple of days that had kept him too busy to do anything about the ghost. When Franjinha was around, which didn't seem to be much these days, he kept whispering in his ear that he was going to lose face if he didn't step up against the ghost. The day before, Anjo had finally agreed that it would be today and Franjinha had immediately announced it to the soldiers. Anjo couldn't back out now. "You'll see, it'll be fine," Franjinha had said to him afterwards, and then he had disappeared again. Gone all night and still no sign.

The muted daytime activity of the favela drifted through the hot metal of the shuttered windows. Even small children were subdued – the threat of a visit from the bogeyman enough to keep even the unruliest of them in line. Anjo's watery guts were telling him it was more like dead of night, terrors creeping, hidden in the shadows. The gentle ticks of the house and electric hum were loud cracks and incessant buzzing. Screams had shaken him from agitated sleep that morning. Just a few doors up, a young woman had woken to find her husband dead on the mattress next to her. His eyes and mouth open. A look of terror in his face, they said. A doctor was called, and heart failure was pronounced the likely cause of death. Natural causes.

But everyone knew. The dead man wasn't yet thirty. Always begging favour with Anjo and Franjinha, he also liked to throw his weight around with people at the bottom of the food chain. He had bullied Vilson.

Outside Anjo's earshot, all anyone could talk about was the ghost and his dead eyes. Stories were going round of people waking in the night to find him standing over them. He bored into them with those sightless eyes, and then he faded silently away. People were now saying that everyone in the favela would receive a visit from him. One by one. He would get to you. You'd better hope you weren't one of those who had done him wrong, even if it was only once that you had shown him unkindness or taunted him. If you had, then he would push his cold, bony fingers through your ribcage and crush the life from your heart.

Few people could remember showing him kindness.

Where the fuck was Franjinha? Things had settled between them since Tôca had died, but Anjo was starkly aware that Franjinha was handling this ghost thing better than he was. He wondered how many others were noticing. Trails of paranoia snaked in, blinding him, confusing him. His head throbbed and there was an itch all over his body that made him want to tear his skin off. His heart sputtered in his bony chest.

All this was happening to him, tormenting him, and the world just spun mercilessly on, threatening to flick him off into the deep, unknown space. He sat down in his leather beanbag, holding onto the sides. He seemed to be sinking into it as the walls yawed away. He was shrinking, becoming the tiniest, most insignificant grub that could be popped beneath a fingernail.

He could blitz all of this with a couple of lines, get relief from the blown wreckage inside his head. The respite was increasingly short-lived these days and the paranoia was claiming more ground every time. But it was respite all the same.

He sniffed and found his nose blocked. He reached up and felt the blockage, pulling out a wad of cotton wool from a nostril. A glob of congealing blood came with it. And then something small and gristly dropped into his lap. He rolled the bloody morsel in his fingers and then folded it in the wad of cotton wool. His nose was falling apart. He got up and went to the bathroom mirror. His nose was changing shape; he had noticed it before, the slow collapse. Pedalling open the lid of the small plastic bin, the wad joined others in it, all soaked in blood and snot.

He pulled the glass vial from his pocket and flipped the lid. Tapping it out on the back of his hand, he got only a dusting. The vial was empty. He licked the harsh chemical taste away along with the salt of his sweat. He didn't have any more coke in either vials or wraps, and neither did his soldiers by the front door. He'd already asked.

But he had to act like the boss before he could go hunting for more coke. He had to get a grip. He strode out of the bathroom, shouting at his soldiers, "I can't wait around all day for Franjinha. Let's go." He hustled the group out of his house, pushing them up the hill ahead of him. He didn't want guns at his back with everyone so jumpy. This bunch was the pick of his lieutenants, older, more level-headed. Some of his most trusted. And a couple he didn't trust so much.

"Hey, man," Franjinha called out behind them. "Wait up."

He was coming around a corner of the narrow concreted alley that jinked up the hill. The steep path was cracked and uneven and had a step or two every few metres. It was hard work and Franjinha was sweating in his regular gangster uniform with the bandana he had adopted to cover the burns on his head. A couple of kids were following him. All three of them had their handguns drawn.

"Where have you been?" Anjo shouted down to him. "I was trying to get you all night."

"Come on, man, I had business with a woman," Franjinha said lightly. "You know you've got to keep them happy."

Anjo didn't know. Women filled a need for him every so often, but there was not very much that he understood about them. He didn't know about keeping them happy. They didn't make him happy; they mostly made him nervous and unsure of himself.

"You two stay here on sentry duty," he instructed the kids who were with Franjinha.

The two kids looked to Franjinha and he nodded. They took up their posts at the front door of the house.

It rankled with Anjo that they had deferred to Franjinha. No one should be questioning his orders. He didn't have time to deal with this right now, but he would come back to it later, that was for sure.

Franjinha drew level with him. "Sorry, man," he said quietly to Anjo, clasping his shoulder.

"You got any powder?"

"No, boss."

That irritated Anjo more.

It was a slog to the top of the favela, the sun frying the back of Anjo's neck. The concrete path started to break up, shrubs and coarse grass sprouting everywhere. The houses were thinning out and the build quality declining. The concrete gutter at the side of the path, stained a greenish-brown, came to an end. There were only houses on one side of the road now. They had come to the outer edge of the favela. The gutter at this point became a shallow, overgrown ditch, diverging from the path. It had once been a stream before getting choked with rubbish.

There was something in the ditch ahead. A body, the top half hidden, the bottom half barely visible in the long grass and thorns.

The point man, a short, garrulous twenty-year-old named Pato, trained his handgun on the body. The others checked all around them, like they'd just stepped into a haunted house.

"Is it him?" Anjo asked, hating the tremor in his voice.

"Don't know, boss."

"Well, go take a look, asshole."

Pato approached fearfully. Filthy legs poked out from the undergrowth, ruined flip-flops hanging off feet that were just as filthy, but rubbed a little cleaner on the balls and heels. The tee shirt and shorts were almost black, the top half of the torso in the ditch, obscured beneath tangled, thorny shrubs and long grass. There was an almost-empty bottle of the cheapest *cachaça* lying next to the body.

Even with the caked-on dirt, the skin wasn't dark enough to be Vilson's and the legs weren't nearly skinny enough.

"It's just one of the alkies, boss. That albino one, I think," Pato said, relieved. "What the hell's he been doing to get like that, though? Can't tell whether he's dead or just passed out."

"You sure it's the albino?"

Pato bent down, trying to peer through the undergrowth without getting too close. He recoiled, holding his nose. "Oh Christ, the dirty old bastard – he stinks of shit."

Pato picked the least filthy part of the torso and dug a toe in the ribs. The body shifted with a distant grunt.

"It's alive. Smells like a fucking drain, but alive," he called back to Anjo.

"Is it the albino?" Anjo said irritably.

"Hey, Osso, that you?" Pato called out.

Some mumbled unintelligible thing came back. He dug his toe in again, harder. Another grunt. More mumble.

"Yeah," Pato said to Anjo. "He's out of it. Looks like he's had a skinful. You want me to shoot him?"

"No, leave him," Anjo said. "Let's go." Most of the drinkers also bought product from the Red Ants, but he wasn't always so considerate to his customers. He was hoping that the ghost might prefer the easier pickings of this pathetic heap rather than coming after him.

They moved on upward through the scrag-end of the favela until they saw Vilson's shack in the shade of the treeline. The soldiers ahead of Anjo faltered, staring at the dark, open doorway.

Anjo shoved the nearest backmarker. "Move. Act like the soldiers you're meant to be." He brought the Beretta up by his shoulder, barrel pointing skywards, showing he was ready for whatever was coming their way.

They crowded to one side of the doorway. The sun struck a clean edge on a shadow cast just in front of the shack, and with the intensity of the sunlight it was hard to make out what lay beyond the doorway.

Anjo steeled himself, pushing through his soldiers. He crouched by the door jamb, gripped his Beretta in both hands and fired six shots through the darkness in an arc. The holes he blasted in the thin walls let a little more light into the shack. He moved in, still at a crouch, making brisk sweeps with the Beretta in the dusty gloom, like he'd seen in the movies. He was showing them all proper soldiering and it bolstered him. He felt a little braver now.

His eyes started to adjust. There was a heap in a corner – his heart skipped and he fired two more shots at it, the muzzle flashes blinding. When his eyes came back again he could see it wasn't big enough to be human. Just sacks.

There was nothing else, no one else, other than an innocuous pile in the middle of the shack that Anjo had almost stepped on. He hadn't noticed it – he had been concentrating on finding something human-sized.

But the others had seen it and, having crowded the doorway after Anjo had entered, they were now backing away, looking around to make sure nothing was coming for them. They crossed themselves and mumbled prayers.

There was a collection of burned-down red candles surrounded by sprigs of leaves, some stuck in the pool of hardened wax. There was also a plastic toy soldier and a small fan of feathers. Peering closer, despite his instinct to run, Anjo saw that it was the wing of a small bird. There was a tiny pile of something twisted and fleshy, bloody and fatty yellow: probably the guts of some small animal. And there were dark blots in the earth around it. An involuntary shiver went through him.

He straightened up and turned on them. "Get a hold of yourselves. This *Macumba* crap is just for simpletons and old women."

Only Pato had remained at the doorway, rooted, unable to take his eyes away from the offering. He shook his head. "No, man, that's the black magic – it's the heavy shit. Christ, this is bad. It's really bad."

Pato's words spooked the others even more.

Macumba was the regular stuff, it came in and out of all their lives. Old folks and sick people, and people with nothing better to do. Getting together, swaying and praying with candles and drums. A spirit might come into someone, often an old woman or an old man. Growing up, Anjo had wandered along to these kinds of evenings when he was younger. They joked about it in the R[...] of it was make-believe to scare little kids or bring som[...] shitty life. But, under the bravado, they had a healthy r[...] the old women knew what they were talking about. Th[...]ings; they had a connection with the other world.

Anjo had said *Macumba* to stop them panick[...] thing inside the shack wasn't an offering, it wasn't som[...] for better luck or better health or for love. It was *Qu[...]* dark stuff. You went down that path and there wasn't a wa[...] might get your revenge, you might reach the place you w[...] ould tear out your soul and feed it to the Devil.

Anjo's mouth was watering. He felt like he was g[...] up. He was standing at the precipice, staring down at a [...] pace. He had to hold his nerve. "Search around this place[...] out."

They picked about in the undergrowth above th[...] vous hens. Just going through the motions, ready to fl[...] hill the moment Anjo gave them the word. Like An[jo...] more time scanning the deep shadows in the undergr[...] than sifting through the ground directly in front. None [...] d it, but they were all convinced that something was w[...]

Anjo counted the seconds, taking deep brea[ths...] wing away the acid vomit that had risen in his throat, be[...] that enough time had passed to show that this stuff had[...]

They needed no second bidding, and it was as [...] ould do to stop themselves breaking into a run to belt ba[...] ill. It felt better to be out in the sunlight but Anjo move[d...] le of the group now. Franjinha stuck to his shoulder. He [...] word since they'd got to the shack. Usually so quick to as[...] vice, he didn't have the stones for this, Anjo realised.

Approaching the area where the path drew clos[er...] Anjo could see that the drunk was no longer there. This [...] lace; he could see the impression the body had made in th[...] They all kept moving. No one mentioned it. No one w[...] bout anything out of place. And Anjo was now beyon[d...] ngth. He just wanted to get back inside his house, pull th[...] cross the door and send someone off to get him some [...]

The point man stopped so suddenly that they al[...] him. "What the fuck are you playing at?" rasped An[jo...] had enough of this shit for one day.

They parted to let him see. Crossing themselv[es...] There was a black cat lying on his raised do[or...] kids they'd left on sentry duty were nowhere to be seen. Anjo felt his stomach lurch and heave again. He had to force his legs forward to take a closer look.

The cat was dead. Ribs sticking out from the emaciated body, limbs rigid, the fur matted and mangy. It looked long gone, save for the thin line of frothy, yellowish–green puke running from its mouth and down the step.

"That thing only just crawled there and died," Franjinha whispered, the only one who would dare. "I mean, like, seconds ago. That's the *Quimbanda* shit, I'm telling you, man. We're fucked."

He was right. Signs didn't get any darker than this. But Anjo screamed in fury, letting all the fear fly with it. "The next one who mentions black magic or voodoo or ghosts or any of that shit is a dead man. You either grow a pair or you can eat a bullet right now. Which is it?"

He had finally caught hold of himself. His black eyes glittered as he looked from one to the other.

A slot in the front door slid open and they saw eyes peering through the spyhole, before the door opened and one of the sentry kids poked his head out. "What's going on?"

"I'd like to ask you that," Anjo said quietly. "You were meant to be on sentry duty."

The kid noticed the cat and recoiled, but he was a lot more scared of Anjo's tone.

"I'm sorry, boss," the kid stuttered, "it was so quiet we just went on the PlayStation for a bit."

Anjo's arms and legs were twitching, the need for a line of coke scrubbing away behind his eyeballs. He really wanted to kill someone.

Chapter 47

Jake

He was wearing the filthy clothes that had got him back to Rio. Stopping at a market, he bought a cheap bottle of *cachaça* with money borrowed from Padre Francisco and doused himself in it. He swilled a mouthful of the harsh spirit before spitting it out. Then, as an afterthought, he took another swig and swallowed. Dutch courage.

On the way to the favela he climbed into a large drainage ditch running alongside a dual carriageway. A pristine, white egret took flight, startled, rising up from the stagnant, rubbish-filled water. There was more rubbish embedded in the soft greenish–black mud at the water's edge. Jake smeared the foul-smelling stuff all over his skin and in his hair, before noticing a concrete pipe poking out of the bank further up the ditch.

Trying to get closer, he lost a flip-flop in the sucking, stinking mud and had to dig around in it up to his elbows to find it. From there, he carried his flip-flops to get to the pipe. When he got closer, he saw that it was pushing out globs of raw sewage. The stench was overpowering, making him retch as he rubbed a handful into his shorts.

It was dark by the time he reached the favela, and the mud was beginning to dry, cracking as it tightened on his skin. Marinho had directed him to the quietest entrance to the favela, which provided a fairly direct route to the top of the hill where Padre Francisco had described the location of Vilson's shack. Marinho hadn't come up with a better idea than Jake's filthy-drunk disguise. Jake psyched himself up, another quick swig of the *cachaça*. It wasn't easy, picking his way up through the favela in the dark through this less densely populated side, with scrubland and rubbish tips amongst the hollow-brick homes, but Marinho was right, the place seemed deserted.

He had assumed that the top of the favela would be a defined line of homes. It wasn't; it was a broken, confusing hotchpotch that didn't match Padre Francisco's description. He spent half the night going up and down the hill as he navigated his way around, and the rest of the night trying to identify Vilson's shack. He could only risk a tiny torch, which he used sparingly. He passed Vilson's shack two or three times before he decided that it was the one. It was the only one that didn't have a door. He stepped inside, switching on his torch for only a few moments. Empty.

He hid himself in the undergrowth up behind Vilson's shack and waited with the biting insects for the sun to come up. When there was enough light he crept back to the shack and took a more thorough look inside. It was a broken-down patchwork of planks, corrugated iron and blue polythene. Garden tools were better housed than this back in England. He saw the candles and bits in the middle of the dirt floor. He didn't know much about Brazilian voodoo, but he knew that they were some of the accessories that went with it. Maybe they were Vilson's; maybe they were someone else's. There was nothing else in the shack that gave him any useful information.

Jake's memories of survival training in the army consisted mostly of wet, cold nights on a Welsh mountainside, but the tracking day had stuck, even though he had only learned the basics. There were paths leading away from the area behind Vilson's shack: a small, well-worn animal path and a couple of wider paths made by humans, neither of them new. He tried the furthest path, looking for signs of more recent activity along it: freshly broken plant stems, trodden-down clumps of grass that were beginning to spring back up. The path ran up the hill into the jungle for fifty metres or so before ending at a dip that was filled with rubbish. Rotting, crumbling and rusting, it wasn't a regular dump, and it didn't look like anyone had walked up here in the last day or so.

Still, he took a good look around before walking carefully back down the path, making sure he hadn't missed anything.

Someone had definitely been up and down the other path in recent days. On a section of bald earth there was scuffed dirt where a foot had slipped. Further up, a weedy shoot was folded over, the tip crushed underfoot, bruised leaves trying to raise themselves from the ground. The path eventually branched in several directions toward clumps of fruit trees, avocados and jaboticaba, the purple–black, grape-like berries covering the trunks and branches.

Any number of people probably came up here to pick the fruit. He retraced his steps back down. He stood next to a strangler fig tree. Something caught his eye in the undergrowth off the path this time, something he'd missed on the way up: the vaguest suggestion of another path.

He stepped off into the jungle and followed. It ran diagonally to the main path. It was old, hardly used. The newly trodden part departed after a few metres, zigzagging and circling. Jake moved slowly, examining everything closely and then stopping every few metres to straighten and scan the bigger scene around him. Trying to picture Vilson here, trying to figure out what Vilson would be thinking, what he was doing up here.

It took him half an hour to find the sapling with the knife mark on it. He had walked past and around it several times before he noticed. He concentrated his search within a five-metre radius of the sapling and it took him only a minute or so to find an area of disturbed ground beneath a shrub. There was a dirty, roughly folded sheet of polythene lying on the ground. He unfolded the sheet carefully and examined it but there was nothing other than dirt and leaves. Jake dug gingerly in the ground with his hands, the freshly dug earth shifting easily. He made a small pile of it, soft and dark, until he reached harder-packed earth, the limit of the hole that had been dug. The sheet and the hole told him that only something relatively small would have been buried here.

He had found no real sign of Vilson. He was going to have to venture into the favela with the benefit of daylight, with the danger that daylight brought. He tried to make his search around the top part of the favela as systematic as possible, looking in the undergrowth, in the ditches, around the homes, hoping that he would somehow stumble across some sign of Vilson, or Vilson himself. Rounding a corner of a small block of homes, he saw a young couple and immediately started reeling from side to side, head hanging down, getting a decent string of drool hanging from his mouth. They were startled initially and then called out an insult once they had passed him. It was working. Hide in plain sight. He carried on looking, daring himself to venture further into the favela.

He heard angry shouts below him and then the approach of Anjo's gang. The drunken, staggering hobo wasn't going to work in the face of that.

Jake ran for the ditch. He only managed to force himself a short way into the thick layer of lacerating thorns on the other side and then had to lie absolutely still.

As Pato stood over him, the feeling of vulnerability had every fibre in him screaming to jump up and run. But he lay still, waiting for the hot stab of a bullet. When the kick in the ribs came it was almost a relief. But when Pato offered to shoot him, time slowed and the whistle of the millions of insects around dropped in tone, it seemed to him.

After they had moved on a good minute ticked by, with Jake remaining absolutely still, before he started to notice the thorns snagging the delicate flesh of his healing scars and stabbing at him from beneath. His hand was stinging like crazy from so   h   lecks of disturbed plant litter were getting in his eyes.

He extracted himself slowly, having to unhook th i   skin, one by one, resisting the urge to jump up and spri   oved along the ditch until he found a less thorny area o   l and long grass. He crossed the ditch and moved into c   t to flatten the grass and give himself away. He foun d   ind a stubby tree and tucked himself in.

He heard a series of gunshots, counting ei   en a momentary lull in the insect chorus following them   eard Anjo's gang coming down the hill shortly afterwa   itoes bit at the already bitten and swollen skin exposed   ts of mud had dropped off. The bottle of *cachaça* was   ench his thirst. He wasn't that desperate yet.

He jumped. Another shot from somewhere bel   vela. He waited it out until dark and then made his w   on's shack. He took another look around with the torch   the floor inside, cross-legged, facing the open doorwa   good a bet for finding Vilson as aimlessly wandering th   the favela.

His nose had become mostly inured to the m   was covering his clothes and body, but the assaults of   shit smell seemed to come more regularly the longer he

He reached for the box of matches he'd found b   ks in the corner and lit the three stubs of candle amongs   that were poking out from the pool of hardened red wa   -out wicks. He stared into the little flames. He found co   the flames draw him in, mesmerise him. Let them pass

Chapter 48

Jake

In the last of the dark hours before dawn, only one of the candle stubs was still burning in Vilson's shack, the flame guttering. Jake felt a buzz in the pocket of his shorts. He pulled out the mobile phone Eliane had given him and took it out of the plastic sandwich bag he had rolled it up in.

A text from Eliane read, "Any sign?"

"Not yet."

"They've taken my dad."

"Don't understand."

"Kidnapped."

He blew out the candle and raced down through the deserted favela.

Back at Padre Francisco's place by mid-morning, he got cleaned up, all the while trying to get hold of Eliane, but her mobile was going straight to voicemail. Finally, he got a text from her telling him to meet her at Marinho's fight venue in the evening.

Padre Francisco rustled up another set of clothes for Jake that was an improvement on his first selection.

The fight venue was a rambling old sports complex near the city centre, an area Jake didn't really know. It wouldn't feature on any tourist to-do list. He queued up in a rowdy line in the lobby and bought his ticket.

The octagon was lit up by a large rig of spotlights suspended from the ceiling. All that kit looked new. Everything outside the island of bright light in the centre of the big sports hall was in a dingy half-light and looked well past its best. There were rows of plastic chairs surrounding the octagon and two sets of tiered benches against opposite walls. Most of the chairs around the octagon were taken, as was much of the standing room to the rear. The male-dominated crowd was noisy and boisterous, a makeshift bar of folding tables selling bottles of cold beer from huge cool boxes.

Wearing a surfer's bucket hat, the frayed brim low over his eyes, most of Jake's face was in shade. He noticed several fight fans milling around who looked nearly as beaten up as he did. No one was paying him any attention. Even so, he found himself a spot high up on one of the tiered benches, overlooking the main entrance from the lobby.

From his vantage point, he could see the brightly lit canvas of the octagon, walled in by chain-link fencing hung on a padded frame. The canvas was covered in logos for MMA brands and Brahma Beer, with rusty patches of long-dried blood that they hadn't quite managed to scrub away.

A gaggle of promoters, announcers and hangers-on trooped in ahead of the first two fighters and their trainers. A couple of girls in sparkly bikini tops and hot pants sashayed around the octagon. The placards they were waving above their spray-on hairdos stated the obvious – Round 1.

Jake had picked up through his TV viewing that the popularity of Brazilian jujitsu had originally been adopted in the sport of *Vale Tudo* – Anything Goes, literally. Brazilians had then introduced their effective fighting style to the nascent MMA scene – mixed martial arts – in the USA. Packaged up with some made-for-TV gloss, it had exploded in popularity, inevitably getting exported back to Brazil.

Some of the fighters went for Lycra shorts, others for baggies, but they all wore fingerless, leather grappling gloves with light padding over the knuckles.

The first bout looked like a mismatch to Jake. It was between a rangy athletic young guy announced as a kick-boxing specialist and a shorter, pudgy, Brazilian jujitsu fighter, who looked very much the wrong side of thirty. Blowing out his cheeks even before the first bell went, he wouldn't have the gas to go the full distance. The crowd knew it, his opponent knew it, he knew it. He would have to finish it quickly with a takedown and a submission choke or lock.

When the referee waved them on to fight, the pudgy fighter tried to keep his distance from the elaborate strikes of the kick-boxer, lumbering around the canvas. He fended shots to his body and legs, before lunging with a messy rugby tackle, staggering his opponent against the chain-link wall.

The kick-boxer recovered quickly, taking advantage of his opponent's low position. He brought his knee up hard into his face, snapping his head back.

The pudgy fighter took another knee to his midriff before the blood exploded from his broken nose. He turned away instinctively to protect his nose. The crowd roared. Attack his exposed back. Choke him out.

He came to his senses just as the kick-boxer was looping an arm around his neck. The panic in his eyes was clear, even as they swelled around his smashed nose. He flicked his head back, catching the corner of the kick-boxer's brow.

Beat your opponent unconscious. Choke him unconscious. Dislocate his elbow or shoulder, blow out his knee. It was all fine. Headbutts were out.

The crowd howled its fury, the referee stepping in to break them up and warn the pudgy fighter.

The kick-boxer dabbed his fingers at the cut in his brow, a thin stream of blood running into the sweat on his face. He was incensed, breathing in the fury of the crowd. When the referee waved them on again, he switched up a few gears. He kept moving the pudgy fighter with feints and jabs.

He put him off balance with a half-formed front kick, then planted that leg to spring load the other for a vicious roundhouse kick. It caught the pudgy guy in his floating ribs, driving the air from his lungs.

The kick-boxer was on him, pummelling him into the octagon wall with a flurry of punches to his face, each one finding its mark. The pudgy fighter tried to make a desperate grab for his body, trying to tie up his arms, trying to hook a leg around the kick-boxer's leg to unbalance him.

They went to the floor in a flailing heap. Even with the punches he'd taken, the pudgy guy was quickest to recover, working to get his weight over the kick-boxer's body to pin him and put a quick lock on an arm.

He was almost there when the kick-boxer responded to the screams from his cornermen. He bridged, launching his hips upward and rolling his shoulder as he thrust his hands as flat blades into his opponent's armpits, flinging him off. He went with the momentum to reverse their positions, scrambling to get on top of the pudgy fighter. He had control now, moving his weight over his opponent's chest, sitting with knees straddled to prevent getting flipped.

The pudgy fighter's arms were still free but they were rendered almost powerless by the kick-boxer's position over him. He could do no more than flap at the incoming fists that rained merciless blows into his face.

His arms dropped as he lost consciousness. The baying of the crowd was undercut with gasps of horror as the kick-boxer carried on using his opponent's lolling head as a punchbag, bouncing it off the canvas. It took maybe a second or two before the referee dived in and got a protective arm in front of the kick-boxer, dragging him away. By then his opponent's face was mush, a gory mask of blood.

The pudgy fighter's body remained limp until a doctor waved

smelling salts under his nose. He came round with a shudder, confused and frightened. His cornermen towelled some of the blood from his face and got him up. Hanging between the two of them, he managed wobbling steps across the canvas, the strength in his legs gone. A bucket and brush were brought in to scrub the blood from the canvas.

The next two fights weren't much less brutal. Halfway through a round, Jake spotted Eliane entering the hall and made his way down the aisle in the tiered benches.

She was checking her mobile when he got to her. She looked pale, scared.

"Have you heard anything?" he asked.

She shook her head. "They must have grabbed him from the apartment when my mum was out. They left a note saying if we speak to the media I'll never see him again. This is Nogueira. God knows how he got wind of the Globo thing. It's all over, Jake. I can't beat this guy."

Jake didn't want to tell her that the media were no respecter of threats of dead bodies. "And nothing more?"

"Just that they would call me with more instructions. It's why I couldn't speak on the phone. But I've heard nothing. Have you had anything on Vilson?"

He shook his head. "No. I don't know whether he would try to come here tonight, but I think Marinho is in danger even if he doesn't. We need to try and get him out of here before the fight." He took her hand and led her through the crowd to the door where the fighters made their entrance to the hall. There were steel crash barriers around it and a whole crowd of burly security guys. Even if he put his crazy head on, Jake wasn't getting through that lot.

He had a look around and thought for a moment. "They must come in a different way," he said to her, backtracking out to the lobby. The only doors were for the box office and toilets, but there was a set of stairs on the opposite side. They led down to a maze of corridors. The only one of significance was long, dimly lit, and at its end there was a small group of men and women smoking, chatting and drinking. Beyond them, two older guys in plain clothes were guarding a double door. They didn't have the look of bouncers. More like cops.

"Okay," Jake said, "about turn. Nogueira's got the place nailed down."

They tried the other corridors but found nothing other than padlocked doors, storerooms and dead ends.

By the time they got back to the main hall, they were announcing Marinho's fight as next up.

Chapter 49

Marinho

It was a pokey room in the bowels of the building, metal shelves lined with cleaning products in economy-sized plastic containers. There were no windows and no ventilation. It wasn't the worst dressing room Marinho had seen.

Beneath the single bare bulb hanging from the ceiling, he was sweating, even in just his fighting shorts. He was jogging on the spot, starting his warm-up routine.

There was a knock at the door and it immediately opened. Nogueira.

"Your opponent has dropped out at the last minute," he said. "But don't worry, we've got you a stand-in."

Marinho knew instantly that it was a set-up. Nogueira was always going to pull some trick or other.

Marinho had his game face on; there was no point in giving Nogueira a reaction. "What do we know about the stand-in?" He needed to know about his opponent's fighting style. Was he a boxer? Did he have a good kick? Was he a groundwork specialist?

Nogueira shrugged. "Never heard of him, never seen him. You'll work him out when you see him."

"Would you put some money on for me, Chief?" It would look odd if he didn't bet on himself.

"Sure, but you'd be throwing it away. You're getting knocked out in Round 3."

"I've never taken a fall."

Nogueira pulled a piece of paper from his pocket and unfolded it. "It's my letter of recommendation to *BOPE*, signed. I've set up your transfer. That's my side of the bargain. Time to move on, uh?"

He handed it to Marinho. It was all there in black and white, with Nogueira's signature at the bottom. After years of waiting, his route into the elite police unit. This was his dream.

"You hold onto that," Nogueira said, "and I'll get around the medical for you – that's my guarantee. But only if you go down in the third. You make sure you hang in there until then, and make it look good. Let him break your face a little."

Marinho looked back at the letter, reading it over again.

Nogueira shook his head. "Always the doubt, uh? Always the weakness. You know, I'm doing you a favour with this fight because although you're good enough, with all the tools to make it, there's one thing missing."

Nogueira pointed between Marinho's eyes and drew a line down his body. "That mean streak in you is too faint. I can barely see it. To really make it in the fight game you need to be willing to destroy your opponent. Willing to kill him. I don't know that you've enough mean in you to make it in BOPE either, but you'll never even get the chance if you fluff your lines tonight. You won't even make it home. And that's not a threat from me. Other people have invested in this fight. Bad people. Understand?"

Marinho locked eyes with Nogueira and gave him the faintest of nods.

"Good," said Nogueira. His tone softened. "We do what we have to do, always remember that. You for your family and I for mine. You know, it was my granddaughter's prize-giving this evening – I missed it and I know she'll be upset. We make the sacrifices, do the unpleasant things in the hope that our children and their children won't have to."

There was another knock on the door. Time to go.

Out beneath the harsh lights in the octagon, Marinho pulled the towel from around his neck and took off his big, loose hoodie. A few jumps – high – tucking his knees almost to his chest with each one. Then he whirled his arms and slapped alternating hands across his body onto his biceps, dipping his head from side to side to keep his neck loose.

He had his mouthguard in and he had the face on, stone-cold ferocity. But Nogueira's intervention in the dressing room had derailed his mental preparation.

Marinho had to shut everything out: the noise, the lights. He focused, getting his head in the zone, seeing himself rising above his opponent, lifting his hands in triumph. He barely heard the announcement over the thumping entrance music and roar of the crowd, but he caught a word, *campeão* – champion. The champion climbed into the octagon and walked slowly and deliberately toward him. No jumps, no shaking out of limbs.

Marinho kept his own routine going – mirroring the guy would show weakness – but his eyes never left his opponent's. He recognised this champion of whatever but the name escaped him. The crowd was going nuts for this guy. They had put money on him.

The champion stopped about six inches from Marinho's face, filling his vision. He was maybe two inches shorter than Marinho with a good fifteen-kilo advantage. There was no fat in that extra weight, just slabs of carved muscle and over heavy bone. Hair spread over his shoulders, down his arms and across his chest in a black haze. His ears were thickened with lumpy scar tissue, the gristle and bone of his nose pounded into something that looked like an impatient child's attempt at making one with Play-Doh.

Marinho tried to hold onto that image. Break this guy down bit by bit.

He looked like a brawler and a grappler rolled up. Dangerous. *Campeão*. Marinho was a middleweight, his opponent looked a heavyweight. This wasn't an officially sanctioned fight; they could get away with this ludicrous mismatch.

Focus, focus, focus. Get back in the zone. Marinho stretched his neck from side to side. This guy had clearly soaked up a lot of punishment in his time, maybe too much. He might be a shot fighter and maybe didn't like getting hit any more. Or, worse for him, he was maybe getting to like it too much. And, strong as he looked, he had a lot more weight to carry around. He would tire if Marinho kept him moving. Marinho had a reach advantage and he was quick. He would make him pay for that. This *Campeão de Nada* – this Champion of Nothing.

His opponent padded away to his corner, turning back when he got there to zero in on Marinho again. His people fussed over him, his trainer leaning into his face to shout instructions, gesturing toward Marinho. The cornerman slathered Vaseline around his eyes and over his ears.

Marinho's trainer came into his vision.

"What do you know about this guy?" Marinho asked.

His trainer shrugged. "Not much. From up north somewhere. Just keep him moving and get in and out quick. Don't brawl. He's a monster but he'll tire."

Marinho nodded. He knew all that already. He shouldn't have asked anything; it had broken his concentration. Nogueira was forcing his way back inside his head.

He was still all over the place when the referee called them together for his let's-have-a-good-clean-fight talk. They touched fists, Marinho's opponent trying to intimidate with a reptilian stillness.

Marinho should have got everything lined up, building to this moment so that he could screw all the fear and apprehension into a hard ball and send it down with the shot of adrenaline that always sent a shiver from the top of his head through to his core.

But he wasn't there and the bell went and the champion flew at him, like a basking alligator bursting in to attack. He came with fists swinging. The brawler. Crowding Marinho, trying to put him on the back foot, get him covering up rather than putting out his own shots.

If he got a sweet connection with just one of those shots it would all be over. Even if he didn't catch him with a good one, his momentum could barrel Marinho over and the champion could then work him on the ground. This guy knew what he was doing. Marinho's mind finally snapped clear of everything other than staying alive for the next few minutes.

All this came in the milliseconds before a fizzing right hook caught his jaw. But he was already swinging his back leg away, his body and head following. The left hook just clipped him, and still it mashed his teeth into his mouthguard and starred his vision. But his mind was still working.

Avoiding the full force of the punch had moved him aside, letting the champion hurtle past him. He tried to grab the swinging right arm by the wrist with his outstretched right and hit the champion just above his elbow with his other fist to dislocate the joint.

The champion was no lumbering dump truck though. Snatching his arm away and dropping low, he threw his left leg out for a back kick. It was ineffective, Marinho blocking with a forearm, but it gave the champion the opportunity to spring around and bring his fists to bear again.

Marinho didn't return his stare; he wasn't going to win the psych battle. He concentrated around the top of his opponent's chest, from where all the movement came. There was a ripple across the shoulders, signalling a lunge and a spray of fists.

Marinho was quicker this time, jinking to the side. The champion had to turn, unbalancing his attack, bleeding off his momentum.

Marinho lashed out a low, roundhouse kick into the outside of the champion's left knee, striking with the bottom of his shin bone. With the swing in his long limb and the solid bone, it was like hitting someone with a baseball bat. The champion's knee buckled inwards and there was a wince, a grunt of pain. There was no amount of muscle that could protect a knee.

But the champion was mobile for a big man, drawing the hurt leg behind him to keep it out of the way. Before, he had just been rushing him and swinging, gunning loosely from a conventional fight stance – leading with his left. Now, he had switched his fight stance to southpaw, leading with his right, no more rushing. Marinho knew he must be badly hurt if he was forced to switch to an unnatural stance. But he drilled out a stiff jab with his right, catching Marinho above the eye.

Marinho only saw it coming late. He jinked to the side again. He had to keep moving out of the way.

The champion had his elbows tucked in, fists up, and he kept moving and drilling that jab, then flashing out the left hand with combinations. He wasn't improvising. He was comfortable. This was his natural fight stance. He was a southpaw. A goddamned southpaw.

Marinho was in big trouble.

He pulled his own elbows in to project his ribs and kept his chin down and kept moving. His hands were up, but he kept them open when he wasn't punching, looking for a chance to grab a stray arm and go for a lock.

He worked his punch combinations and followed with kicks. He didn't manage to trouble the champion with any of his kicks, landing on muscle and thick bone. He got a messy uppercut through, snapping the champion's head back. But the eyes stayed clear. He could take a punch, this champion. And he could box.

The champion went for the odd kick, but there wasn't much to that side of his game. At least not with one bad knee. Guys who didn't have kicks hated getting kicked.

Marinho flicked out with his leading foot, his left. Catching the champion in the hard muscle of his belly, it pushed him off balance. Marinho got a quick combination of punches in, one marking up a cheekbone. He jinked sideways and around came his vicious low roundhouse. It struck just above the bad knee. It didn't give, but he had softened it some more.

The champion grinned, a distorted grimace with his mouthguard, and shook his head. You didn't hurt me.

Meaning that he had. Good.

The champion came back hard with the jab again. Marinho was able to slash it away, but he didn't see the thundering left cross that followed it into his ribs. And then came a clubbing right into his ear that made his hearing whistle as if a bomb had gone off. The crowd sounded like it was roaring from the bottom of a well. He staggered. His thought process disintegrated into a thousand fragments.

The champion rushed him, windmilling the punches in, looking for the finish. Marinho could only cover up as he was forced against the chain-link wall. The blows that were landing rattled his brain. His thinking scrambled, he didn't know what to do next. He [...] the overwhelming awareness that he was in a place close [...].

The bell went for the end of the round, a couple [...] ches flying in before the referee dragged the champion off him.

"You okay?" the referee asked, looking into Marinho's [...]

He nodded and gave a thumbs up. He hoped [...] walking straight when he turned to go to his corner, slumping [...].

"A southpaw, I can't believe it," his trainer shouted [...] crowd, pulling Marinho's mouthguard out and squirting water [...] plastic bottle into his mouth. "Your boss really screwed us."

The cornerman pressed a small eye iron beneath [...] eye, with downward movements. It was painful. He was trying to [...] the swelling away from the immediate area.

"Your left eye is beginning to close," the cornerman [...]

If his left eye closed completely he was done. The [...] swelling or cut around his right eye, but he could only see a grey blur [...] moving shadows from it. He wasn't able to see all the big effects [...] coming.

The detached retina was his secret, Nogueira's [...]. The condition was an automatic medical discharge from [...], no insurance backup, no pension. He was an invalid and he [...] never make it into *BOPE* without Nogueira oiling the wheels.

A southpaw would always be landing the bombs [...] blindside. He had always made a point of avoiding fighters [...] the unconventional stance.

The champion stood beside his stool as his corner [...] him. He wanted to show that he didn't need the rest. [...] it might be because his knee was stiffening and unwilling [...].

The bell went and Marinho did what the champion least expected. He rushed from his stool. Catching him off guard, he landed a couple of punches in and swung a decent kick, slapping in [...] of muscle over his ribs. He couldn't box this guy and he [...] him enough to risk taking him to ground, even with the [...].

Marinho kept flying in and out, taking care to protect [...] side from the heavy left-handers. But the champion was [...] secret. Nogueira must have filled him in. Of course he had, even [...] Nogueira after all, Marinho thought bitterly. He kept moving [...] Marinho's blindside.

Marinho was only able to half block a fierce left that [...] exploded beneath his right eye.

His brain shorted out – milliseconds – and [...]. The champion rushed him, lunging high, leading with an elbow to catch him in the face. Marinho dipped his shoulder to avoid the elbow but the champion collected him up and crashed him into the chain-link wall.

Marinho managed to keep his feet, turning a hip into the champion's midriff as they both fought for a hold, hands and arms slipping on sweaty skin. Preoccupied with getting his hold on, the champion didn't notice Marinho bending his knees. Marinho sprang up, levering the champion over his hip. Launching forward, pulling the champion with him and kicking out his back leg, he swept away the champion's legs.

The crowd roared for Marinho now. It was a clean throw, the champion sailing over his shoulder. Marinho followed him, diving off his feet, driving all his weight through his shoulder into the champion's ribcage. He felt the give as the air whistled from his lungs in a painful gasp.

But he rolled Marinho with the momentum of the throw, getting some of his weight on top. He worked his arms around Marinho like a coiling anaconda. Marinho needed to break free of the weight crushing down on him. He shrimped – curling up and then thrusting out straight – but the champion had anticipated it, letting his body turn away, snaking a forearm under Marinho's chin. He wasn't perfectly set up but he had the brute strength to make the choke.

It came on fast, even as Marinho used everything – his arms, his legs, his body – to break out. He had only seconds before he would lose consciousness. The sound changed in his ears. The colours flaring around the blinding floodlights were dimming. He softened his body for a moment before bunching all that remained of his strength. Thrusting, he tried to twist free.

It didn't work. He was done. The champion was able to wind his anaconda squeeze tighter.

The referee was on all fours, his face close-up, looking into Marinho's eyes, waiting for the tap out – for Marinho to tap a hand on his opponent or on the canvas to submit – or for his eyes to roll up and close.

There was no way Marinho was tapping out.

And then the pressure eased very slightly. Marinho was confused, not enough blood getting back to his brain for him to react. The champion kept the choke on but now he was shifting his weight to better pin Marinho rather than tightening the squeeze.

The bell went. End of Round 2.

Now Marinho understood. The champion needed to take it to

Round 3 to get his payday.

The referee slapped the champion's back and he released his hold. He feigned a slip as he rose, digging a thumb in Marinho's closing left eye. He jumped back up, raising a fist aloft to claim the round as he strolled back to his corner stool and stood beside it, looking down on Marinho.

Marinho regained his feet, coughing.

"You want to throw the towel in?" the referee asked, peering into his face.

Marinho shook his head. "He caught me in the eye. I just need to clear it." The referee was just a watery, red blur. He was struggling to counter the reflex that was shutting it, trying to protect the delicate tissue.

"Okay son, but you look like you've had enough to me and if you're shipping any more punishment I'll stop it, whether you're down or not. I don't want to see you die in here, understand?"

Marinho nodded. His trainer grabbed him and got him back to his stool.

"You've got to keep away from him," he shouted in Marinho's face, "he's killing you with that left. You just attack the knee – it'll go if you keep at it. You've got to at least TKO him to win – the judges will give him the first two rounds."

His cornerman was working on his right eye. "This one's closing up too." That eye didn't really matter.

The champion stood off from Marinho when the bell went, giving him a little wave of his left fist. It was coming for him again.

Marinho was blinking some focus back into his left eye as he shimmied around the champion. Staying out of range, keeping his feet close to the canvas for maximum stability. A feinted front kick, quick punch combination, another kick. It was cagey stuff. Ineffective.

The crowd were getting restless. They could whistle and boo all they liked. Marinho needed to find the right gap.

The champion was paying attention to the crowd, and he surged with a tight combination. But he was just a fraction slower than before, tiredness seeping in. Marinho ducked and lunged for the bad leg. He got his shoulder into the femoral crease at the champion's hip joint, the sweet spot, and he folded and went down.

It was messy, the suddenly frantic champion grabbing for a hold as Marinho fought to lock the knee. He was getting there and the champion panicked. Releasing his hold, he managed to kick Marinho off to roll away and scramble to his feet.

On his side Marinho saw the target. Flicking onto his front, forearms down on the canvas, he drew both knees up beneath him to raise his hips and then drove one leg out like a piston. His heel caught the inside of the champion's knee. He screamed and hopped back, unable to put his full weight on it.

Marinho sprang up and went after him with more kicks. He landed another roundhouse in the ribs with enough force to break a couple in a regular guy. The champion just grunted.

Marinho was also tiring, losing just that fraction of speed, not snatching his leg back sharply enough. The champion grabbed it, Marinho flailing to keep his balance.

The champion should have kicked his other leg away and taken him to the ground, but he was angry. He wanted to take Marinho's head off. His left arm out grazed Marinho's jaw, the movement swinging his shoulders to load his right. Letting go of the leg, he swung a powerhouse hook aimed at Marinho's chin. The knockout button.

Marinho turned his chin, the punch slamming into his cheek. He felt the crunch of breaking bone, fiery tracers stabbing behind his eyelids. The crowd erupted in a roar that sounded like petrol thrown on a fire.

Marinho staggered back, desperately trying to keep his feet. He kept moving to the side, then turning, then stepping back to keep clear of his opponent without trapping himself against the cage wall. His vision wouldn't clear, just swimming shadows. The left eye was gone, same as the right. He was finished.

He didn't feel fear. Instead calm descended over him. Lucidity. He could hear someone calling to him, a clear voice over the screams from his corner and the baying crowd. It was a young voice. A girl's. He didn't recognise it and yet it was familiar. It was at once the craziest thing in the world and the most natural. The voice was calm and soothing.

"What has gone from your sight is given to every other sense," the girl's voice said, and he knew instinctively that he had to absorb the words, believe them. It was his only chance of surviving this.

The champion, hobbled by his damaged knee, was lurching toward Marinho with his head dipped to drive him into the canvas.

Marinho felt the air around him change, the rush and swirl of tiny particles moving through the hairs on his skin as the champion came at him. He smelled the different odour of the sweat on the champion's head, levelled at his chest. The sour blow of his breath. Closer.

Marinho put everything through his right hand, the punch

detonating on the champion's temple. He jinked to collect the champion's head under his left armpit and whipped his arm under his chin to snare his neck. He bent his knees and launched backward and down, taking the champion's head with him into the canvas. The champion's momentum somersaulted his legs over his head and he crashed down on his back behind Marinho.

Marinho let the momentum carry him too, releasing the neck to make a backward roll, finishing astride the champion's belly. Marinho could feel the champion moving beneath him but he wasn't yet fully plugged back in after the shot to his temple. Marinho shuffled up to his chest to get control before the champion managed to put his hands up or draw in his legs to attempt to dislodge him.

In the box-seat, Marinho didn't need his senses to tell him where the champion's head lay and he milled in his ground-and-pound blows hard and fast. The body went limp beneath him and he felt the grind and crunch of gristle and bone as he connected with the champion's nose. He could smell the champion's blood.

The pitch of the crowd changed. A howl of anguish and disbelief and fury, and another note, deeper. Blood lust.

Something big hit Marinho, bowling him off the champion's chest, his arms trapped by a bear hug. A clean, aftershave smell with sweat.

"That's enough, son," the referee was shouting. "It's over. It's all over."

Chapter 50

Jake

He and Eliane had found some standing space in one of the aisles running through the rows to the octagon. Hoarse from shouting, he had been scared for Marinho, watching him battling someone who looked more troll than man. Blood lust had displaced the fear as Marinho had triumphed, raging as hot in Jake as in anyone else in the crowd. Then it had evaporated.

There was pandemonium all around. It was turning ugly already, furious guys screaming and gesticulating. Others shouting and gesticulating back. He saw one guy grab another. A scuffle was breaking out to his right.

People were flooding into the octagon, remonstrating, shoving each other, shoving the referee. A group formed a protective circle around Marinho's opponent. He was still laid out on the canvas, unconscious. A couple of thuggish young men pushed Marinho's trainer and cornerman away from him, backing them up against the chain-link wall. A fight broke out. The two old boys were game but they were getting a hiding.

Marinho just stood there, staring blankly, seemingly oblivious to what was happening to his guys. There were other men crowding Marinho, gesticulating, jostling, shoving, shouting in his face.

"We've got to get him out of there," Jake shouted to Eliane.

She was already on her way.

There were two lumpy-faced bouncers standing at the top of the steps into the octagon. They had obviously decided that there was enough mayhem inside the octagon already, and were swatting away anyone trying to enter.

Eliane didn't break stride, running up the steps and flashing an ID card at them. "I'm a doctor, let me in," she demanded. "This is my colleague." She waved behind at Jake.

One of them was buying the story but the other looked past her at Jake. He wasn't convinced and he didn't budge. "There's a doctor in there already," he said.

"And is he a consultant neurologist too?"

Now he wasn't so sure.

Eliane kept going. "If he has bleeding on the brain, every second counts – you must know that, don't you?"

He came down the steps, ushering them past with [illegible]ead. There was another hopeful coming up behind Jake [illegible] ncer straight-armed him in the throat with the heel of his [illegible] ictim flew back onto a couple of guys below.

Inside the octagon it was chaos. Jake barged [illegible] nelee ahead of Eliane. Bottles were flying in from the cr[illegible] end over end, spraying beer over the knots of fighting m[illegible].

"Stand back, let the doctor through," Jake sh[illegible] men jostling Marinho. It checked them for at least a few [illegible] rinho was looking right at him, but there was no recogni[illegible] bbed him by the shoulders. "Come on, man, let's go."

Flashing his hands up defensively, Marinho check[illegible] his ear. "Jake?"

"Yes. Of course. Let's go."

"I can't see you, Jake. I can't see anything." H[illegible] llen and his eyes were closing up.

"You'll be all right when the swelling goes down."

"No, it's gone, I felt it go."

Jake was having to hold onto Marinho, the [illegible] them pushing and hitting. Most of the blows were wild, [illegible] s in close confines, but Jake caught one in the back of the [illegible] rted out his lights momentarily. A peal of sparks in the d[illegible] last of a fading rocket.

No one had got around to paying Eliane any atte[illegible] was still getting thrown around in the crush.

Jake took one of Marinho's hands and placed it [illegible] er as he turned. "Keep your hands on my shoulders and [illegible] We need to get out of here right now."

Marinho did as he was told, head down, close to [illegible] liane tucked in close to Marinho with her arm around h[illegible] vered through the crowd, chopping aside anyone who di[illegible] f his way quickly enough. Marinho's trainer and corner[illegible] oing and were able to thrash their way through to follow, [illegible] king them now having to fend off their own attackers.

A young guy blocked Jake's path, waving a crum[illegible] lip in his face, jabbing a finger at Marinho, shouting abo[illegible] the result.

Jake aimed his punch carefully, angling down in[illegible] exus. The guy crumpled immediately, winded. "You've g[illegible] ver a body," he shouted over his shoulder to Marinho. [illegible] than going around.

Jake caught a glimpse of Marinho's opponent, still an unconscious hulk on the canvas, men crowded around him. It was astonishing that Marinho had managed to beat him.

There was a startled scream from Eliane behind him.

A cop-looking guy of maybe thirty had hold of her ponytail. She was wincing, trying to hit out as he twisted, pulling her to him.

"Not so fast," he shouted at Marinho, "the boss wants you. And the *gringo*, and this little bitch." He lifted the hem of his tee shirt to show them the butt of the semi-automatic sticking out of his waistband.

Marinho didn't see the warning. Instead, he cocked his ear to the voice, letting go of Jake's shoulders. He flashed a straight right. It caught the cop sweetly on the chin. Poleaxed, his grip on Eliane's hair relaxed and he keeled over, knocking into guys behind him before smacking down on the canvas.

Eliane was on him instantly, pulling the handgun from his waistband and ramming it under his chin. She slapped him around the face to bring him to. "Where's my father?" she shouted in his face.

The cop looked at her groggily. "I don't know."

She slapped him again and moved the barrel of the handgun over his eye. "Tell me, you shit, or so help me God, I will blow your brains right through this canvas."

"I don't know. I swear it."

She spat in his face and rose, tucking the handgun into the waistband of her jeans.

"Okay," she shouted to Jake and Marinho, "keep moving, keep moving."

Marinho hooked back on Jake's shoulders.

Jake shouted back at him, "I thought you said you couldn't see?"

"I can't, but there's nothing wrong with my ears."

Jake was no longer fighting against the tide but riding with the throng going out of the octagon and down the steps. Everyone wanted out now rather than in.

Chapter 51

Vilson

The underground garage was a small concrete space with room for maybe fifty cars. Dull strip lighting overhead. Vilson was crouched behind a concrete pillar next to a car. A vantage point, looking through the side window at a doorway at the opposite end to the exit ramp. Beyond the doorway was a concrete stairwell that led up to the main hall above. An angry rumble of booing and catcalls rolled down the stairwell.

He watched as Nogueira made his way down the stairs, mobile phone in one hand, rubbing at his belly with the other and grimacing. Vilson didn't scrunch himself down further in fear as he might once have done. He held the old revolver in his lap, ready. He felt nothing other than resolve.

Nogueira stopped just inside the garage and dialled a number on his mobile. Putting it to his ear he waited, looked at the screen again and then cursed and called on.

"Not so fast Chief," a voice called out from the stairwell behind Nogueira.

Nogueira turned slowly, unhurried. He was practised with the tough-guy show, thought Vilson.

Franjinha came down the stairs, wearing his hip-hop city gear, and Vilson saw the anger flare in Nogueira when he saw him. "Idiot. You don't follow me down in here."

"I lost a lot of money tonight. What are you going to do about that?"

"I lost more too. Everyone did."

They were talking more quietly now, Vilson straining to hear.

"Are you double-crossing me?" Franjinha asked.

"Pull yourself together. Leave the paranoia to your boss." Nogueira turned on his heel.

"I'm not finished with you yet," Franjinha shouted.

Nogueira wheeled on him, drawing his open hand back, as if to slap a kid.

Franjinha stepped back.

"That's better," said Nogueira. "My patch, my rules. Remember? Just do what I told you earlier, and let me do my thing. They think they've got the better of me but all they have is a house of cards. I pull one out from the bottom and the whole thing comes down. And I'll get to each fallen card and burn it at my leisure, believe me. Now go. Go on and disappear."

Nogueira turned and walked to his old VW. Franjinha stared at him for a few moments, a half-hearted show of defiance before he sloped off and went back up the concrete stairs. Nogueira opened his car door, pulled a handgun from the waistband beneath his loose shirt and reached in to place it on the driver's seat before he got in. Vilson had heard that cops were in the habit of driving around with their handguns lodged beneath a thigh for quick access. They had a lot of enemies.

Nogueira got in, the engine started and Vilson saw the front windows opening with an electronic whine. He came out from his hiding place, taking care to stay out of the view of Nogueira's mirrors. Nogueira was leaning across the car. It looked like he was trying to get something from the glove compartment. He came back upright, and then Vilson saw a jet of cigarette smoke coming through the open window.

Vilson edged closer, stopping at the rear bumper of the car parked next to Nogueira's side. He saw Nogueira smack the wheel. Frustration or anger, maybe both. More smoke drifted out the window and then the gearbox clunked and the reversing light came on. Nogueira reached an arm behind the passenger-seat headrest to look out the rear window as he edged the car backward. Vilson knew he had seen him then. He pointed the revolver at Nogueira. "Kill the engine and get out of the car," he commanded. The brake lights bathed Vilson in red as the car halted.

Nogueira took his hand off the headrest and turned his head toward the driver's window, trying to get a better look at Vilson. "I've got money, here," Nogueira said, the cigarette bobbing on his lips.

"Both hands on the steering wheel," Vilson said.

Nogueira obliged but lifted them to gesture as he spoke. "I can't pass you the money with my hands on the wheel, son. We could be here all night if we don't put a little trust in one another."

"I said keep your hands on the steering wheel." Vilson knew Nogueira was trying to test him by lifting his hands from the wheel. But he was not playing with the old Vilson. Things were different now. "And kill the engine. Do it slowly."

"Look, son," Nogueira said, "hands on the wheel or turn off the engine – which is it? And I really need to get rid of this cigarette, the smoke is getting in my eyes. Would you mind?"

"Kill the engine or I'll kill you," Vilson said calmly.

"You know it wasn't me who shot your friend? It was young Marinho who killed him."

"I know."

That was Nogueira's last card. Vilson knew it; Nogueira knew it.

The engine roared and the tyres squealed on the shiny concrete surface as Nogueira snapped the clutch and ducked down. Vilson jumped back as he saw him haul the steering wheel down. Nogueira was trying to crush him.

The front passenger wing caught a concrete pillar as the car swung round, bouncing the front of Nogueira's car back into the car on Vilson's side. Slewing violently out of the space, Nogueira still had the steering hard in lock.

Vilson held the heavy old revolver with both hands, aiming through the driver's window at Nogueira's crouched upper body. The gunshot cracked loud over the sound of the revving engine. He couldn't see if he had hit. The car kept going, the front whipping round as it came clear of the parking space, clipping the line of cars opposite. The car bounced from side to side with the inertia of the suspension. Close to the dead end of the small concrete garage, Nogueira was taking the only option open to him – backing out between the two lines of cars to the exit ramp.

Careering along in reverse, Vilson saw Nogueira's head come up to look out the rear window, trying to correct, trying to veer away from the line of cars. He looked back at Vilson for just a moment and then glanced at something in the rear-view mirror. For just a millisecond, Vilson saw horror fill Nogueira's face before he hauled on the steering wheel, his head snapping back to look behind again.

The car swerved violently, rolling on its suspension, stacking into a concrete pillar and flipping round, the driver's side smashing into the line of cars. A hammer blow of metal against metal. Breaking glass. It settled with the bonnet wedged beneath a fancy pickup with jacked-up suspension.

The wheels were spinning on the concrete, acrid smoke billowing up from the burning rubber. It was stuck fast, twisted metal trapped beneath twisted metal. Vilson approached, unhurried.

He heard the revs drop for a moment and then the clunk of gears. Nogueira wasn't dead yet. The car jumped and bucked in first gear and then back in reverse, grinding metal, groaning as it tried to tear itself from the big pickup.

The revs fell away to idle as Vilson approached. There was a small gap between the mangled driver's side of Nogueira's car and the line of smashed-up cars. Nogueira was thumping his shoulder against the door, but it refused to shift. He gave up and was trying to get across to the passenger's side as Vilson got to that door.

Catching sight of Vilson, he looked frantically around for his handgun. He looked in the back. The only thing there was the smouldering cigarette that had flown from his lips. He sat back in the driver's seat.

Vilson pointed the revolver at him. It didn't look like he'd hit Nogueira. There was no blood, save for some nicks on his face and forearms from the smashed glass. If he wasn't hit, Vilson couldn't understand why he had swerved and crashed.

Nogueira looked up at him, anxiety in his face. "Is she OK?"

"What are you talking about?"

"You didn't see a girl?"

"Cut the bullshit, there's no girl here."

"I thought I saw my grand—" Nogueira stopped himself. "I thought I saw someone, but it couldn't have been." The fear went from him. There was no fear to replace it. "Now I think of it, she wouldn't dress like that. All in white. Huh, I really thought it was her, but there was no one. Good. That's good. She's safe."

Nogueira brushed little cubes of the smashed glass from his shirt and trousers, and examined one of the nicks on the back of his hand. He seemed to notice then that the car's engine was still running and he turned off the ignition.

"You killed my best friend, my only friend," Vilson said. "You probably don't even know his full name. Jose Carlos Pereira da Silva – Babão to me. He was a good kid and he didn't deserve it."

Vilson pulled the hammer back on the old revolver. Nogueira nodded, looking Vilson steadily in the eye.

Vilson fired once.

He wafted at the tyre smoke that was drifting in around the car in heavy layers and peered inside at Nogueira's slumped body, thrust the revolver closer and fired once more into his head.

Hatred coursed through Vilson, but he was willing to give the cop one thing. He had met death with courage.

Chapter 52

Jake

The crowd moving toward the lobby wasn't so hostile, focused instead on escaping the chaos inside. Mostly. Men were still shouting insults and threats, and jostling. Marinho's trainer and cornerman were now protecting his flanks, with Jake still the buffer upfront.

The stream mushroomed around the single door that led into the lobby and they had to wait a couple of minutes with people pressing up behind them. Once through the door, people raced through the open lobby and out the multiple doors at the entrance.

The air outside was sticky and hot but free of the febrile atmosphere inside. Any remaining anger seemed to have evaporated from the crowd. Out of the bear pit, angry guys were back to being the ordinary guys they had been before they had entered.

"My car's a block down that street," Eliane said, pointing to a side street along from the building.

They didn't need to huddle now, but Jake only picked up the pace a little – Marinho still had his hands on his shoulders and his steps weren't confident.

They heard two dull reports.

Marinho tilted his head. "That's gunfire."

"It's okay, we're here," Eliane said, clicking the doors open on her car with her key fob and running a few metres ahead to open the passenger door for Marinho.

Jake got him in and pulled the seatbelt across as Marinho's guys got in the back. Eliane was turning over the engine as Jake closed the passenger door on Marinho, the guys shuffling up on the back seat to make room for him.

Marinho hit the window from inside. "Jake!" he shouted.

He'd heard them coming before Jake did.

Jake only managed to half turn before they hammered him into the side of the car.

There were four of them, a couple of them nearly as tall as Jake. He covered up to take the punches, pistol whips and kicks, lashing out a few shots of his own.

Keep your feet. Jake knew that going to the ground with this bunch kicking at his head would be fatal. He used the car to prop himself up, pushing his back against the passenger door to prevent Marinho getting out.

Another guy came running up behind the others with a handgun. His arms and face had reddish–pink patches of healing skin. Jake remembered him from before his burns.

Marinho's trainer and cornerman were scrambling to climb out the back of the car.

Franjinha pointed his gun at them. "You get back in and stay there," he shouted. They shuffled back in and he slammed the door.

"Good," said Franjinha. "I like sensible people. Now let's get those two chumps out of the front."

Jake turned his back on the group, scarcely registering the blows to his spine and kidneys. Marinho's face was tilted up, his sightless eyes screwed shut. Eliane had the gun she'd taken from the cop in the octagon in her hand, going for the door handle.

Jake slammed his open hand on the window. Eliane's face was filled with fear but her eyes were sharp on him.

"You drive this car now," Jake shouted fiercely. Franjinha's boys were still hitting him but they were also trying to drag him away now to get to the door and to Marinho.

Another of them was running around the front of the car to get to Eliane.

Her eyes stayed locked on Jake's, even as she pushed the gearstick forward and hit the accelerator.

Taking off with stuttering wheelspin, the car collected the kid at the front, rolling him over the bonnet. He went off the passenger side, hitting the kerb.

Jake spun around and hit the nearest boy as hard as he could. He caught him on the side of the jaw with the flat smack of fist on flesh. One of the biggest, he went straight down, clattering to the pavement. Franjinha fired a shot at the car. There was no shattering of glass. He'd missed. Jake lunged and swung again, catching Franjinha on the brow, knocking him backward before he could fire another shot.

Something hard hit Jake behind his ear with a sickening thud. The power went out from his neck down and he went to the pavement. He wasn't out cold but the blow shorted him out. He only had an awareness that they were hauling him up and carrying him along, his feet trailing along the pavement. The iron tang of blood seemed to fill his head and he felt sick.

They bundled him into a rusty old VW Kombi van. It had double doors. He hadn't seen one like that before. He liked it. He wondered whether he ought to be thinking about more important things. The driver turned to look at him. He looked scared. Jake thought he should remember why.

"Drive," Franjinha instructed the pressganged driver, gesturing forward with his handgun.

The Kombi van pulled away to the rough buzz of the air-cooled engine. Jake took a few punches as he lay on the floor pan between two rows of seats. They rolled him onto his front and grabbed his arms. There was a strong rubber smell in his nostrils from the floor mats.

It was only when someone pulled a plastic bag over his head that the fear kicked back in. The plastic was sucked into his mouth and nostrils each time he tried to drag in a frantic breath.

There was too much weight on his arms and legs for him to get free. And every time he tried, they stamped on him and punched him, draining his strength.

Jake had to get hold of the panic or he would suffocate under the feet of these little psychopaths. They probably wouldn't even notice and they wouldn't care less.

He turned his head and dipped his chin, trying to work the bag upward with his lips and tongue. He breathed in, very gently, through his nose. A thin but steady stream of air. Long, shallow breaths. It was hard to control his body screaming for great lungfuls of oxygen.

It took a minute or so for Jake to get his breathing under control. To feel like he wasn't dying.

He could hear the loud and aggressive banter amongst the gang now. Jokes and insults, jacked up on adrenaline, with quick-fire slang that he found difficult to follow. It felt like an hour, but it was probably closer to twenty minutes when the Kombi van pulled over. The inside of the bag was running with sweat, Jake's hair soaked.

Franjinha and his boys were clearly of the opinion that he was capable of moving under his own steam now. They tipped him out of the van, kicking him to encourage him to find his feet.

The condensation inside the bag made it difficult to see. Jake staggered forward, guided by kicks and shoves. They were going uphill. They were in the favela. The effort and panic were breaking the rhythm of his breathing, the polythene stoppering his mouth and nostrils every couple of breaths with a nasty, rustling pop. It was an exhausting climb, his lungs bursting. He was nauseous and disoriented.

When they finally stopped and pulled the bag from his head, the relief only lasted a second. He saw where he was. The scrubby hilltop, the burned trees. It wasn't set up with the paraffin torches but he knew that this was the Burning Hill.

He was a dead man. It wasn't the dying that frightened him so much as what was going to happen before that.

Chapter 53

Jake

More boys arrived. Some were in their teens, some were youngsters. A boy of around eight came with a small gas lamp that he placed on the dirt. It burned its white light with a ferocious hiss.

"See the smart guy?" Franjinha said. "Nuno brought light."

Franjinha took a pistol from one of the teenagers and gave it to Nuno. "There you go, now you can cover this *gringo*. You're the official security detail tonight."

The pistol was so heavy for the kid that he had to prop his elbows on his hips and hold it close to him.

"You keep that away from your body if you fire it," Franjinha instructed, "otherwise the hammer will dig a hole in your chest." He was trying to keep it light but all the other kids were tense, staring fearfully into the dark spaces around them. And then Jake understood. The last time most of them would have seen Vilson was here. They had executed Vilson and turned him into a ghost here.

Nothing happened for over an hour. Jake thought about running, but there were too many guns. One of them would hit him. The law of averages. There were a lot of murmured questions amongst the kids. Agitation. Franjinha was the only one who didn't look bothered. They were waiting for something. It turned out they were waiting for someone.

Another teenager finally strutted in, flanked by a gaggle of his soldiers. He was slight, no older than Franjinha, but he was clearly the leader. A Beretta hung loosely in his hand.

With his skinny frame and the constant nervy twitch running through it, he didn't cut a very imposing figure. He looked like a frightened kid trying his best to show he wasn't. He was a head shorter than Jake but, when he came close, squaring up, Jake saw. There was pure sparkle-eyed psycho behind the fear.

Anjo tilted his head to one side and then the other, and put the barrel of the Beretta to Jake's forehead. Getting no reaction, he traced the barrel down the scars on Jake's cheek. He sniffed and wrinkled his nose, flecks of white paste in his wet nostrils.

"So," he said, stepping back and looking at the soldiers fanned out around him. "The *gringo*, huh? Where all this started."

THE BURNING HILL

He looked back to Jake, dried spittle at the corners of his mouth. "Welcome to the hill, *Senhor*," he said, making a bow. "I'm sure a bunch of uneducated favela soldiers like us could benefit from some cultural exchange, but I'm afraid your stay can only be short, though probably longer than you would like. And very painful. You see, your idiot cop friend wasn't meant to win that fight tonight — that was a lot of money. Unfortunately for you, you're the only one we picked up for our party tonight, so you're going to have to tell me what the hell is going on."

Jake let the fear show. He was playing the meek prisoner. Don't antagonise or play the tough guy. Survive. Every minute he could add to his life was precious. "I hardly know that cop," he said. "I really don't know anything about what happened."

"Yeah, they all say that to start with. You'll amaze yourself with how much more you'll remember before the end. You and I are gonna have a whole stinking pile that we need to get to the bottom of. The quicker you tell me, the quicker it will be over. Understand, *amigo*?"

When the time came, right at the end, Jake wasn't going to give the grey man. He was willing to sacrifice a few minutes. He would play into the anger, plunge the thermometer into the boiling water and let it explode. He wasn't going to beg for mercy from this fucker either.

A frightened murmur rippled through the gang. One by one they looked at Jake.

Jake saw the whites of Anjo's eyes as they widened. Then his face slid to a waxy mask of terror. His knees gave way and his hand to the earth.

It wasn't Jake they were looking at. They were staring past him. They started crossing themselves.

Someone was coming through the tall grass on the other side of the clearing. Walking slowly, purposefully. His skin was bone grey, his matted shock of hair the same colour. Emerging from the trees, his skin started to glow almost white in the flare of the gas lamp.

This wasn't Vilson as Jake remembered him. This was not a lope-shouldered gait, his eyes no longer darting about nervously. The soft parts of Vilson had been cut away.

Anjo opened and shut his slack mouth a couple of times before he found his voice. But it betrayed him, quavering and small. "Help me, God." He lifted the Beretta.

Vilson stopped around five metres short of him and shook his head slowly. "You cannot kill a dead man." His voice was clear and near. It went through the gang like a shockwave.

THE BURNING HILL

The Beretta wavered in Anjo's hand and then fell back to his side. He was unable to get it to do his bidding.

Vilson pulled the old revolver from the back of his shorts. He lifted it and swept it around in a slow arc. And then he came back the other way, dipping the barrel momentarily.

Everyone understood the signal and those holding a gun dropped it on the ground in front of them.

Chapter 54

Vilson and Jake

Vilson pushed the cylinder out from the revolver, pulled three empty shell cases from it and dropped them into the turf. He pulled the two remaining live bullets out, holding them up between his thumb and forefinger as he looked at Jake. "Hey *gringo*, two bullets left. One for you and one for me.' His voice was cold, detached. All those lies and broken dreams and distrust, all the misery of his life, slowly crushed into a ball of steel from that moment they had walked into one another on Copacabana.

Vilson put one of the bullets back in the cylinder, spun it and then put the other in without looking. He closed the cylinder back into the barrel and spun again. "Or maybe one for him and one for him," he said, pointing the revolver first at Franjinha and then Anjo.

Still on his knees, Anjo clasped his hands together, begging. He whimpered some inaudible prayer.

Vilson fired.

The bullet hit Anjo just beneath his collarbone, rocking him back. He screamed, putting a hand to the wound and slumping to the ground. Conscious, not fatally wounded.

Jake caught the movement before Vilson did, Franjinha reaching for the pistol tucked in the back of his waistband. Jake launched at him. He put a shoulder into Franjinha's chest, hard, to flatten him, but he was concentrating on the pistol. Grabbing the barrel with both hands, wrenching and twisting it out of Franjinha's grip. They both went sprawling, but it was Jake who came up with the pistol.

None of the other kids moved. They could barely look away from Vilson. Jake stepped back from Franjinha, training the pistol on him. It took him a second to realise that Vilson was aiming his revolver not at Franjinha, but him.

"So, one bullet was destined for him," Vilson said, gesturing at Anjo, now moaning with the pain of his wounded shoulder. "Just one left." Vilson lifted his aim from Jake and put the revolver to his own temple, never taking his eyes off Jake. He started squeezing the trigger, slowly. The hammer drawing back.

"Don't do it, Jake pleaded with him.

Click.

There was no change in Vilson's expression, no look of relief. "See? You can't kill a dead man." He took the revolver away from his temple and pointed it back at Jake. He nodded to the gun that Jake was still pointing at Franjinha. The invitation for him to go for it. Take his chance.

Jake let the gun drop to his side and shook his head.

Vilson drew back the hammer on the revolver with his thumb. "Go on, *gringo*."

Jake didn't move. He wasn't going to.

Vilson kept the revolver levelled at Jake's chest. There was no tremor in his hand. He moved it a fraction away from Jake's chest. Squeezed the trigger. *Click*.

"Huh. Death didn't want you after all," he said. He looked at Jake for a long moment before he spoke again. "We're okay, *gringo*, you and me, yes?"

Jake nodded.

Vilson turned the revolver on Franjinha. "The last bullet is for you, then." Franjinha shifted, but his face was empty of expression.

Blam. Blam. Blam.Blam. The shots rang out.

Little Nuno was holding the heavy pistol Franjinha had given him away from his chest, his head pulled back to keep it as far from the danger of recoil as possible. No one had seen him pick it up.

For a few moments, nothing happened. It seemed like the bullets had had no effect. You cannot kill a dead man. The soldiers stared, transfixed, the words echoing in their head.

Then Vilson's revolver dropped to the ground. He touched his chest and looked at the blood on his fingertips. Two of Nuno's bullets had found their mark.

Sinking to his knees, Vilson crossed himself, leaving a dab of blood on his pale forehead. He rolled gently onto his side, head turned to stare up at the sky. Just for a moment, something came back into his eyes. The life. "Hey Gabriel, hey Babão. *Eu tou chegando ai, irmãos*," – I'm coming, brothers – he said, and then his last breath slipped away and his eyes went blank again.

Slowly, the realisation began to dawn on the members of the Red Ants that he wasn't a ghost. He was just another kid who could be shot.

"Put it down," Jake commanded Nuno. He had Franjinha's pistol trained on the kid. The kid was still aiming at Vilson. Nuno looked to Franjinha and got the nod. He dropped the pistol.

Jake swept around the others to discourage them from going for their weapons lying on the ground. He glanced at Vilson's body one last time, and then started backing away.

"You go, *gringo*," Franjinha called out. "Run back to the city. I can get you there. I have my people down there."

Jake kept on backing away to the cover of the first buildings. Getting to the first house, he ducked behind its corner and held his ground for a moment, to see if they were going to give chase.

Franjinha was no longer interested in him, turning instead to Anjo. His boss seemed to be slowly recovering from the terror that had paralysed him. A couple of his soldiers went to him, gently helping him up. "I knew there was no ghost," he winced.

Franjinha came over and picked up the Beretta. Anjo held out his good hand to take it.

"You knelt in the dirt, snivelling like a baby," Franjinha said to him, "while a little kid had the balls to step up and kill it."

Jake felt the collective intake of breath, the tension in the gang. He could see the edge return to Anjo, the sparkle-eyed psycho. Anjo gestured with his outstretched hand. "Give."

Franjinha shook his head. "You're done, brother." The bullet hit Anjo just below the eye, snapping his head back and throwing him into the dirt.

"I'm boss, now," said Franjinha. "Anyone got a problem with that?"

None of the gang did.

Jake turned and ran. Once he had gone a hundred metres down through the alleyways he made his way to the edge of the favela, out into the long grass. He started creeping slowly back up the hill. It didn't matter how long he had to wait it out amongst the rotting corpses in the undergrowth before Franjinha's gang dispersed, he wasn't leaving Vilson's body up there.

Chapter 55

Jake

Stepping out of the shower, he towelled off and looked in the mirror. His skin was a camouflage pattern of bruises and wheals. He was stiff and sore all over. He turned away from the mirror and looked over his shoulder. His back was worse.

Going through to the bedroom, the floor fan swept across the room and chilled the still-wet skin on his back. He had returned to the same cruddy motel outside Cruzeiro that he had stayed in when he was first searching for Vilson's mother.

He had slept the sleep of the dead on the marshmallow bed and thin, lumpy pillows. He was feeling halfway to human again.

There was a light knock on the door. He wrapped the thin, scratchy towel around his waist.

It was Eliane. She was barefoot, wearing a cropped vest and jogging bottoms. He was trying not to notice the shape of her through the thin cotton of her vest or the smooth skin of her belly. She was scrubbed of make-up, her hair loose. He wanted to tell her how beautiful she was. It probably wasn't a great idea.

He sat on the edge of the bed and gestured for her to sit on the cheap chair in the corner.

"Seen the news?" she asked.

"Try to avoid it if I can."

The release of Eliane's father had not made the news – she hadn't reported him missing. Her father told her that when his captors were unable to contact their boss they had panicked and then fretted over whether or not to kill him before letting him go. They hadn't even known who he was or why they were holding him. Chaotic video footage from the mass brawl at the end of the fight had made the news, as had shots of Nogueira's wrecked car in the underground garage. The media had latched onto the narrative of the hero police captain murdered while trying to take down a drug gang. A couple of outlets, including Globo, had hinted at a story that lay behind that, but there was no enthusiasm for it. Eliane's reporter contact had told her that she just couldn't get it to catch. The moment had gone.

"Is there anyone else you can try?" Jake asked.

She thought for a moment before shaking her head. "I don't think

I want to. Going by the book goes out the window when it's your family – I would have gone to any length to get my dad back. Maybe we lost the war, but we won a battle. It's the wrong way round but it's all we've got. Is that good enough?"

"It is if you're doing what you're doing now."

She nodded. "And maybe I need to pick the right kind of battles. I found a lawyer in town who's willing to help me with Vilson's mother and Toninho."

Both Jake and Eliane had gone to the farm to bury Vilson. His mother decided on a shady spot on the edge of some woodland, close to a stream. She had wept silently at the graveside as Toninho hugged her. She said without self-pity she had been a bad mother to Vilson.

Eliane had also come back to follow up with the ILO on behalf of the farm workers. A few of them wanted to stay on; they had nowhere else to go. Goretti had offered to give them a wage and that would count in her favour in the fight with Torquato's son over the division of the farm. He was already making moves to get Goretti and Toninho evicted.

"I need to stick around here for a few days," Eliane said.

"I'm getting a bus back to Rio today – Marinho wants me to take him to see Yara."

"I thought he didn't go for all that stuff."

Jake shrugged. "He won't say exactly what, but something happened in that fight just after his sight went. It changed his mind."

"And after that, what then for you?"

"There's a battle back home that I never finished."

"Back in England?"

He nodded.

"Straight away?" she asked.

"Well I need to get dressed and maybe get some breakfast first."

She didn't smile, her head dropping for a moment, and he wished he hadn't cracked the lame joke.

When she looked up again, she rose from her chair. Coming to him, she bent to kiss him gently on his scarred cheek.

He felt her soft hair falling on his shoulder, and he could smell something subtle and wonderful on the warmth of her body. She was everything good. All the death and ugliness disappeared in that moment.

He pushed himself from the bed to his feet, his limbs and back stiff, and she stepped back, placing a hand on his chest, holding him at a distance. Like she'd made a decision.

She glanced at the bruises on his body. "I'm sorry. I did wonder what it might be like with you around when there was no trouble," she said, and sighed. "But I think if you stayed trouble would find you."

"I could behave." It was worth a go, even though it seemed the moment had passed.

"If the trouble didn't find you, I think it wouldn't take long before you went looking for it. And until that changes you're not a healthy person to be around."

"We could talk about it over breakfast," he said, lightening the tone, despite himself.

She smiled. "Sure. I'll get breakfast with you, but let's not talk any more about that. Let's part on good terms."

As much as he wanted to make some grand statement of intent to change himself, to change her mind, he knew she was right. A more easy-going, socially acceptable version of himself was way over the horizon. He couldn't really see what that person looked like.

Her hand dropped from his chest and he immediately missed its warmth.

She went to the door, "Get dressed and I'll see you out front."

And then she was gone.

Epilogue

Up on the hill, people still believed that the ghost moved amongst them. And it was hard to find anyone who would speak about Vilson in anything but hushed tones. Different stories flew around. Almost no one outside the Red Ants believed that little Nuno could have rid the favela of the ghost or that it was Franjinha who had killed Anjo. They believed it was the ghost that had killed Anjo. In a way, they were right.

People who had known Vilson always made sure that everyone else knew about it. Many of them said that they had always known there was something different about him. Anyone who had seen the ghost was given extra kudos, a special status. The number of people claiming to have seen it ran into the hundreds. As time went by, it became thousands.

And Vilson moved beyond the hill and into the city below. People living on the hill who had jobs down there took the stories with them. Maids would use them to get spoiled kids to behave. City people went to parties and dinners and shared the stories that their gardener or security guard had told them.

To many on the hill and beyond, Vilson was a part of their lives.

THE END

I hope you enjoyed my book. I would be so grateful if you would, please, spread the word by leaving a rating/review on Amazon (or other retailer) or Goodreads.
Thank you,
Dom (A.D. Flint)

The book you are holding was first published via Unbound, and was partly funded by readers. Without these readers it would not exist.

Peter Allport
Alison Ascough
Magda Ashley
Peter & Carolyn Barry
Adam Bates
Fabia Bates
Vanessa Boer
Michael Brooks
Hamish Calder
Glenn Campbell
Grace Clark
Peter Dale
Chris & Deirdre
Juarez Durigon Lemes
Teresa Earle
Julie Exley
Jane Fletcher
Helen Flint
Helen & Roger Flint
Juka Flint
Esme Flint
Léo Flint
Raquel Garcia
Jamie Goold
Ray Goold
Ian Graham
Juliet Hammond
Giles Harding
Tony Hudson
Ogg Ibrahim
Ney Ibrahim
Eth Ibrahim-Flint
Robert & Inge
Kate Innocent
Wendy Jane Jackson
Sarah Jenner
Marjorie Johns
Daniel Johnson
Chris Jones

THE BURNING HILL

Michael Jubb
Slawek Jurczyk
Andrew Kemp
Sophie Key
Dan Kieran
James Langton
Kim Laws
S Lawson
Francois Margottin
Ruth Martin
Andrew Mcbeath
Sarah McCulloch
John Mitchinson
Carlo Navato
Lesley Onyett
Kwaku Osei-Afrifa
Melody Paradise
Julia Park
Annie Parnell
Tim Pass
Maddy Pass
Tim Percival
Martin Percival
JD Pink
Justin Pollard
Clive Ponting
David Pringle
Charles Rae
Martin Reid
Stuart Richardson
Justine Robinson
Anne Rose
Matt Scott
Jon Scurr
Michael Sleet
Paul Smith
Victoria Smith
Margaret Steel
Phil Steel
Charlotte Steel
Jo Taylor

THE BURNING HILL

Aliff Turner
Russ Veduccio
Hazel Ward
Rebecca Wild
Jason Wild
Richard Willis
Rosemary Willis
Michael Willis
Judith Wraight

Printed in Dunstable, United Kingdom